INROADS

The Killing of Callie Shane

LINDA AMEY

HIDDEN VISTAS PUBLISHING

AUSTIN, TEXAS

PUBLISHER'S NOTE

Published in the United States of America
HIDDEN VISTAS PUBLISHING
Austin, Texas

Cover Design by Kimberly Greyer

Library of Congress Cataloging-in-Publication Data

ISBN: 979-8-9929451-6-4 (paperback)
ISBN: 979-8-9929451-7-1 (e-book)

DEDICATION

To victims and survivors of violent crime,
And to those who love them.
To the wrongly imprisoned,
And to those who fight for their freedom.

PROLOGUE

Callie reached between the front seats of the dimly lit car, then snatched a folded bill from her sister's hand. She was beyond annoyed with Nichole. She was angry. It was nine o'clock. They were supposed to have started home from Galveston by mid-afternoon. If they had left the island on time, they would have been home in Sparrows Cove hours ago.

But no. Nichole and Jessica had spent the afternoon on the beach with their friends. Now they were stopped at a crummy convenience store on Interstate 10 with a hundred and eighty miles ahead of them. A few minutes ago, Callie had sent her mom another text. Stopping for gas. Nearly to Katy. Sorry.

Fed up, Callie shouldered open the rear door of the SUV. A gust of thick, humid wind shoved it back against her. Stiff arming the door, she climbed out, then let the wind slam it shut. Nichole and Jessica would think she had slammed the door on purpose, but Callie did not care. She was exhausted, hungry, and mad. And maybe a little hurt. Jessica and Nichole had invited her to the beach house with them, but they had left her behind most of the weekend with Jessica's parents and a family next door. "Never again," Callie muttered, rounding the rear of the Mazda.

Battling another gust of wind, she trotted away from the gas pumps toward the store, her long hair swirling. A black car was parked near the end of the building, to the left of the door. A dark-haired young man sat in the driver's seat. He and Callie exchanged glances. Her inner-warning system sounded. Would he follow her into the store? Should she go inside alone? No, her mom would say. Always stay with a group. Uncertain, Callie looked over her shoulder at Nichole standing between her SUV and the gas pumps. She was talking to the driver of the Mercedes she had parked behind. If Callie returned to the car, Nichole would laugh and say, "Really, Callie? Are you seven or seventeen?"

After an agony of indecision, Callie walked on. She stepped onto the raised sidewalk, then muscled open the heavy glass door. The store was small, stuffy, and smelled of tangy mustard and wieners cooking on a roller grill. A few steps ahead stood a waist-high barrel of beer on ice. She wished it was filled with bottled water. She was eager to get out of there. The check-out counter was to her right. The clerk, a young Black man, said hello. The name on his white shirt read Derek. Callie returned his greeting, then asked where she could find cold, bottled water.

"On the back wall." The clerk smiled as he pointed toward the far corner. "Fourth door from the left."

"Thanks." Callie walked around the barrel, then took off down the center aisle, her flip flops squeaking on the floor tiles. At the rear of the store, she skidded to a halt in front of the refrigerated cases. "Fourth from the left." Tugging open the glass door, she propped it back with her hip, then scanned the shelves. Nichole drank nothing but Ozarka. "There it is." She grasped the plastic bottle, but then let it go. Dasani was cheaper.

Nichole would complain, but Callie did not care. She could drink it or not. Yanking two bottles from the dispenser, she tucked them in the bend of her elbow, stepped back, then let the door swing shut.

A buzzer sounded. Callie looked toward the front of the store. A customer lumbered through the door, then began digging around in the barrel of beer. In the harsh overhead lighting, the man's face looked like a graveled parking lot. Tattoos of some sort snaked up both sides of his neck. He was a big man, not tall, but fat and clumsy looking. He was sloppily dressed in a red tee shirt and black gym shorts that reached almost to his ankles.

If I hurry, Callie thought anxiously, I can get to the check-out counter before he does and get out of here.

Snugging the bottles in the bend of her elbow, Callie clenched the five-dollar-bill in her right hand. As she made her way up the aisle, the shelves seemed to close in around her. Perspiration dribbled down her back and dotted her forehead and upper lip. Had the man noticed her? She wasn't sure. She picked up her pace when he pulled a can of beer out of the barrel, then disappeared from Callie's sight.

A furious voice lifted in a shout. "You! Put that back and get out of here! Now!"

Callie froze, her feet fastened to the floor, her left arm locked around the water bottles. Every nerve in her body shuddered. She heard a loud crash, then more shouting. But now there were two voices. Men. Yelling, cursing, and smashing into things. Callie's heart hammered in her chest. She had to get out of there. A deafening blast bounced off the walls. Then another. A wave of terror surged through her. Gunfire. Callie's entire body stiffened. The bottles pressed hard against her ribs. Frantic questions streaked through her mind. What should she do? Should she hide? Should she run? Yes! She had to get out of there.

Dropping the bottles to the floor, Callie raced toward the mouth of the aisle. She was almost there when the fat man stumbled backward into the beer barrel. The clerk, his white shirt now stained with blood, charged the man, pounding his head and shoulders with a baseball bat. Blood streaked down the man's pocked face, contorted now with pain and fury. His arms flailed, the gun wobbling. Shielding his head with one hand, he pointed the pistol with the other, then squeezed the trigger. Callie screamed despite herself. The clerk swung the bat again, but it flew from his hand. He lunged at the shooter, pounding him with his fists.

For a pulse-pounding instant, Callie and Derek exchanged glances. "Go! Run!"

Callie lurched forward. A shot rang out. Then another. A bullet ripped into her neck. Blood spurted. Her head erupted in blinding white pain, and her knees buckled. Collapsing against the barrel of beer, Callie slid to the floor, unable to move, lids open, eyes fixed. A pool of blood bloomed around Callie's head. Her clenched fingers went limp. A five-dollar-bill lay crumpled in her palm.

CHAPTER 1

TWO YEARS LATER

Rebecca Grant had overseen few disinterments in her twenty years as a funeral director. She was here today in a rural cemetery west of Austin at the request of a friend. The casket in the small rectangular grave held the body of a little girl named Nina Jones. Last year, her older sister, unaware that the adventurous child had toddled out the door, had backed her car over little Nina in the family's driveway. Now the parents wanted their child's body moved to a cemetery near Waco where the family had relocated.

When Rebecca had agreed to oversee the disinterment, Jake Spencer had offered to stand in for her. Jake worked for Rebecca at Baker and Grant Funeral Home. He was a professional in every respect, earnest and caring. Jake had been a godsend to Rebecca when her daughter Callie had been killed. Although he and Rebecca had never discussed the subject, she knew that preparing Callie's body and directing the funeral had been excruciating for Jake. He had watched Callie grow from a shy ten-year-old into a lively, engaging girl of seventeen. Then she was gone.

Rebecca battled back the thought, unthinkable even after nearly two years, then focused on the task at hand. Funeral records indicated that the flock-covered, wooden casket had been buried without a vault. Rebecca had explained to the parents as gently as possible that the casket had likely deteriorated to some extent, and that removing it from the grave was an uncertain process. "We can't leave Nina here by herself any longer," the child's father had insisted. "Just do the best you can and be careful with her."

As Rebecca looked on, two men from a local grave service company carefully shoveled soil from where the casket rested, within a foot or so of Nina's pink granite monument. About two feet below the surface, their shovels scraped the casket lid. Switching to small hand tools, the men got on their knees, then continued to work. Minutes later, Carlos and Rebecca moaned in unison. Just as she had suspected, the lid had partially collapsed. Soil had rained into the casket, concealing its tender contents but for a small triangle of lace-trimmed fabric. Carlos crossed himself, then continued to work, scooping earth away from the sides and ends of the fragile casket, working slowly and deliberately. The men were as concerned as Rebecca that at any moment the sides could give way, and the entire casket would collapse.

The grave was shaded by an oak tree, but the canopy did little to offset the morning's smothering warmth. Perspiration trickled down Rebecca's back. She unbuttoned her suit jacket, resisting the urge to remove it. "Respect," her father had explained when she first started working at the funeral home. "The way we dress and present ourselves is a way of showing respect."

Like her father, Rebecca was a funeral director and embalmer, her mother JoAnn an accountant. Nelson Grant and his partner had established Baker and Grant in Sparrows Cove, a small town on Lake Travis, fifty miles west of Austin. Her parents had stepped away, as they called their attempt at retirement, four years ago. They had traveled extensively, primarily in the states, and taken several long-awaited cruises. On day six of a seven-day Alaska cruise, life as the couple knew it had ended with a single emergency phone call. "Mom, it's me. Adam. I have terrible news. You must get home right away. Rebecca needs you. It's Callie, Mom. Our Callie. She's dead."

Rebecca had still been in shock by the time her parents returned home. It was a merciful psychological state, she believed now. Without it, she could not have survived the hours and days after Callie's father had appeared at her home without phoning first. The contorted look on Russell's face had screamed that something was wrong. A hard fist of panic had formed in Rebecca's stomach. It was Callie. Something had happened to Callie. Rebecca had wanted to slam the door and not open it.

For twenty hours after Callie's death, Rebecca had warded off the brutal truth as if it were an attacker or an intruder. She had kept Russell at arm's length too. Even if they had not been separated at the time, she would not have turned to him for comfort. It was Nichole, his daughter. Rebecca could not bear to think of her. The girl had always been impulsive and unreliable. It was her fault that Callie was dead.

Oddly, it had been her mother's reassuring words and her father's embrace that had jarred Rebecca from the protection of shock-imposed oblivion. She had not felt safe until her parents had returned home.

Rebecca rarely relived that horrifying moment when Russell stood in the door opening, tears glistening in his eyes, his lips quivering. But when she did, she recalled the roar in her ears before he had said a word. Even now, almost two years later, memories could come flooding back like a current hidden in the cove. Callie's dead. She's been shot.

"Miz Grant," Carlos said quietly, "excuse me. You're standing on my strap."

"Oh, I'm sorry." Rebecca stepped aside. "You're ready to lift the casket."

Carlos and Tim, still on their knees, worked straps under Nina's fragile casket. Then Carlos grasped the ends of both straps and stood. Easing the casket inches off the floor of the grave, he created clearance for Tim to slide a section of canvas beneath it. Once done, Carlos settled the unstable box back into place, then removed the straps. Now, if the casket came apart, the canvas sling would preserve its precious contents.

Watching the men inch the casket from the grave, Rebecca stood next to a polystyrene vault. She was thinking how well the canvas was working when the head end of the casket gave way. Rebecca tensed, knotting her fists. Chills rose on her arms as a curve of bone, like an upturned seashell, protruded from the shifted soil. "It's all right," she assured, reacting to the distress on the men's faces. "We did the best we could."

Moments later, the fragile casket and Nina's remains were secure in the vault. The men were preparing to seal the container when Tim whispered, "Would you look at that?"

Tangled in a clump of soil was a broken piece of delicate gold chain. Rebecca reached into the debris, then flicked dirt from around it. "Oh, my," she whispered. "Look at this." Attached to the broken chain was a tiny gold heart. Rebecca picked up the pieces, then polished the little heart with her thumb, slowly restoring its sheen. "Nina," she read, and from the back, "Love, Mom and Dad."

Rebecca started to return the necklace but reconsidered. "Wait to seal the vault. I need to make a phone call." She stepped away to speak with the child's father. "I wanted to let you know that the disinterment is complete. As we expected, the casket had deteriorated a bit, but Nina's little body is safely in the vault. I know this because I found something very precious in her casket. It's a necklace."

The father was silent for a few seconds, then sighed loudly. "Oh, God. The little gold heart we gave her. I can't believe it. My wife has always regretted burying that necklace with Nina. This is a miracle. Thank you, Rebecca. You can't know what getting that necklace back will mean to my wife."

With the vault sealed and placed in the funeral coach next to the granite marker, Rebecca thanked the men for their competency and their kindness. At last, with the air conditioner on high, she began the forty-mile drive back to Sparrows Cove. When she reached the edge of town, a black Mazda SUV sped past. Rebecca's hands tensed on the steering wheel. It was Nichole. Although they lived in the same small town, Rebecca attempted to avoid the girl and deliberately tried not to even think of her.

Why had she allowed Callie, only seventeen, to go out of town with Nichole and her friend Jessica? And why had Nichole not bought gas before leaving Galveston? How massively idiotic to wait until dark and pull into a convenience store on an interstate highway.

Three people had died that horrific night. Two of them, Callie and the store clerk, were innocent victims. Derek Jaxson had been shot twice in the chest, but the courageous young man had summoned the strength to bash the gun-wielding meth addict in the head with a bat. Rebecca hoped Calvin Canon died in excruciating pain as he bled out on the grimy sidewalk. A Harris County jury had decided that Canon's accomplice should meet the same fate, but the state of Texas would employ a less brutal manner of death. Six months ago, Calvin Canon's accomplice had been sentenced to die by lethal injection.

CHAPTER 2

As far as Mac McKeon could see, acres of ranch land sprawled under a glaring afternoon sun. From the cool comfort of his Chevy Tahoe, he watched a man on horseback emerge from a grove of oak trees. His western-style straw hat was sweat stained, the brim pulled low in front to block the glare. The sleeves of the man's pale blue shirt were rolled up to his elbows, and the toes of his work boots rested in the saddle's stirrups. He and the jet-black horse moved in familiar unison toward the fence at the edge of the property.

The man was Lester Donovan. He and his wife Emma were putting their three-hundred-acre ranch on the market. The property was located on the edge of Kerrville, a small town a hundred miles west of Mac's hometown of Austin. If all went well, Lone Star Land and Ranch would get the listing. Mac had the prepared agreement in his briefcase. All he needed were the couple's signatures.

At the fence, Lester Donovan crossed the bridle's reins, then rested them on the horse's neck, the leather straps dangling freely. Dismounting with ease, he patted the animal's shoulder. Muscles rippled in the dazzling sunlight. After retrieving a tool from a saddle bag, he walked to the fence, then tugged the top strand of sagging barbwire. The horse shifted his weight from one hind foot to the other, swished his long, silky tail, then sniffed the thick afternoon air. The scene, Mac thought, could have been the subject of a Charles Russell painting.

The Donovan home appeared up ahead, positioned well off the county road. It was a single story, sandstone and stucco ranch house with a metal roof and a spacious porch. The front door was paneled oak with heavy, oil-rubbed bronze hardware. It swung open when Mac stepped onto the front porch. "Afternoon, Emma." He extended his hand. "Good to see you again."

"Likewise," the woman answered, shaking Mac's hand, then stepping aside. "Come in."

Emma Donovan was a petite woman, perhaps five feet four. Mac guessed her to be in her mid-fifties, a few years younger than Mac and his wife Catherine. She wore her auburn hair in a low ponytail just above the nape of her neck. Her smile seemed a little forced, but her tone was gracious when she invited him to sit, then offered iced tea. Mac accepted. "You've got a fine home here, Emma," he commented, taking in the spacious great room with its high ceiling, exposed beams, and wide-plank oak flooring. "Remind me how long you and Lester have lived here."

"Nearly ten years. We bought the ranch land from my grandparents. They used to live in a house just up the road." Emma crossed the room while talking. "As we mention, Lester is an architect, so we designed the house together." At a granite-top island, she poured glasses of tea, then rejoined Mac. "Lester should be back any minute. He's checking a fence somewhere."

"I saw him," Mac said, reaching for the glass and thanking her. "I was surprised when Lester told me he's an architect. I assumed he was a rancher."

"Primarily evenings and weekends." Emma's smile relaxed a little, tilting the corners of her lips. She sat in a worn leather armchair next to the sofa, sipping her tea. "The cattle on it are not ours. They belong to a rancher down the road."

"And the black horse Lester is riding?"

"He's ours. I have one too. A beautiful chestnut mare."

"Do you ride a lot?" Mac asked, settling comfortably on the sofa.

"Almost every evening. I'm the office manager for a physician in Kerrville. It's a hectic office, so I can hardly wait to get home." Emma looked over her shoulder when the back door opened. "Lester, Mac is here."

Lester Donovan, although not a rancher, certainly looked the part. Western style shirt with grippers, not buttons. Well-worn Wranglers with an equally worn leather belt. He had removed his hat, but the band left an impression in his thick brown hair and across his forehead. He washed and dried his hands at the kitchen sink, then joined them in the living area. Mac stood to shake the man's hand, not the battered hand of a rancher.

"Well, Mac, where's the helicopter?" Lester asked, taking a leather armchair opposite his wife.

"It's in Austin," Mac answered. "My partner is headed to the Panhandle as soon as the weather clears."

"Seeing the ranch from the air last week was quite an experience," Lester remarked. "We enjoyed meeting your partner too."

"Don's a good man. We've been in business for a long time. Haven't sued each other yet, although I've been tempted to push him out of the helicopter a few times."

Conversation among the three was easy. The Donovans had located Lone Star Land and Ranch on the Internet. Lester had checked out the company thoroughly, had spoken at length with former and existing clients, then finally with Mac by phone. Several weeks passed before he and Emma had met Mac and Don, that being the day they enjoyed the aerial view of the acreage. It was clear to Mac that the couple loved their home, the ranch, and their neighbors. They had not disclosed why they were putting the place on the market.

When the conversation slowed, Emma set her glass on a coaster. "Mac, would you excuse us for a minute? Then I guess we should review the listing agreement."

"Of course," Mac said. "There's no pressure. If you need more time to—"

"Time won't make it any easier." Emma's lids drew down for a flutter of a moment. "It's what we have to do."

Mac rose to a half-stand as the couple walked away. It's what we have to do. What had Emma meant by that?

While his clients spoke quietly at the breakfast table on the far side of the great room, Mac gazed at framed photographs on the mantle, a massive slab of oak stained the same deep brown as the floors and beams. There were three pictures. The one in the middle was a snapshot of a slightly younger Lester and Emma. They were sitting side by side on the front porch swing. Lester's arm was around Emma's shoulders. Her hand rested on his thigh. It was the picture of a contented couple. To the left was a photo of a young man in his late twenties or early thirties. The resemblance to Lester was astonishing. He was clearly their son. The photo on the right was of a younger man, perhaps a second son. His hair was less full and a shade lighter. Mac detected little resemblance.

It was the same with his own daughters. Sierra looked much like Mac, particularly the almond shape and color of her eyes.

She even had Mac's broad shoulders and square chin. Sierra was five-nine, with light brown hair, and a trim, graceful form. Her daughter Michaela, almost five now, had overheard Catherine say that Sierra was just like her father. Michaela had quipped, "No, she's not, Gran. Mom lets me do nearly everything I want. Granddad does not."

Mac's younger daughter Brooke, twenty-nine, had chocolate brown hair and a heart-shaped face like Catherine's. Mother and daughter were the same height—five feet six—but that was where their resemblance ended. Brooke was perpetually tan, athletic, and loved the outdoors. Catherine was equally close to both of their daughters, but Mac was clearly closer to Sierra, a fact that Brooke acknowledged, but did not seem to care.

Catherine had worked for twenty years at Texas Times Monthly, many of them as editor-in-chief, and now as president. The magazine chronicled contemporary life in the Lone Star state, a must-read for people who wanted to stay atop anything of significance in Texas.

That morning, Catherine had insisted that her staff work from home. Just after midnight, a thunderstorm had descended on the Texas hill country. Lightning cracked and dazzled. Thunder rolled. Rain, sharp as a lance on the windows of their home, had lasted until dawn. Five counties had been under a flashflood warning, and this morning low water crossings in and around Austin were closed. Morning traffic, always a headache, would have been a nightmare. Catherine had followed her own advice and worked from their west Austin home.

Mac had asked his wife to join him on the trip to Kerrville, a pleasant drive from Austin. The invitation was an olive branch of sorts. They had quarreled again last night, violating their practice of not going to bed angry with each other. It was Graham Hollister, Sierra's estranged husband. Mac and Catherine had argued about what tack to take with the man until the custody agreement was signed, and their mess of a marriage was finally over. "I loathe the man, too, Mac," Catherine had snapped. "But Graham is Michaela's father. We cannot antagonize him." Mac had blazed like a grassfire. "Antagonize him? You're playing right into his hands, Catherine. The man is a manipulator and an overbearing bully, but he has intimidated my daughter for the last damn time."

The rhythm of the conversation at the breakfast table changed. Emma and Lester pushed back their chairs, then returned to the living area. Mac rose, walked to the cold fireplace, then stood by the mantle. "Are these your sons?"

Emma stood next to him, nodding to the photo on the left. "That's Lester Jr. He goes by Les. He got married last month, and I'm waiting on a wedding photo." She adjusted the angle of the photo on the right. "This is our younger son Jude. Named after my father."

"Where do Les and his wife live?"

"Saint Louis. Les is with the Cardinals organization. Looks as if they will be staying there."

"And Jude?"

Emma paused momentarily. Lester answered the question for her. "East Texas. Livingston."

When neither elaborated, Mac said, "Catherine and I have two daughters. Sierra, our first, is going through a divorce, so she and her little girl are living with Catherine and me. Brooke and her husband live nearby. She's all about her dog. He's a champion Boston terrier, so they travel all over the country to compete. Brooke has loved animals all her life. For now, she and Bryant have no children."

"Would you like to see ours?" Lester offered. "Not our children. Our horses."

Mac chuckled. "Lead the way."

The men left through the back door, then struck off together down a stone path angling gently across the fenced backyard. It ended at a wooden gate which Lester opened and motioned Mac through. The barn was situated next to a stand of mature, well cared for live oaks. It was a large structure painted tan with the same metal roof as the ranch house. Mac was commenting on how well maintained the property was, but his words were drowned out by a prolonged whinny from inside the barn. "Someone hears us coming."

"That would be Gracie. I'd recognize that call anywhere."

The men entered the shade of the barn. Mac detected the strong smell of sweet hay and the faint scent of leather and manure. Black dirt and coarse sawdust muffled the sounds of their footfalls.

Lester paused at the first stall. "Hello, Gracie. You were hoping I was Emma, weren't you?" He patted the chestnut mare's broad cheek, then stroked the white blaze stretching from between her eyes to just above her velvety nose. "Gracie is her nickname. Her real name is Graceful Lady. And she is that. Do you like to ride, Mac?"

"If you mean a golf cart, the answer's yes."

Lester grinned as they moved in unison to the adjacent stall. "This is Jet. He's mine. Handsome, isn't he?"

"Beautiful animal. I saw you riding him in the pasture." Suddenly another horse poked its head over the door of the fourth stall. "Oh, you have three horses. And who is this?"

Lester patted Jet heavily, then walked past an empty stall. "This is Reno. He and Jet are not exactly friendly, so we keep a stall between them. Reno is Jude's horse."

Reno was smaller than Jet, about the same size as Gracie. He was honey colored, and his mane was the shade of pale straw. "Good looking boy. Does your son visit often?"

"No, but we visit him when we can."

"Who rides Reno?"

"Emma and I both do," Lester answered, smoothing a tangle in the horse's mane. "We should have sold Reno when Jude left, but we just couldn't part with him." With his gaze still on the animal nuzzling his hand, he continued, "Jude doesn't actually live in Livingston, Mac. He's in prison there." The man's voice was flat, inflectionless. "That's why we're selling the ranch. Legal costs." When he turned to face Mac, Lester's eyes squinted and glistened with moisture. "Our son is on death row."

CHAPTER 3

Rebecca Grant felt obligated to attend her former father-in-law's birthday party. Her relationship with August Shane had always been close, even during her separation from Russell, and since their divorce. August was a solid man, hardworking, and humble. Callie had been his youngest grandchild and would probably be his last. August and his late wife had been as attentive to Callie as possible, while living a hundred fifty miles from Sparrows Cove in the town of Hillsboro.

Last week, Russell had asked Rebecca to travel with him and Nichole, but she had declined. The prospect of spending even half a day with her ex-husband and his daughter was Rebecca's idea of a road trip from hell. She had told Russell that she would need to leave the party by two-thirty, which was true. There was a rosary service at the funeral home that evening, and she wanted to be there when the family arrived.

The party was held at a Mexican restaurant called Lupe's. Guests, about forty in number, were family and close friends. The meal was served buffet style, standard Tex-Mex fare, but exceptionally tasty. Chips and salsa. Guacamole salad. Chile con queso. Tamales, enchiladas, rice and beans. Russell and Nichole arrived late, typical of them both. Nichole craved the attention of a grand entrance and had dressed for the part. In sleek black ankle pants, strappy bejeweled sandals, and a flowing silk blouse, the girl was ridiculously overdressed for a casual birthday celebration. The fuss she made over her grandfather was nauseating.

Rebecca sat at a table for eight with an assortment of relatives, across the noisy room from Russell and Nichole. It occurred to her that everyone at the table had attended her wedding. It seemed a lifetime ago. The conversation was at first stiff and awkward. Rebecca was no longer part of the Shane family, and she did not want to be. Callie's name was never mentioned, and that was to be expected. Long after her daughter's death, Rebecca had interpreted every expression of concern and compassion as pity. Poor Rebecca. She can hardly keep herself together. That sweet little Callie. Such a tragedy. Such a waste.

The conversation rightly focused on August, how well he looked, and what a good man he was. As dessert was served — warm, honey-drizzled sopapillas — Rebecca excused herself from the table to steal a few words with August. "I think you'll enjoy the gift I got you. It's in a very small box."

"Let me guess." He grasped Rebecca's wrist in feigned anticipation. "A handmade lure from that shop in Sparrows Cove."

Rebecca elbowed him gently. "How did you guess? Maybe because I've given you a dozen over the years."

August chuckled while patting her hand. "You're looking so good, dear. You could stand to gain a little weight, but you look much better than the last time I saw you." Frowning, he gazed across the room at his son who was ordering another margarita. "I wish I could say the same for Russell. He's drinking too much. I'll have to make sure Nichole is driving." August shook his head and grimaced. "What a tragedy. That whole awful mess." He leaned close to Rebecca, speaking softly. "Russell is obsessed with that Jude Donovan. He cannot understand why the execution date hasn't been set. Always saying that the man should be dead by now."

"I try to avoid the subject."

"Sometimes it's just not possible. I wish my son would get some help."

"I've suggested it again and again."

"But he just gets angry."

Rebecca stroked the dear man's thin shoulder, then pressed energy into her voice. "Let's not do this, August. This is a happy day. A celebration." She pecked his soft, lined cheek. "Enjoy yourself. You deserve it."

An hour after arriving, Rebecca was eager to leave. Never again, she vowed. I will keep in touch with August, visit him from time to time, but never again will I attend a family gathering. I do not belong here, and I do not want to be here. She picked up her purse and was making her way toward the restroom when Russell intercepted her.

"You're not leaving, are you?"

"Shortly, yes."

Russell was almost finished with his second margarita. His eyes, once as clear blue as a summer sky, were watery and streaked with red. His cheeks and nose looked sunburned, and he had lost weight. Russell had never paid particularly close attention to his attire, but today he looked almost disheveled. His jeans were too loose, his plaid cotton shirt needed pressing, and his hair, which was thinning on top, was in desperate need of a trim.

"August looks well," Rebecca commented. "So nice to see him again."

Russell nodded in a disinterested way, finished his drink in a single swig, then raised the empty glass toward a server.

"Like the margaritas, do you?" Rebecca made no attempt to hide her sarcasm. She was fed up with the man. Falling apart did nothing to honor Callie. Nothing.

The server delivered another margarita. Russell thanked her, then took a swig, swaying slightly as he tilted back his head. Had he been drinking before arriving at the restaurant? Rebecca fretted. Two margaritas would not otherwise affect him. Her anger began to boil. Drink yourself to death if you want. But I will not stand here while you make a fool of yourself at your father's birthday party.

When Rebecca turned away, Russell grasped her arm. "I called my contact at Victims Services. There is still no execution date for that worthless thug." He took another drink. "It's been six months, Rebecca, and Donovan is still breathing."

"Stop it." Rebecca yanked her arm away. "The appeals process will go on for years. You know that, Russell, yet you bring it up anyway."

"Then where is your outrage?" he demanded, his speech slurred. "My daughter is dead in her grave, and Jude Donovan is still alive."

People had begun to stare. Rebecca felt her face reddening as she struggled to maintain her composure. If only she could grab the glass from Russell's hand and hurl the drink in his face. Calvin Canon and Jude Donovan had killed their daughter. Her death had been a dagger in the heart of a failing marriage. Now Russell was allowing those men to ruin his life too. Did he think that the intensity of his suffering was somehow a measure of his love and devotion to his daughter? Rebecca had no clue what the man was thinking anymore, and she did not care.

Rebecca's heart had begun to pound. She took a deep breath, but before she could speak, Nichole strode quickly across the room. "Dad, are you okay? What happened?" She turned on Rebecca, her voice low, accusing, and dramatic. "What did you say to him? What are you even doing here?"

Rebecca choked back a response. Beats the hell out of me. Summoning what was left of her composure, she told them to have a safe drive home. As she walked away, she heard Nichole comforting her father in nauseatingly solicitous tones, certain that anyone standing nearby could hear her. Was that how Nichole had sounded to Callie as she lay dying on the floor of the convenience store?

The ambulance is on the way, Callie. Please talk to me. I love you, Callie. You're going to be okay. I'm right here, Callie.

Rebecca rushed from the restaurant to her car. She would call August later. "But not tonight." The interior of her car was a sauna. She started the engine, lowered the windows, then turned the air conditioner on high. Her head was pounding as she dug her sunglasses and a bottle of aspirin from her purse. A half empty bottle of Dasani sat in the drink holder. She popped two pills in her mouth, then swallowed them with a gulp of warm water.

Bottles of water. Callie had entered the convenience store that night to buy water. Nichole, Jessica, and Callie had been on their way home from Galveston. They had spent two nights at Jessica's family's beach house. Nichole had promised that they would leave the island by mid-afternoon. Rebecca had warned,

"We don't want you girls on the road at night." But that was exactly what happened. At nine o'clock, on Interstate 10, east of Katy, Nichole had pulled into a convenience store. "I'll pump the gas while you go inside and get us some water." Rebecca's precious Callie had been shot in the head and neck. She had died with five dollars still clutched in her hand.

CHAPTER 4

The McKeon family had been members of Westwood Country Club for decades. Since 1955, the Club had been a focal point of life in the west Austin community. The heart of the complex was a medieval-style French mansion. The masterfully built structure housed the main clubhouse. To some extent, each expansion had stayed true to the charm of the home's early 1900's architecture. The result was a celebrated private club nestled on live-oak covered acres hugging the shoreline of Lake Austin.

Mac was meeting his daughters and granddaughter by the pool. His wife Catherine had a business dinner at a restaurant downtown. It was six o'clock, and Mac had just driven in from Kerrville. The listing agreement for the Donovan ranch was signed and in his briefcase. On the way home, he had thought of little else than the cruel fact that Lester and Emma's son was on death row. When Lester had first said that his son was in Livingston, the possibility that Jude was imprisoned there had not crossed Mac's mind. And why should it have? Five thousand law abiding citizens made their homes in the pleasant, east Texas town.

Staggering, Mac thought, that one of the nearly two-hundred inmates on death row was Lester and Emma's twenty-five-year-old son. Mac did not know how it was possible, but he wished there was some way he could help, other than finding a buyer for a home the couple obviously did not want to part with.

The pool at Westwood was comfortably crowded with two lifeguards on duty, red whistles at the ready. Mac spotted Sierra, Brooke, and two friends chatting in the shade of an umbrella on the near side of the pool. He scanned the area, looking for Michaela. On the far side, kids were lined up at the diving board ladder, squirming, laughing, and dripping wet. But where was Michaela? He spotted a couple of her little friends in the deep end, not far from a lifeguard stand. The girls had gathered every available noodle and fashioned them into a makeshift raft, but Michaela was not with them.

Mac continued scanning the area, but he still could not spot the child. Was she in the café? Or the restroom? And why weren't Sierra and Brooke keeping a closer eye on her? She was not a good swimmer and, yes, it was a private club with security at the gate, but anybody could walk onto the property, including Graham Hollister.

Mac walked briskly toward his daughters. They were still chatting away, not a care in the world. With each passing second, his annoyance grew, and he still did not see his granddaughter. Sierra had to be more cautious.

"Where's Michaela?" Mac's gruff tone silenced the conversation. "I don't see her anywhere."

Sierra's wide, warm smile dissolved. She leaned to the side, looked around her father, and pointed. "She's right there, Dad."

Mac looked over his shoulder. Michaela and a cluster of other youngsters were splashing around in the shallow end of the pool near the steps. Her orange goggles dangled from her hand. Her hair was plastered to her skull. Had he walked right past her? She was wearing a black and white polka dot suit that he had not seen before. Maybe that's why I didn't spot her right away, he thought, acknowledging a level of relief that the situation did not warrant.

"Granddad! You're here." The child's face lit up like a struck match. Michaela threaded her way among the children, her sturdy little body rising out of the water in increments. Scrambling up the steps, she rubbed her eyes and squinted from the sting and the glare. "I'm hungry, Granddad. Are you?"

"Not yet, but I'm really thirsty."

"How about a lemonade?" she suggested, smiling up at him.

"I'll order you one." Mac smoothed the child's straggly hair. Her long eyelashes were bunched and spiky. Cute little mess. "So you're hungry, huh? You want your usual?"

"With chicken, please. And carrots." Michaela shuddered and grimaced. "No broccoli."

"I'll let you know when your meal's ready. Hop back in the water before you get cold." Mac patted his granddaughter's back, then nudged her toward the pool. "Did Mom put sunscreen on you?" When the child held up two fingers, Mac assumed that was an affirmative.

The door to the pool's Lakeview Cafe opened, and two men emerged. Phil Kuykendall spotted Mac, then motioned him over. After exchanging words with his companion, he signaled for Mac to join him at a nearby table. Phil was a mover-and-shaker in the state. To say the man was gregarious would be like characterizing Donald Trump as fairly self-confident. Mac spoke briefly to his daughters and their friends. He considered apologizing for his gruff tone but didn't bother. His daughters understood, but if they didn't, then they should.

Mac walked behind a long row of chaises to where Phil was standing. The guy looked ridiculously well-groomed to be toting a gym bag, and Mac told him so.

"I work out, but I'm not a fanatic." Phil dropped the bag at his feet, then collapsed into a chair. "I talked to your girls earlier. Brooke said she and Sydney are off to Chicago soon for another dog show. Sierra's looking better than the last time I saw her. Divorce final yet?"

Mac shook his head and sat. Austin was a major city now, but west Austin was like a small town. People talked. He detested the fact that his daughter's personal life had supplied grist for the gossip mill.

Phil waved over a server, then gave the young woman his member number. "Kettel One and tonic for me. No lime. Mac?"

"Your coldest beer in a can."

Phil scribbled his signature on the server's tablet. "I'll have it right out, sir."

"Just a second, Carly." Mac supplied his member number. "Michaela wants her usual. Pasta with butter sauce. Grilled chicken. Carrots. No broccoli."

"Yes, sir." She presented the device for his signature. "Thank you, Mr. McKeon."

Mac nodded, then thanked Phil for the beer. The man smirked and settled into the metal chair, adjusting his sunglasses. "So how's business?"

"Staying busy," Mac answered. "Don and I flew to Floresville a few days ago. Showed a fifteen-hundred-acre ranch to a man from Boston. The fellow was nice enough, but he didn't know a sheep from a white tail deer. The trip was nothing but a fuel burn."

Phil laughed. "Take me up in that thing sometime, would you?"

"Sure," Mac answered. "Be glad to."

The men continued to chat, then Carly returned with their drinks. Phil stirred his cocktail with a finger, took a swig, then asked Mac if he and Catherine would be in town next week.

"I'll be in and out." Mac took a long drink of cold beer. "Can't speak for Catherine."

"Check your schedules and get back with me, would you? I need to talk to you about something." He assumed an under-oath pose. "I won't be asking for a donation. I swear."

"Count me out of the next gala too," Mac said, not at all joking.

"I hear you. Too damn hot to put on a tux." Phil propped one sneakered foot on the opposite knee and grinned. "Well, look who's here."

Michaela was making her way across the pool deck, fast-walking to avoid a caution from a lifeguard. She ducked and shrieked when a grackle swooped close to her head. "Granddad, is my dinner ready?" Reaching Mac's side, she skidded to an abrupt, sliding halt.

"Michaela, we were talking. Say, 'Excuse me.'"

"Excuse me, Granddad. Is my dinner ready?"

"Say hello to Mr. Kuykendall."

"Hello, mister … mister …"

"Just call me Mr. K. It's nice to see you, Michaela."

"Nice to see you too." She hugged her arms around her shoulders, dripping and starting to shiver. "Can I talk now?"

The men laughed. Mac assured the child that he had ordered her dinner. "Go sit with Mom and Aunt Brooke. I'll be there in a minute. Put your cover-up on. Say goodbye to Mr. Kuykendall." Michaela wiggled her little fingers and said goodbye. Mac grinned as she padded away, her bare feet splashing through puddles on the stone.

When Carly returned, black plastic tray in hand, Mac asked her to deliver Michaela's dinner to his daughters' table, then took another long swig of beer. Phil finished his drink in a satisfied gulp, picked up his gym bag, and stood. "I'll call you tomorrow, Mac, and see when you and Catherine are free."

"Sounds good," Mac answered, wondering briefly what Phil wanted to talk to them about. "See you sometime next week."

With the sun dropping slowly behind the clubhouse, Mac sank deeper into the chair and massaged the knotted muscles in his neck. It had been a long day. His eyes felt sandy, and he was tired to the bone. Maybe that explained his short fuse when he hadn't been able to spot Michaela. But no. Sierra and Brooke had to learn. They could not let down their guard. Graham Hollister had taken Michaela out of the country without her family's knowledge, much less permission. Mac could not let that happen again.

Memories of those brutal ten days came crowding in, but Mac battled them back. The fact that Michaela's passport was in his office safe was of little comfort. If Hollister was determined to get the child out of the country again, getting a passport might not stop him.

Wearily, Mac pushed himself up from the chair, then joined his family. Michaela was digging into her pasta as if she had not eaten in a week. She declared it awesome when her mother asked how she liked it. Chuckling, her Aunt Brooke tucked a tangle of hair behind Michaela's ear.

"So what did Phil have to say?" Sierra asked, inching her chair closer to the table, shielding her fair skin under the umbrella.

Mac shrugged. "You know Phil. He always has something on his mind." He told Michaela to use her napkin, then said to Brooke, "So where is Sydney's next beauty pageant?"

Brooke rolled her eyes in reply. "Michaela, tell Granddad it's a conformation show, then give him a smack on the arm for me, would you?"

Relaxing with his family, listening to his daughters chat with one another and with Michaela, Mac thought back to earlier in the day. He had been sitting on a hay bale next to Lester Donovan, listening as the man choked his way through an explanation of how his son had ended up on death row.

CHAPTER 5

Rebecca stood next to the casket of James Underwood, then pulled on a single latex glove. His lips had dehydrated during the night, causing a narrow separation between them. The funeral mass was scheduled for two o'clock at a Catholic church in Marble Falls. The family was due shortly for their final viewing, giving Rebecca just enough time for the touchup.

From a small container, she dipped a dab of flesh-colored wax onto the tip of a spatula. Depositing the wax onto the heel of her gloved hand, she kneaded it with the blade. The action and the warmth of her skin quickly rendered the wax soft and pliable. With the edge of the blade, she scraped off a thin line, then pressed it into the narrow gap. Easing the man's lips together with her fingertips, she held them in place until the wax adhered. Finally, with the gap closed, she feathered the edges until its flesh color blended perfectly.

James Underwood was ninety years old. His hands, dotted with age spots, were crossed comfortably on his abdomen. Someone had placed a rosary between his thumb and index finger. The casket's gray velvet interior complemented the rich charcoal color of his suit. His tie was perfectly knotted. His cuffs extended beyond the sleeves of his jacket in a narrow, uniform strip of white. The man's reddish hair was neatly combed, his glasses free of smudges, his nails trimmed and filed. Not even a piece of lint from the velvet interior dotted the suit's dark fabric.

When the Underwood family arrived, Jake Spencer escorted them to the chapel. The daughter tucked her hand in the bend of Jake's arm as they proceeded up the aisle. Two generations of Underwoods trailed behind. As the group neared the casket, one of the grandchildren sighed, "Oh, Papa."

Rebecca and Jake stepped aside while the family said their goodbyes. When the tearful process was over, Rebecca lifted the spray of red carnations. In a practiced movement, Jake removed the velvet overlay, folded it, then tucked it out of sight inside the casket. As the family watched, he unpinned a small envelope attached to the underside of the casket's valance. On it, Jake had written, Remove tie clip. Leave wedding ring and rosary. It was a fail-proof procedure meant to avoid a dreaded error, burying a personal item that should have been removed and returned to the family.

Jake placed the tie clip in the envelope, then handed it to the daughter. Then he tucked the valance inside the casket and closed the lid quietly. Rebecca returned the spray, positioning it in the center of the casket. Finally, with the pallbearers walking alongside, they rolled the casket out the side door of the chapel to the porte-cochere. The family and close friends walked behind. The silent procession halted at the rear of the funeral coach where the pallbearers placed the casket inside.

Minutes later, as Rebecca looked on, the procession crept off the parking lot. Her cell phone vibrated in her pocket, but she let the call go to voicemail. Returning to the chapel, she locked the heavy double doors behind her. She was turning off multiple banks of lights when Kevin Murray, a newly hired funeral director, approached. "There's a gentleman here to see you. He's waiting in the reception area. I'll finish up in here."

The visitor was Liam Montoya, a longtime acquaintance, and a deputy sheriff. He was dressed in uniform—tan shirt and pants, brown boots, and a western hat which he had removed and held at his side. Rebecca was surprised to see the deputy. Law enforcement officers never made death notifications in person, not to funeral homes anyway. "Afternoon, Liam. What brings you here?"

"Have I caught you at a good time?"

"You have." The two walked side by side past the arrangement office and the door to the casket selection room, chatting about the heat and the unlikely chance of rain. In her office, Rebecca offered the deputy iced tea which he declined. They sat on a sofa positioned under a window. "I don't see any papers in your hand, Deputy Montoya. Is it safe to say you're not here with a warrant?"

Liam chuckled. "No, Rebecca. Despite your vast criminal record, I'm not here to arrest you."

"So what's going on?"

"About an hour ago, dispatch got a request for a welfare check. It was from Nichole. Apparently, she's out of town and hasn't been able to reach her dad. She asked us to send a deputy by his apartment to check on him. I was nearby, so I took the call. Russell's SUV was in the parking lot, but he didn't answer the door. He still drives a white Tahoe, right?" Rebecca nodded. "I called Nichole with an update, but she insisted that something is wrong."

Rebecca sighed. "Liam, you know how Nichole is."

"Oh, yes. If I had to give the girl an alias, I would pick Drama Queen. That's why I didn't go kicking in the man's door."

Rebecca's phone vibrated again. "Excuse me." She retrieved the device from her pocket and frowned. "It's Russell's dad." She accepted the call. August, too, had been unable to reach his son and was growing concerned. "I'll go to his apartment, August, and check on him. I know where Russell hides a key." She promised to phone him when she knew more, then ended the call. It was then that she remembered the call that had gone to voicemail. It was Nichole making a tearful plea for Rebecca to check on her dad.

Fifteen minutes later, Rebecca and Liam were standing outside the door of Russell's apartment. It was an old complex, only forty units, but was clean and well maintained. Russell's apartment was a ground floor unit at the end. His vehicle was parked nearby, but the door went unanswered when Rebecca knocked repeatedly. She retrieved a key from a hiding place on the lantern next to the door and used it.

"Russell," she called through the narrow opening. "Are you here?" Easing open the door, she peeked around the edge, calling to him again. When he still did not answer, she and Liam entered. "Russell?"

The apartment was dark, and the air was stuffy, although the air conditioner unit hummed. Blinds and curtains were closed, and all the lights were off. Rebecca's eyes adjusted to the dimness, then she spotted him. Russell was either asleep or passed out in a recliner, a closed notebook computer in his lap.

"Russell," she said softly, not wanting to startle him. She felt badly for the man. He looked vulnerable stretched out in the faded chair, snoring quietly. He wore black gym shorts, a wrinkled white tee shirt, and leather sandals. Clearly, he had not shaved for days, and his thinning hair looked drab and dry. A beer can sat on the chairside table. Rebecca felt a sense of relief that there was only one, but then noticed more in the trash basket. She said his name again, touching his shoulder.

The sleeping man's eyelids fluttered, then popped opened. His fist shot out, grazing Rebecca's thigh. "What the hell? Get out of here!"

Rebecca jerked back, shocked. "Russ, it's me. I'm sorry." He struggled with the chair, trying to stand, but the footrest was engaged. "I didn't mean to startle you."

Liam stepped between them. "Hey, man. It's okay. Calm down." He placed his hand on Russell's shoulder. "It's okay. Sorry to barge in on you." Russell stopped wrestling with the chair, but his chest still heaved. "Nichole has been trying to reach you. She's worried."

"So she called the Sheriff's Office?" Russell yanked the lever and disengaged the footrest, popping the chair noisily to an upright position. "Damn. That girl. She is driving me crazy. So what are you doing here?" he demanded, as if he were just then noticing Rebecca.

"August called me."

Russell cursed under his breath. "Apparently my dad hasn't heard about the divorce." Noticing the computer in his lap, he tossed it onto the end table, knocking the empty beer can to the floor. "This is just great." Annoyed but calmer now, he picked up the can and dropped it in the trash. "I wish those two would back off."

Liam opened the curtains on the front window, then turned on the ceiling fan. "It's like a cave in here." He sat on the sofa, positioned close to the recliner. "People are worried about you, man. You need to answer your phone. You had anything to eat recently?"

"Not today." His composure regained, Russell rubbed his eyes and blinked repeatedly. "Nichole brought a bag of stuff over here before she left town." He twisted his lips in disgust. "What the hell is hummus anyway?"

"Beats me." Liam laughed. "Sounds like you need to get out of here and go grocery shopping."

As the men talked, Rebecca turned on a table lamp, then walked to Russell's desk to turn on another. Next to a stack of unopened mail were two letters, each marked COPY, both from Russell. The one on top was addressed to the Board of Pardons and Paroles, the other to the governor's office. "Do you mind?" she asked, pointing. When Russell shrugged, she picked up the letter to the Board and read it. The wording was initially crisp and professional, but then began to ramble. A similar version had been sent to the governor. They were letters of protest against a moratorium on executions. Below the signature line was an Enclosure designation. "What did you include with the letters?"

Russell looked up at Rebecca, his eyelids heavy. "A picture of Callie, and one of Derek Jaxson with his family." He took a deep breath, then his eyes blurred with moisture. "They have to see them. Without pictures, Callie and Derek are nothing more than names." He sat silently for a moment, then reached for his computer. "Look at this." He opened the device in his lap and clicked a few keys. "It's this damn bunch. Texas Innocence Initiative. They're behind all this talk about halting executions."

"They've been pushing for that for years," Liam said, patiently.

"I know that," Russell barked. "But some lawmakers are starting to listen to them now. And they are getting a lot of media attention. Oh, and guess who's one of their mouthpieces, Becca. Emma Donovan. Could anybody be more biased than her?" He closed the computer and set it aside. "Innocence Initiative." Russell spat out the words. "Jude Donovan is not innocent. He is an accomplice in a double murder. If it wasn't for pressure from groups like that, he'd be scheduled for death by now." Russell slumped forward, running his hands through his unkempt hair. "I don't know how much more of this I can take, Becca. I miss her so much. It will be two years next month, and I still have this picture in my head. Callie lying on that filthy floor. Scared. Bleeding. Dying." His face collapsed in misery. Tears streamed down his face. He wiped them away, carelessly and angrily.

For once in her life, Rebecca conceded, Nichole had not overreacted. Her concern about her father was justified. Rebecca had never seen Russell in this condition. Grief and frustration. Anger, prescription drugs, and alcohol. I don't know how much more of this I can take.

Rebecca returned the letters to the desk, next to the stack of mail. "I'll get you some Kleenex, Russ."

She walked down a short, dim hallway. It was a two-bedroom apartment, but Rebecca had no trouble determining which was Russell's room. The bed was unmade, the linens crumpled, a pillow on the floor. The closet door stood open, its contents a jumble. The trash can overflowed with balls of crumpled paper and beer cans. On the dresser, two prescription bottles stood next to a half-empty bottle of Ozarka. Russell had never been neat and organized, but this level of disarray was out of character.

"But I'm not here to snoop." Rebecca went directly to the nightstand and opened the top drawer. There it was. A black, nine-millimeter Glock pistol. She picked it up, then ejected the magazine into her hand. Fifteen rounds. Also in the drawer were a box of ammunition and another loaded magazine.

Frowning, Rebecca weighed her options. Sneaking the pistol out of the apartment was impossible. She had no place in her clothes to conceal it. Leaving the firearm in the drawer and saying nothing was unacceptable. With no other clear option, she returned to the living room and stood next to Russell's chair. The tears were gone, his emotions tamped down again. She held out the gun. "This was in your nightstand. Do I need to be concerned?"

"Well, that's just great," Russell snarled, then yanked the chair lever with his right hand. The footrest popped up noisily. Crossing his arms across his abdomen, the man shook his head, appearing disgusted and annoyed, even insulted. "You think I'm suicidal? Really, Becca?"

"I don't know, Russ. You're in a lot of pain, I know that. You're mixing alcohol and prescription drugs. My guess is that you are isolating yourself. So I'm concerned, yes. And so are your daughter and father." She held up the gun. "Having this in the apartment is not a good idea. For now, anyway."

He shrugged. "Take it, if it'll make you feel better." When a voice crackled over Liam's radio, Russell said, "Looks like the deputy needs to get back to work. You do too." With the remote, he turned on the television. "And I'm done talking."

Rebecca placed the pistol and magazine inside her purse. When she and Liam reached the door, she paused, the bag weighing heavy on her shoulder. "Callie loved you, Russ. You loved her with all your heart, but this is not the way to show it."

"Don't lecture me," he said flatly, staring at the television. "I'm making sure that my daughter gets justice. That is more than you can say." Resigned, he increased the volume. "And, Becca, you don't think that's the only Glock I own, do you?"

CHAPTER 6

To avoid the IT-expert his partner had hired, Mac McKeon was working from home again. The guy and his jargon grated on Mac's nerves, but he had to admit that the company's website had never looked or functioned better. Earlier that morning, Mac had scheduled a trip to the Donovan ranch with a topnotch photographer, then emailed Lester for approval of the date and time. Then he had contacted a select group of high-volume land brokers. Mac didn't want a bunch of lightweights wasting his time or intruding on Lester and Emma. He had also emailed several of his own clients looking to buy. Each had expressed interest, but an oil and gas man from Dalhart was eager for a tour.

Mac looked up when he heard a tap on the door trim. Catherine entered with a mug of coffee in her hand. She was dressed for work, but obviously not in a hurry to get there. The morning was practically over. She had a speaking engagement that night, but Mac couldn't remember where. For years, his wife had traveled throughout the state promoting Texas Times Monthly. She served on advisory boards and was a trustee for several foundations. Now she was a sought-after speaker and panelist, addressing topics related to business, politics, workings of the legislature, and criminal justice. His wife was an impressive, accomplished woman.

"Can you take a break?" Catherine set the mug on a Texas Longhorns coaster next to Mac, then took a chair in front of his desk. "We've been spread a little thin lately. We hardly have time to talk these days."

Mac removed his glasses, set them aside, then leaned back in his chair. "I agree."

"Do you have time for lunch?"

"Sorry, honey. I have too many emails and phone calls out." Mac gave his wife a warm, admiring smile. She was wearing a black and cream silk dress. The abstract pattern was subtle but eye-catching. The simple gold necklace and earrings were a gift from him. The pieces were her favorites, and she wore them often. "You look pretty. I like that dress. Where are you speaking tonight?"

"Headliners Club," she answered, her tone unenthusiastic. "It's a Chamber of Commerce deal. I'd love for you to go, but don't feel obligated. You have a lot on your plate."

Mac took a drink of coffee. "Can I let you know later?"

"Sure. Attire is business casual." Catherine checked her watch. "Sierra should be arriving for her interview about now. What do you think about her going back to work?"

"It's not a good idea. Not until the divorce is over."

"You're probably right," Catherine acknowledged. "But I guess we need to support her decision."

"I don't," Mac snapped. "I'm her father. I'm not about to stand by and let Sierra Catherine make a mistake if I'm sure that's what she's about to do."

"Point taken."

"Getting her resumé out there is one thing," Mac continued, "but accepting an offer is another." His wife's nod was almost imperceptible. "Starting a new job is hard enough under the best of circumstances. Sierra has to worry about Graham Hollister lobbing a grenade into the middle of her day."

An email appeared in Mac's inbox. It was from Lester. Emma and I are scheduled to see Jude that day. How about the following? Same time. Mac typed out a quick response. Of course. Have a safe trip. Jude is fortunate to have parents like you and Emma. He released a deep, protracted sigh and pressed send. "A man can't protect his family from everything, but he has to do what he can."

"Are we still talking about Sierra?"

"What?"

"Is there something troubling you, honey? You haven't been yourself the last couple of days."

Mac pushed the keyboard out of the way, then settled his forearms on the desk. "Are you familiar with a death penalty case in Harris County involving a man named Jude Donovan?"

Catherine's brows narrowed in a frown. "Jude Donovan. Nothing comes to mind. Did we cover his case in Texas Times?"

"I don't know. It involves a double murder at a convenience store on Interstate 10."

Catherine shook her head slowly. "Maybe if I had a few more details. Why are you asking?"

"Jude Donovan's parents are my clients. They own the ranch I listed near Kerrville."

"Mac, no." Catherine's eyes widened in shock. "Your clients' son is facing capital murder charges?"

"The trial is over. Jude's been on death row for six months."

"How dreadful." Catherine's tone was low and breathless. "How did you find out?"

"Lester told me. That's why he and his wife are selling their ranch. To pay attorneys and hire an investigator. They're convinced their son is innocent."

"Did they speak with you in confidence?" Catherine asked, always respectful of privacy concerns.

Mac leaned back in his chair, swiveling it at an angle. His conversation with Lester the day in the barn had not been confidential, but it had an emotional resonance that lingered. Initially, Mac had been reluctant to ask questions. Then it had become clear that Lester wanted, needed to talk. For half an hour, they had sat side by side on a hay bale.

"The murders happened two years ago," Mac began. "A thug named Calvin Canon went into a convenience store to rob the place. The guy was a career criminal out on parole. The clerk recognized him, and when Canon pulled out a gun, the clerk went after him with a baseball bat. There was a violent fight. Canon got bashed in the head multiple times, but the clerk was shot during the struggle. There was a customer in the store at the time — a teenage girl named Callie Shane." Mac paused, allowing the image of Lester's suffering expression to surface. "Canon shot the girl twice, most likely by accident. She died on the scene. The clerk died on the way to the hospital."

"What a tragedy. And Canon? What happened to him?"

"He collapsed outside the store and died on the sidewalk."

"Unbelievable. An armed robbery and three people end up dead." Catherine stared out the window, her eyes narrowed in thought. She appeared puzzled when she looked at Mac again. "How was Jude Donovan involved?"

"If you believe him, Jude wasn't involved at all. He was brought in for questioning after eyewitnesses provided the police with a vehicle description and a partial license plate number."

"So he denied being there?"

"No. Jude admits to being parked outside the convenience store, but he denies having anything to do with Calvin Canon or the robbery. He was getting ready to go inside, but he sped away when he heard gunfire."

"And somebody got his license number."

Mac nodded. "Callie Shane's sister. She was putting gas in her car."

"How awful. She heard her sister being shot. That poor girl."

"Her name is Nichole Shane. At Jude's trial, she testified to seeing Canon near the passenger side of Jude's car, before Canon entered the store. But another witness testified that Canon actually got out of Jude's vehicle."

Catherine rolled a tiny gold bead on her necklace back and forth between her thumb and forefinger, the picture of intensity. "The witnesses couldn't have been standing that far away," she said, more to herself than to Mac. "Canon either got out of Jude Donovan's car, or he didn't."

"The prosecutor convinced a grand jury that Jude was Canon's accomplice."

Mac recalled how Lester had closed his eyes and pressed his hand to his forehead. The district attorney's words are etched in my mind, Mac. 'Jude Donovan is a party to the offense of a murder carried out in the course of a robbery. Therefore, he is being charged with capital murder in the deaths of Derek Jaxson and Callie Shane. My office intends to seek the death penalty.' Eighteen months after his arrest, Jude had been tried, convicted, and sentenced to death.

The trial attorneys, according to Lester, hadn't been worth half the fortune he and Emma had paid them. With their cash all but depleted and their retirement accounts drained dry, they saw no other option but to put the ranch on the market, land that had been in Emma's family for seventy-five years.

"What Jude Donovan said could be true," Mac continued. "It could be untrue. One thing is certain. Continued investigation into the case and the appeals process will be massively expensive and could be heartbreakingly disappointing."

Mac pictured Lester rising from the hay bale to scoop up oats and let Reno nibble them from his palm. Jude is giving up hope, Mac, but Emma and I are not. We never will. Our son is innocent. Jude was not with that SOB when he murdered Derek Jaxson and Callie Shane.

"Unthinkable," Catherine said. "Their son is on death row. And ironically, Mac, if the crime had occurred somewhere other than Harris County, there is a good chance that Jude would not have been charged with capital murder at all. If I'm not mistaken, there are more inmates on death row from Harris County than from anywhere else in the state."

"And Jude is only twenty-five, Catherine. Younger than Brooke." Mac looked at the email still open on his computer. "Emma and Lester are going to Livingston to visit Jude at the end of the week. Those good people are living a nightmare with no end in sight."

Mac's cell phone rang. He retrieved it from under a stack of papers. It was Sierra. Was she finished with her job interview already? He put the call on speaker. "How did your interview go?"

"Dad, where are you?" Sierra's tone was brusque with urgency.

"I'm at home. What's wrong?"

"Get to the club right away. Graham's there — or he will be any minute."

Mac popped out of his chair. "I'm on my way." With the phone on speaker, he rushed through the house toward the garage, Catherine close behind. "Talk to me, Sierra."

"Graham is in town on business. I had no idea. He left a message on my cell that he was picking up Michaela for lunch."

"He knows she's at the club?"

"Yes, Dad," she snapped. "They talk, you know."

In the garage, Mac pressed a button on the door opener and spoke over the rumble. "What time is her swim lesson over?"

"Eleven-thirty. You need to hurry, Dad."

There were three traffic lights between their home and the club. Mac caught each one on green. He nodded to the security guard at the entrance, then drove through without slowing. The Tahoe bounced over a speed bump and lurched to a stop in the first available parking spot. He and Catherine rushed down the sloping sidewalk to the fenced pool area. It was eleven-forty.

Mac yanked open the tall metal gate, ignoring the young man at the check-in table. He and Catherine rushed down a short corridor between the bathhouses, emerging into the glaring sun. The pool was crowded with children and adults. He scanned the area, searching. Just as before, he could not spot Michaela. "Where is she? Catherine, I don't see her."

Mac spotted a friend of Sierra's sitting on the edge of the pool, her feet dangling in the water. "There's Jenny. Maybe she's seen her." He and Catherine threaded their way through a cluster of children. Mac's pulse was racing. He did his best to sound calm. "Jenny, have you seen Michaela?"

The young woman looked up and shielded her eyes from the glare. "Hi, Mac. Catherine. She was in the café a few minutes ago."

"Who was she with?" Catherine asked.

"Anna Rose and her nanny."

Catherine walked away without a word. Mac calmed himself, then asked if Jenny had seen Graham.

"Graham? No." Jenny's expression suddenly changed. She nodded in the direction of the gate. "There he is. He just walked in."

Mac looked over his shoulder just as Graham Hollister emerged from the shadows. He sauntered toward the lifeguard stand. Heads turned his way. The man had a strong, dauntless air about him. He was on the tall side of six feet and powerfully built. As always, he was well dressed, today in gunmetal jeans and a pale gray shirt. On the surface, Graham Hollister appeared relaxed, easy going, approachable. The truth was that the man was overbearing, manipulative, and as hard as nails.

Mac walked briskly back toward the lifeguard stand, determined to intercept Graham. He would keep his composure, avoid a confrontation. People were looking, and there were children everywhere. He waited until Graham was a few yards away before acknowledging him. "Well, look who's here. What are you doing in town?"

"Hello to you, too, Mac." Graham nodded and grinned. "I came to take my daughter to lunch."

"That's too bad. Michaela already has lunch plans."

"I'm sure she'll change them when she finds out her dad's here." Graham continued walking toward Mac, hands in the pockets of his jeans.

"Did you clear this with Sierra?"

"Why so hostile, Mac? We're staying right here in Tarrytown." Graham's smile was smug. "I'm not taking her to Vancouver."

Mac's right arm shot out. He jabbed the man hard in the chest with his palm, pushing him against a towel bin. Graham stumbled but recovered quickly. He took a single step toward Mac, but then stopped when a passing lifeguard approached cautiously. "Is everything okay, Mr. McKeon?"

"Yeah," Mac answered. "Sure. Everything's fine."

Smoothing his shirt front, Graham smiled at the lifeguard. "We're good. No problem here." He nodded in the direction of the café. "There's my daughter." Brushing past Mac, he clipped him with his elbow.

Mac watched as Catherine and Michaela walked toward them, hand in hand. Michaela looked upset. The child flinched when a grackle darted past, snatching a French fry from an abandoned basket. Her hair was tousled and windblown. She was barefoot and wearing a turquoise cover up. What is Catherine doing? Mac thought, more than irritated. Why hadn't she kept Michaela in the café? Why was she bringing her out to see him?

Graham was a few yards ahead of Mac. He greeted Catherine, then ran his hand over Michaela's head. "How's my girl?"

"Hi, Dad. I didn't know you were coming for a visit."

"I didn't know either until this morning. I came to take you to lunch."

Michaela looked up at her grandmother. "But I'm having lunch with Anna Rose."

Graham stroked her head again. "You can change your plans, though. Right? I'm sure your friend would understand."

"But, Gran, we just ordered chicken tenders."

Reassuringly, Catherine squeezed Michaela's hand. "That sounds delicious. And it wouldn't be polite for you to cancel on Anna Rose." She cut Graham a look. "Your dad understands. Don't you, Graham?"

Aware that people were watching, the man flashed a smile. "Of course, I do. Your mom must have forgotten about your lunch plans."

Mac fumed. Sierra didn't forget, you sonofabitch. You didn't even talk to her.

Catherine squeezed Michaela's hand again, then let go. "Mom will be here at one o'clock. Enjoy your lunch. Say goodbye to your dad."

The child offered a tight, nervous smile, and wiggled her fingers. "Bye, Dad."

"Bye, Sunshine."

When Michaela was out of earshot, Catherine said tersely, "She saw what just happened between you two. And so did everyone else. Graham, you need to go."

"Not a problem." Walking away, he said over his shoulder, "Michaela will be with me in a few days anyway."

Catherine put a restraining hand on Mac's forearm. "Let it go."

"You should have kept Michaela in the café. Why did you put her in the middle of that?"

"Your little shoving match, you mean?" She released Mac's arm and spoke in a low voice. "Go check on your granddaughter. She is obviously upset."

"I noticed." Mac took a deep, calming breath. "I'll be right back."

"Mac, wait." Catherine stood close, so as not to be overheard. "It wasn't the scuffle that upset her. I told her you and Graham were just kidding around. She got upset when she found out Graham was here." She touched his arm again, this time tenderly. "Go talk to her. No one can reassure Michaela like you can."

Mac cupped his hand over his wife's, squeezed it, then handed her his car key. "I won't be long."

Three orders of chicken tenders were being delivered when Mac approached the table. Michaela's face lit up when she saw him. He said hello to Anna Rose and introduced himself to her nanny. "I need to talk to Michaela for a minute. We won't be long."

At a corner table, away from the din, Mac lifted the child onto his lap. "Those chicken tenders look good, huh?"

She nodded. "Is my dad gone?"

"Yep. Headed back to Plano. Gran said you seemed upset when she told you he was here." Michaela nodded reluctantly, almost undetectably. "Mind telling me why?"

The child spoke so softly, Mac had difficulty hearing her over the racket. "I was afraid."

The words jabbed at Mac's heart. "Afraid of what, sweetie?"

"My dad." Michaela leaned close, putting her lips to her grandfather's ear. "I'm afraid he'll take me on vacation again."

CHAPTER 7

The Highline Grill was situated on the water's edge, so close that once in Rebecca Grant's memory the place had all but washed away when Lake Travis rose above flood level. The owners had threatened to tear the building down, but everyone knew it was just frustration talking. The Highline was George and Addie's private fishing hole where they snagged all the area gossip, then served it hot and spicy to the Highline regulars.

In the foyer, Rebecca walked past the Seat Yourself sign, crossed the nearly empty dining room, then sat at a table for four by the lake view windows. She was meeting her friends Bob and Myra Perriman for dinner. As soon as Jake Spencer could slip away from a visitation at the funeral home, he would join them too.

Rebecca checked her watch. She was early, but grateful for some alone time. She was still tired from the trip to Hillsboro for August's birthday party. The drive home had seemed interminable. What a disaster, the confrontation with Russell. And if Rebecca never saw Nichole again, it would be too soon. *What did you say to him, Rebecca? What are you even doing here?*

Rebecca shoved aside the memory and gazed out the window. She had an unobstructed view of the lake. Blue-gray water rippled gently toward the shoreline. Wet leaves and the debris stirred by recent rains piled against smooth oval rocks and jagged boulders. Dusk powdered the hills across the lake with a silvery mist. Next door at the marina, boats of varying kinds and sizes rested motionless in their slips. George and Addie's weathered sign welcomed boaters to the Highline Grill. Shirts, Shoes, and Smiles Required. At the bar near the far wall, three men were perched side by side on sturdy oak stools, their sandaled feet resting on a brass rail in need of polishing. Rebecca was reminded of how Addie and George had come up with the name Highline Grill. "When we decided to buy this old building and put in a restaurant, we could just imagine the music playing, the tables full, and folks lined up at the bar, like birds on a highline."

As Addie approached, Rebecca wiggled a greeting with her fingers and smiled. Addie was a pudgy little woman in her late sixties with sternly styled red hair, and a face that had wrinkled like an orange left out in the sun.

"Where's that handsome Jake Spencer?" Addie asked, smiling. " We had coffee together this morning. Said he was meeting you here tonight."

"He'll be here shortly. He's overseeing a visitation. The Perrimans are joining us too."

"Great. I haven't seen Bob and Myra in a while. What can I get you to drink, hon?"

"Iced tea, I think."

"I'll bring it right out. I have your favorite tonight," Addie said, penciled eyebrows rising. "Fried catfish. Nice and crispy. Just the way you like it. I tweaked the tartar sauce," she announced, walking away. "Let me know what you think."

"Will do." Rebecca put an elbow on the table, dark oak and marred. She propped her chin in her palm and sighed. Her workday had started obscenely early. At three in the morning, she had made a death call, then waited on the family in the afternoon. The deceased and his wife had bought a vacation home in Sparrows Cove less than a year ago. "We came as often as we could," the widow had said with regret. "I just wish we'd had more time."

Addie returned with Rebecca's tea, dark as caramel, and a tiny bowl of freshly sliced lime. "Here you go, hon."

"Thanks, Addie." Gazing out the window, Rebecca caught her reflection in the glass. Her image reminded her that she was forty-five years old, but that she looked far better than even six months ago. Grief had exacted not only an emotional toll, but also a physical one, obliterating her appetite and her strength.

Myra, soon after Callie's funeral, had said, "Becca, you know more about grief than I do, for sure. You also know how I hate to read self-help books. But because I love you, I'm reading a book about grief." She had gone on to summarize what she was learning, that the process takes about eighteen months, that grief comes in stages. "Four or five, maybe." She admitted to forgetting what the stages were called but said that the last one was resignation. "Or maybe it's called acceptance. I'm not sure." Then she had promised to be at Rebecca's side through all the stages, no matter what they were called, and that when Rebecca reached the final stage, they would mark the milestone in some very special way.

And so they had. On a blustery afternoon last winter, Rebecca and Myra had driven to the cemetery together. Bundled in heavy jackets, warm boots and scarves, they had stood at the foot of Callie's grave, arms linked and eyes watering.

Rebecca had waited three months after the funeral to order her daughter's monument. She had wanted something special, but she had not had the strength to take on the task of designing it. Russell had pressured her for weeks, offering to take care of it himself. The last time he brought up the subject, she had turned on him and shouted, "Stop it! Do not mention the monument to me again. I will take care of it. Now leave me alone!" And in her own time, she had.

Consistent with many monuments in the cemetery's old section, the granite stone Rebecca had chosen was nearly square. The edges were roughly chiseled, not polished like the front and back surfaces. The images carved on the stone were recognizable to anyone familiar with the cove. But Rebecca held the engravings close to her heart. The scene captured her view from an expanse of windows in the rear of her home.

In the gently flowing water, in perfect script, were inscribed the words Callie Mae Grant. The reverse of the monument read SHANE. Below Callie's name, in smaller block letters etched amidst the waves, were her birthdate and date of death. In the foreground, the engraver had etched stones and boulders along the shoreline. On the left, he had captured the majesty and the intricate beauty of a towering tree known as the Lone Oak.

Callie had loved the tree, marveling at the way it drew boaters to the inlet just to get a look. Its long, sturdy branches soared and reached and bent. Numerous times over the years, Callie had sketched her treasured view of the cove, growing more pleased with each result. The final drawing had been completed the last week of her life. Each time Rebecca had gazed at the drawing, she could almost hear the branches of the Lone Oak creaking as a gust of wind whipped across the lake.

Before leaving for the cemetery that frosty winter day, Rebecca had placed the folded sketch inside a crisp linen envelope. Myra had sealed the envelope in plastic and then tucked it in the pocket of her jacket. At the cemetery, they had buried the treasure in precious Callie's grave. Often irreverent, Myra had wiped tears from her cheeks while offering a brief prayer, ending with, "Your mom is not alone, Callie. You can rest in peace."

As a funeral director, Rebecca had often encouraged those closest to the deceased to place a memento in the casket or in the grave. But not until Callie's death had Rebecca even begun to appreciate the comfort that simple gesture brought with it.

The hollow clatter of footsteps on the oak floor caught Rebecca's attention. She looked away from the window and instantly tensed. Her hand, where her chin still rested, tightened. Her nails pinched her cheek. It was Nichole. She and Addie were making their way across the dining room, chatting amiably. Nichole looked striking. Her black hair was pulled back and twisted into a casual up-do. She wore slim white jeans and a pale blue blouse that accentuated her shape.

"Rebecca is over there by the window, if you want to say hi," Addie said cheerfully.

"Thanks. I will." Nichole's smile had dissolved by the time she reached Rebecca's table, and her amiable tone had vanished. "What are you doing here?"

"Meeting friends for dinner," Rebecca answered coolly, not motioning to the chair opposite her or inviting Nichole to sit.

"Have you talked to Dad since you went to his apartment?" Nichole asked, standing with her hip cocked. "He's not doing well, in case you didn't know."

"So I gathered."

"Do you care?" she asked snidely.

"I'm not having this conversation with you, Nichole." Rebecca glared at the girl, refusing to look away.

"After all this time, he still misses you. God only knows why."

Uninvited, Nichole sat, turning sideways in the chair, strappy sandals flat on the floor. She looked as if she might need to make a run for the door at any minute. If only she would, Rebecca thought. Feeling no inclination to initiate chat, she sipped tea and gazed out the window.

"I stopped by his apartment this afternoon, just to check in with him. It wasn't even four o'clock and Dad was already blitzed." When Rebecca did not react to her dramatic word choice, Nichole continued. "He was slurring his words, raging about Jude Donovan. I know mixing alcohol with anti-depressants can be dangerous, but I don't know what to do."

"He needs professional help, Nichole." Rebecca offered nothing more, determined not to be dragged into Russell's problems yet again. If he were struggling with grief alone, she would have more compassion for him. But mixing drugs and alcohol was reckless and self-destructive. Russell knew better.

"We were watching the news together a few nights ago, and Dad got so upset." Nichole swiveled in the chair, facing Rebecca. "They were doing a story about some group in Austin. Texas Innocence something-or-other. They want to stop executions of people on death row." She leaned forward, her dark eyes widening. "Dad went into a rage. What if it was your loved one that got shot by one of those killers? What would you be saying then, you bunch of bleeding hearts?" Nichole turned toward the window to watch a sleek ski boat sidle up to the pier. "Rebecca, do you think Jude Donovan will be put to death?"

The question caught Rebecca off guard. It was the last thing she had expected Nichole to say. "I have no idea. And I refuse to dwell on it. It's up to the justice system to give Jude Donovan what he deserves."

"But I'll never get what I deserve, right?" Nichole's voice cracked. Still facing the window, she said, "That is what you think, isn't it?"

"Stop it," Rebecca demanded, her voice dropping to a harsh whisper.

"If we had left Galveston when we were supposed to, then we wouldn't have been at that convenience store at all." She looked directly at Rebecca, her tone now high-pitched, as if she might start crying. "It was just one in a long string of times when I didn't do what I was supposed to, right?"

Exactly, Rebecca thought bitterly, choking back the words. Only this time it cost Callie her life.

CHAPTER 8

The helicopter was a Bell 407, black as night with Lone Star Land and Ranch emblazoned in bold red letters. The aircraft had been repossessed by a bank in Dallas, so the lender had been more than eager to get it off the books when Mac made them a low-ball offer. At Austin Executive Airport, the pilot set the aircraft down, then taxied to the nearby hangar. Mac thanked him and apologized for the delay leaving Lufkin. "Damn lawyer. The closing could have been wrapped up in half the time if the buyer had left that guy in Memphis."

Traffic was heavy, so the drive to Tarrytown would take half an hour. He called Catherine and told her he was en route. Brooke and Bryant were coming for dinner. Phil Kuykendall would stop by later for coffee and dessert. The man still had not hinted at what he had on his mind.

Mac had just crossed over Interstate 35 when his cell phone rang. Three letters appeared on the touch screen. TWI. He frowned, then his brain engaged. Travis Wheeler Investigations. He accepted the call. "Evening, Travis. How are you?"

"I'm well, Mac. Have I caught you at a convenient time?"

"I'm alone. You can speak freely. What do you have for me?"

"I spoke with my associate in Dallas. His name is Caleb Baker. He can definitely handle the job for us. In fact, he said he will handle it personally."

"Are you sure he's reliable?"

"Guarantee it. Caleb is a father. He has a little girl about Michaela's age. When your granddaughter is in Plano with Hollister, Caleb will know where she is every second of the day."

"And what about when he comes here for visitation?"

"I'll handle the surveillance myself."

"I appreciate that, Travis. So what is our next step?"

"I'm picking up the watch in the morning. You'll be pleased. I'm sure. How do you want me to get it to you?"

"Deliver it to my office. Around ten?"

"Perfect. I'll download the app on your phone, then set up everything for you. Of course, Caleb and I'll do the same on our designated phones. As long as Michaela is wearing the watch, you have nothing to worry about, Mac."

"You're the expert," he said. "That's why I hired you." Mac ended the call, regretting that he had not hired the private investigator months ago. If he had, Graham would never have been able to sneak Michaela out of the country and into Canada. We stayed at Cynthia's house. She's my Dad's very close friend. She tucked me into bed every night.

◆ ◆ ◆

THE FAMILY GET TOGETHER was just what Mac needed. Sierra had a brisket in the smoker. The aroma made his mouth water. She had also picked up potato salad, beans, and coleslaw. Catherine had assembled a tray of pickles and onions, and made macaroni and cheese for Michaela. Brooke and her husband brought Mac's favorite beer, and a chocolate cake from Russell's Bakery. "For you, Catherine," Bryant had said, kissing her on the cheek. "But we are all hoping that you'll share."

Bryant Kittrell was an attorney in private practice. He specialized in estate planning and did some probate work as well. Mac directed clients to his son-in-law when he could, and so far he had not regretted it. Bryant's mother had died when her children were young. His grandparents had raised him. Lela Kittrell was still living, and Bryant was devoted to her. Being part of the McKeon family meant a lot to Bryant, and he made no effort to hide it. Mac did not have a lot in common with his son-in-law, but they shared the things that mattered. They would do whatever it took to protect the people they loved, and they both loathed Graham Hollister.

July in Austin did not invite outdoor dining, so after drinks on the terrace the family gathered inside for a casual meal. Sierra's brisket was exceptional. Perfect bark, juicy, and falling-apart tender. Brooke assembled Michaela a brisket fold-over, then put it on her plate with macaroni and cheese. Mac piled thick slices of beef on his plate, leaving just enough room for the sides.

Conversation bounced around the table like a ping pong ball. Sierra's job interview had gone well, although she did not have a feel for whether or not they would offer her the position. For her sake, Mac hoped they would, but for hers and Michaela's, he hoped she would turn it down. Catherine asked Brooke about the next dog show. It was coming up soon in Chicago. She and Bryant, along with another couple, would travel by private jet, a Citation XLS they owned with two additional couples. As was his habit, when there was room aboard the jet, Bryant asked Sierra and Michaela to join them.

"Uh ... let me think." Sierra pressed her index finger to her lips and pondered. "Private jet. Watching my four-legged nephew compete. Try to keep us away. Right, Michaela?"

Listening to the pleasant banter, Mac's thoughts returned to the confrontation with Graham Hollister. Shoving the man had been a reflex. Truth was, he had been as shocked as Graham by his reaction. Hopefully, only a handful of people at the club had witnessed it. Unfortunately, one of them was Michaela. Mac doubted that she believed her gran's explanation that they had been kidding around.

I have got to get control of this situation, Mac thought. One way or another, Graham Hollister is going to sign the custody agreement. The man has jerked Sierra around long enough.

Mac looked across the table at Michaela. Her eyes looked tired. He crooked his finger at the child, motioning for her to sit in his lap. "Are you ready to call it a day?" Michaela nodded, yawned, and nestled her head on his shoulder. Her whispered words still haunted Mac. I'm afraid of my dad. I'm afraid he'll make me go on vacation again.

◆ ◆ ◆

PHIL KUYKENDALL SET HIS empty dessert plate on the coffee table, then flicked chocolate cake crumbs from his shirt front. "Bryant picked that up at Russell's, huh? Delicious." He took a quick drink of coffee, then set the cup aside. Tonight, he was not a man given to chitchat. "About the reason I wanted to talk to you. First of all, I'm not here to ask for a donation to anything. And I'm not going to ask you to buy a table at next month's gala. Mac has already made it clear that he's not putting on a tux until the first cold front hits."

Catherine chuckled. "And surely you wouldn't eat my cake, Phil, then complain again about Texas Times Monthly being too hard on the governor."

"Of course not." Phil grinned. "You made it clear the last time I griped about an article that you're the president now, not the editor. I get that." He took another quick sip of coffee. "Ironic, though, that you would mention the governor. As you know, he'll be announcing in the next few weeks that he won't seek re-election. He has had a successful term by any measure, and he wants to leave office on a positive note. Forrest would be a fine governor, but his health is an issue."

Forrest Vinton was lieutenant governor. Mac and Catherine knew him well, and what Phil said was true. Forrest had suffered a heart attack recently. He had recovered well, but he and his wife had decided it was time for him to step away from state government and to spend more time with family. Normally, that particular reason for not running was code for the likelihood that the official either was not confident of re-election or that some really bad press was in the offing. But in Forrest's case, it was fact. The man wanted to spend more time with his family.

It was rare for the governor and the lieutenant governor to both be stepping aside, leaving fields wide open. Mac assumed that Phil was about to inform them as to who might be stepping onto the field, and to ask for their support.

"So to my point." Phil leaned forward, then looked from Mac to Catherine. "We've known each other for a long time. You know that I have the greatest respect for you both. You are pillars of this community. You have been for years." He turned to Mac. "I don't need to tell you what an impressive woman your wife is. Her intellect is as sharp as my mother-in-law's tongue. She's well versed on an array of issues and passionate about critical ones. She's persuasive and gracious, and she has a great sense of humor." The man shrugged his shoulders and raised both hands, palms up. "Like I said, Catherine is an impressive woman."

Mac pierced the final bite of cake with his fork. "I get it, Phil. I married up."

"That goes without saying." He waggled his head. "I did too."

No question, Mac thought. The man's wife was a justice on the Texas Supreme Court. "So where are we going with this, Phil?"

Propping both elbows on his knees, Phil laced his fingers. "Hopefully to the governor's mansion." He paused for effect. "Catherine, we want you to run for governor."

Stunned, Mac casually set his plate aside. We want you to run for governor. Phil had come here to ask Catherine to run for governor. Mac looked at his wife. Outwardly Catherine remained calm, but he knew that the effect of the words had to be physical. He tried to read her face, but it was impossible. What was she thinking? Governor. It did not cross Mac's mind to say, "You're kidding, right?" Catherine's name had been mentioned before for statewide office, but not for governor, as far as Mac knew.

When neither Catherine nor Mac responded, Phil said, "While you're absorbing what I said, I'll keep talking."

"Imagine that," Mac teased, attempting to relieve the tension.

Phil grinned and talked on. "No doubt you know that Ty Dixon is testing the waters, and he may decide to jump in at some point. But Ty is no competition for you, Catherine. First of all, he's a Democrat." The man waved off the fact with a flick of his hand. "Texas is a red state. Dixon can't get the job, Catherine, but you can."

When Catherine finally spoke, she took a stab at humor. "In case you aren't aware, I already have a job."

"And a fine one it is," Phil joked. "You've done yeoman's work at the magazine, Catherine. For twenty years. It's no secret, though, that you tried to step down last year, but the suits in Fort Worth talked you out of it."

Phil was right. Over Mac's objection, Catherine had agreed to a one-year extension of her employment contract. The magazine had experienced some turnover in management, and Catherine had concluded that her experience was needed until things settled down.

"Catherine, you are what the people of Texas want and deserve," Phil insisted. "We don't want a career politician this go round. We want a citizen governor. And I promise you," he said with total confidence, "the money will be there to assure that yours is an efficient, professional, and victorious campaign. Think about it. Texas has had two female governors. Miriam Ferguson and Ann Richards. Both Democrats. Catherine McKeon will be the first female Republican governor in the history of the Lone Star state. Governor McKeon. Nice ring to it, right? Seriously, Catherine, you are the ideal candidate for all the reasons I just mentioned. You know Texas business, politics, criminal justice, workings of the legislature. You have name identity and instant credibility." He looked at Mac and raised an eyebrow. "Admit it, Mac. The woman's perfect."

"Catherine is everything you just said and more," Mac agreed.

"Indeed, she is."

"You said we want her to run for governor. Exactly who is we?"

"People who matter," Phil said emphatically. "People who make things happen."

Phil left a few minutes later. Catherine saw him to the door while Mac checked on Michaela. The door to her room was ajar. Quietly, he nudged it open and peeked in. A nightlight glowed in the corner. As always, one of the child's bare legs was crooked over the jumble of bed covers. Her face was buried in her pillow, and her hair was a mess. Tomorrow morning, he would take receipt of a tracking device. He would learn how to use an app so he could keep his grandchild safe. A tracking device for a five-year-old. Damn you, Graham Hollister.

Walking down the hallway, Mac tugged his shirttail out of his pants. Unbelievable, he thought wearily. A bunch of the state's heavy-hitters had handpicked his wife to run for governor. There was no doubt Catherine could do the job. But would she be interested? Mac wasn't sure. He was certain, though, that her first words to him would be, "I can't believe this. They want me to run for governor. So what do you think? I have to consider it, don't I?"

The truth was, Mac admitted, tossing his shirt into the hamper, if he were forced to give her an answer tonight, it would be, "Tell them thanks, but no thanks." His family was in turmoil, and it would stay that way until everything was settled between Sierra and Graham. Mac wanted normalcy for his family, not the spotlight, particularly not for his innocent granddaughter.

CHAPTER 9

Gerald and Susanna Hewlett had lived in Sparrows Cove all their lives. They were high school sweethearts and had been married for twenty-five years. Now they were in the arrangement office at Baker and Grant Funeral Home. Rebecca sat opposite them securing vital statistics that would be needed for their daughter's death certificate. Zoe was not deceased, but she was on life support. Tomorrow, the machines keeping her alive would be turned off.

Zoe was twenty-three years old. Ten days ago, her roommate had found Zoe unconscious on the floor of her bedroom. Next to her body was the shaft of a ball-point pen and a small bag of light brown crystalline powder. Meth use was rampant in the county. Recently, twenty people were arrested in a multi-agency investigation of methamphetamine distribution and trafficking. Investigators had identified more than fifty individuals who sold or used meth that had been purchased from the ring. Zoe Hewlett had been among them.

Gerald Hewlett was a short, plump man with thinning hair and rounded shoulders. His expression was pained when he said that there was little chance Zoe would be able to breathe on her own when she was taken off the ventilator. "She could live only a few minutes, maybe a few days. No one knows."

Susanna Hewlett was a bulky woman. Her tone was devoid of emotion. "Even if she is able to breathe on her own, Zoe will have severe brain damage. Better that my daughter just slips away than to spend what's left of her life in a nursing home." Smoothing a tissue repeatedly between her fingers, she took in a deep, ragged breath. "So we need to get things in order."

"I'm so very sorry," Rebecca said.

"If anyone understands what it's like to lose a child, it's you."

"There's nothing worse." Rebecca nodded faintly, refusing to allow thoughts of Callie to fully surface.

"I read somewhere," Susanna continued, still smoothing the tissue, "that when a girl loses her parents, she's called an orphan. When a woman loses her husband, she's called a widow. But when a mother loses her child, there is no label. It's so unthinkable that no one knows what to call it."

"That never occurred to me," Rebecca responded. An uncharacteristic feeling of impatience was surfacing, and she made sure to hide it. She wished she had asked Jake to wait on the Hewletts. Worrying about Russell last night, Rebecca had slept poorly. Now her head was pounding, and she did not want to wander down an emotional path.

"I know what I would be called," Gerald said, reaching for his wife's hand. "Failure. I let my daughter down."

"No, you didn't," Susanna protested firmly but gently. "You recognized the signs right away. Weight loss. Nervousness. Anxiety. Even that Zoe's hair was thinning, for heaven's sake. You persuaded Zoe to go to rehab twice. You did all you could, Gerry."

"And so did Zoe," he said, defeated. "She just couldn't beat it."

"Those degenerates wouldn't give her a chance." Susanna released her husband's hand, then removed a folded paper from her purse. "We've decided against a traditional funeral. Zoe wanted to be cremated, so we'll honor her wishes. We'd like to have the memorial service here in your chapel. This is what we want on the memorial folder." She handed the paper to Rebecca. "My brother will preside. I guess that's what you call it. And those are the two songs we want. Zoe's cousin will sing them and play guitar."

Gerald turned to his wife and said, "What did we decide about Jessica?"

"Jessica is not speaking at the service." Susanna was adamant. "Jessica was Zoe's roommate, Rebecca. She found her the night Zoe overdosed."

"Jessica Hart?"

Susanna nodded. "Yes. Nichole's friend. Have you seen Jessica recently?"

Rebecca shook her head. "I've only seen her a few times since she testified at Jude Donovan's murder trial."

"You might not recognize her. She looks terrible." Susanna set her purse on the floor, then crossed her arms across her chest. "Jessica denies using drugs, but I don't believe her. Her mother says Jessica has never been the same since the night your Callie was killed."

"It was a horrific time," Rebecca responded, bristling at the suggestion that Jessica's problems, whatever they were, hinged on Callie's death.

"I don't know if you know this, Rebecca, but Zoe was supposed to have gone to Galveston that weekend, but she was just getting over a summer cold. I told her I didn't think it was a good idea and, to my surprise, she listened to me. Otherwise ..." Susanna allowed the words to trail off.

Otherwise, it might have been Zoe, Rebecca thought, who went inside to buy Nichole a bottle of water.

After Gerald and Susanna left, Rebecca was suddenly flooded with nagging questions and self-doubt. "Did I miss something?" she worried, returning to her private office, then dropping into her chair. Two years ago, the use of methamphetamines had been on the rise, but there had been no reason to suspect Jessica was involved, certainly not Nichole. Surely Nichole would not have invited Callie to go with them to the beach house if Jessica had been on drugs. "Oh, God, why did I let her go?"

Rebecca sealed off regrets and questions, then picked up her cell phone. Her parents were on a road trip to Jackson Hole, Wyoming. They would be gone for a month. She sent her mother a short text. I miss you. Where are you? She waited for a response. When none appeared, she set aside her phone, then picked up a bundle of mail. The mindless act of opening envelopes allowed her thoughts to wander.

Jessica has never been the same since the night your Callie was killed. Rebecca tried to distance herself from a growing sense of resentment. If Jessica Hart was making a mess of her life, it was her fault. Not Callie's death.

"I'm her mother," Rebecca muttered, ripping off the end of an envelope. "If anyone has a reason to run her life into the ditch, it would be me. Not some whining, weak-willed twenty-year-old with her whole life in front of her."

Rebecca tossed the letter back onto the stack. She was massaging her temples when her office manager, Karen Reynolds, appeared at the door. The title office manager was wholly inadequate to describe Karen's position at Baker and Grant. Not a day went by that Rebecca did not think to herself,

"What would we do without her?" Karen was a petite woman with strawberry blonde hair and a warm, genuine smile. Her personal qualities were many, but the most admirable, in Rebecca's view, was her demeanor. Karen was always pleasant, and nothing rattled her. Not ringing phones, a relentless flow of paperwork, or funeral directors appearing at her desk with one request or another.

In Karen's hand was a thick stack of cash. Rebecca glanced at it and said, "Been to the casino again, I see."

Chuckling, Karen thumbed the end of the bills, then handed the stack to Rebecca. "Mr. Terry paid the balance on his preneed contract. Twenty-two hundred."

"I'll put it in the safe." Rebecca set the cash next to the stack of mail. She handed Karen the paperwork detailing the prearrangements for Zoe Hewlett. "Mark this an imminent death, would you?"

"I'll take care of it." Karen glanced at the papers. "So young." She lingered a moment, then said, "Is something bothering you?"

Rebecca dropped the letter opener noisily into a cup of pens, then motioned to the chair in front of her desk. "Zoe overdosed on meth. She's on life support."

Karen sighed. "Just dreadful."

"Jessica Hart found her. They were roommates. Susanna suspects that Jessica does drugs too. Probably meth. Hearing that caused me to wonder if she was doing drugs when I let Callie go to Galveston with her and Nichole."

"It's reasonable to wonder about that," Karen responded. "But that's something you'll never know, Rebecca." She spoke tenderly, but with total conviction. "This you do know, though.

You were a loving, attentive, involved mother. You did everything you could to keep your daughter safe. It's easy for me to say that you can't blame yourself, but it's unjustified."

Rebecca nodded, then leaned back in her chair, grateful for this time with Karen, but noticing her furrowing brow.

"I'm remembering a young couple we served last year." Karen looked toward the ceiling, searching her memory. "The name is not coming to me. Their toddler fell down the back steps at their home."

"Madsen." Rebecca wondered where Karen was going with this. "Matt and Sara."

"That's it. What was the baby's name?"

"Umm." Rebecca frowned at her own failure to recall, but then said, "Was it Caitlyn?"

"Yes. Caitlyn. Sara left the baby on the back porch to get cinnamon rolls out of the oven. I remember her saying, 'Cinnamon rolls, for God's sake. I left my baby alone to keep cinnamon rolls from burning.' Do you recall what you said to her?"

Rebecca shook her head.

"You said, 'Sara, parents take their eyes off their children all the time and nothing happens. Tragedy does not strike. Caitlyn was napping on the porch in the sunshine. If you had known she would awaken, you would never have left her, not even for a second.'" Karen looked squarely into Rebecca's eyes. "Parents allow their seventeen-year-old daughters to go to the beach all the time, Rebecca, and tragedy does not strike. You did nothing wrong. You are not to blame."

"Thank you. I'm getting there." Resigned, she smiled at Karen. "It's only taken me two years."

"Time is the only healer." Karen stood. "If you don't need me for anything else, I'll be leaving for the day."

"Enjoy your evening. See you tomorrow."

Picking up the stack of bills from her desk, Rebecca secured them with a rubber band and a sticky note. $2200. Mr. Terry. Preneed contract. The safe was housed in a closet in her office. She pressed six digits on the keypad, pushed down on the lever, and swung the heavy door aside. Rebecca flinched, startled momentarily at the sight of a pistol atop a stack of files. The Glock.

You don't think that's the only Glock I own, do you, Becca?

She slid aside the loaded magazine, making room for the bills. "Oh, Russell. Please don't do anything you can't undo."

CHAPTER 10

Travis Wheeler described it as a super-smart watch as he removed it from the box. "This is the best of the best, Mac, and you paid a pretty penny for it. It's ideal for a child Michaela's size because of the slim design." He handed the watch to Mac. "You don't want a tracking device to draw attention to the child wearing it."

"Good point." The watch was as light as a feather. Mac ran his thumb over the face. It was not a digital screen. The face was round, white, and the numerals were in assorted colors. "Perfect look. Michaela doesn't like girlie clothes or jewelry. And the band is turquoise. You found her favorite color."

"Took me a while, but I got it done."

"Tell me how it works, without getting too deep in the weeds."

"Well, not sure if you know, but GPS works most effectively outside. But the technology in this watch enables tracking inside some buildings as well. It has extended battery life, and the software has all the features we need. The app is simple to use. You'll like it. You track her movements and location on Google maps. As long as Michaela is wearing this watch, you will know precisely where she is."

Travis spent the next half hour familiarizing Mac with the app he had downloaded onto his iPhone. "I think I've got it," Mac finally said. "All I have to do is sign in with my password and follow the prompts."

"Simple as that. And when Michaela is in Plano with Hollister, Caleb Baker will track her every movement. And when she's with Hollister here in Austin, I'll be all over it."

Mac put the box in a desk drawer. Travis had bought a small, velvet gift bag. Mac placed the watch inside it and pulled the drawstring. "Be sure Caleb understands. I'm not paying him to monitor Michaela's movement remotely. I expect him to be in striking distance in case something happens."

"He understands, Mac. Believe me." On the way out the door, Travis said, "In case I didn't mention it, that genius little watch is as waterproof as a Rolex."

Mac put the velvet bag in his briefcase. He would give the watch to Michaela tonight. He had not decided if he would tell Sierra that it contained a tracking device. Hollister intimidated her. If she knew, she would worry about him finding out and becoming more vindictive than he was already.

Mac's assistant stepped into his office, then laid a stack of well-organized mail on his desk. "Ben Morrow called while you were in your meeting. He's available to tour the Donovan ranch any time next week."

"I'll get in touch with Lester and set it up."

Mac reached his client on his cell phone. The background noise signaled that he was mobile. "Good afternoon, Lester. Have I caught you at a good time?"

"Sure, Mac. We're actually on our way to Austin." Lester explained that Emma had been asked at the last minute to fill in for another spokesperson for the Texas Innocence Initiative. "It's a panel discussion at Saint Edward's University."

The event was at four o'clock. "If Emma's up to it, maybe we could meet for drinks afterwards?" Mac suggested. "Or dinner? I'd like for Catherine to meet you."

"Emma is nodding her head. We'd like that. Things should wrap up about five o'clock. Text me the address, and we'll meet you there."

"Sounds great." Mac paused, then said, "Emma?"

"Yes, Mac."

"You're a courageous woman."

"I'm doing my best."

How did they bear it? Mac wondered, as he ended the call. Their son had been on death row for six months. Sometime in the next few days, they would drive to Livingston to see Jude. From what Mac understood, they would be confined to a cubicle and separated from their son by a sheet of Plexiglas. Death row offenders were allowed no physical contact. How did a man survive? Why would he want to?

♦ ♦ ♦

MAC HAD EXPECTED to see several panelists seated at the front of the classroom at Saint Edward's University, but there were only two. Emma and a gentleman named Clay Borger. He was a pleasant looking man, wearing a gray blazer over an open-collar blue shirt. His salt-and-pepper hair was short and neat. His dark frame glasses gave him a thoughtful look. Emma looked small sitting at the table next to Clay Borger, but there was something about her that was instantly credible.

Mac had phoned Lester again after their earlier conversation, asking if he could sit in. When Catherine wrapped up things at the office, she would meet them on campus, then the four of them would have dinner. Catherine had wanted to hear Emma speak, too, but could not break away. "I have so much work to do," she had said, uncharacteristically bewildered. "But I can't concentrate. They want me to run for governor, Mac." Phil had not set a deadline of any kind for when he needed an answer, but Mac was sure that sooner was better than later. The fundraising machine would have to fire up and kick into full speed.

Mac had known, when he asked Catherine to marry him, that she would not be a traditional wife. She had more drive than any woman he knew. He liked to think that he had supported her, that he had helped her achieve her professional goals. But could he do it now? No. Not if supporting his wife meant spending even a single day on the campaign trail. He had a company to run. Beyond that, he had a family to protect, and politics was a nasty business.

Before leaving his office, Mac had visited the Innocence Initiative's website. On it, he had found a link to details about Jude Donovan's case, and another link to details of the shooting at the convenience store. The shooter, Calvin Canon, was no doubt a thug and a career criminal. The store camera showed him brandishing a handgun, and the clerk striking him repeatedly with a bat. It didn't, however, capture the shooting of Callie Shane as she made a run for the door.

Mac shifted focus to the front of the classroom. After a brief welcome, the instructor introduced the guest speakers. At his conclusion, he invited the guests to make opening comments. Clay Borger spoke first, thanking the professor, then telling Emma that he was pleased to meet her.

"I'm a retired police detective," he began. "My father, Clayton Borger, was a cop too. He was part of a team that helped put a serial killer named Kenneth McDuff on death row. McDuff murdered between nine and fourteen innocent people. He was known as the Broomstick Murderer. He was put to death by the state of Texas because he deserved to die. Kenneth McDuff was a vicious predator, a brutal, hated man." Borger paused for emphasis, making eye contact with students in all parts of the room. "But McDuff's execution was not about revenge or vengeance, as death penalty opponents often claim. His execution was a matter of retribution, and there is a difference. Death was the price that McDuff paid for the murders he committed. Forfeiting his life was proportionate to the gravity of his crimes. I favor the death penalty for a number of reasons. One is that a killer like McDuff should not be allowed to lie around in a Texas prison, eat three meals a day, get medical care, sleep on clean sheets, and have visits with his family. Killers like him deserve to die. I take a lot of satisfaction in knowing that my father played a part in seeing that the Broomstick Murderer got what he deserved."

Borger's statement stilled the room. He spoke with reason and passion. Mac wondered how Emma would respond. The issue of revenge versus retribution, because it was based on morality or religious beliefs, was more difficult to address than other arguments for and against the death penalty.

Emma did not address the issue of retribution. Instead, she shifted the focus to the matter of deterrence. To Clay Borger she said, "Society owes a debt of gratitude to your father, Mr. Borger, for what he did to get Kenneth McDuff away from society and to put him behind bars where he belonged.

Everything you said about the man is true. Do I care that Kenneth McDuff is dead? No, I don't. But do his and other executions serve as a deterrent to murder?" Emma turned from Clay Borger and spoke directly to the students. "There is no conclusive proof that the death penalty is a better deterrent than life imprisonment. People who commit murder don't weigh different punishments before they act. McDuff certainly didn't. Fortunately, most states now have a sentence of life without parole. Prisoners who receive this sentence will never be released. Thus, the safety of society is assured without employing the death penalty."

Clay Borger waited courteously until Emma had finished her remarks. "I agree with Ms. Donovan that there are no conclusive studies that the death penalty is a deterrent to murder. But clearly, the execution of Kenneth McDuff deterred him from killing again. He's dead. If McDuff had been given life without the possibility, who's to say he wouldn't have attacked a corrections officer, or medical personnel, or another inmate. The death penalty made sure that no one would be harmed by the Broomstick Murderer again."

The discussion continued for another half hour. The students were attentive and took copious notes. A young man near the front recorded the event. Emma Donovan and Clay Borger were respectful of one another, informed, and passionate. They discussed the constitutionality of the death penalty, whether or not it was cruel and unusual punishment. Emma raised matters of race and income level of death row inmates, as well as the cost to taxpayers of the death penalty as compared to life without parole.

As time wound down, Emma was invited to speak last. She spoke to the issue of irrevocable mistakes. "Since 1973, almost 200 people have been exonerated and freed from death row in the United States. They were freed because they were later proven innocent. In the view of many, that is an alarming error rate. But I am not here to place blame. Jurors do the best they can with the evidence before them to arrive at a just verdict and an appropriate sentence. However, mistakes are made. If a mistake is made in a death penalty case, it could be irrevocable." She paused, her gaze scanning the room. "At this time, more than 180 inmates are on death row in Texas." Emma's voice wavered. Seconds passed before she recovered. "The Texas Innocence Initiative is calling for a moratorium on executions, allowing the state time to review its application of the death penalty. A growing number of fair-minded Texans are joining our movement. We invite you to be a part. If your time permits, become a volunteer. If not, write letters to the Board of Pardons and Paroles, to state lawmakers, and to the governor. I encourage you to let your voices be heard."

The applause from the students was vigorous and lengthy. Mac watched with growing admiration as Emma extended her hand to Clay Borger. It disappeared when both his hands closed around hers. Leaning close, the two exchanged obviously pleasant words. Clay Borger stood and helped Emma with her chair as the applause continued and the students rose from their seats.

Catherine was waiting outside the door when Emma, Lester, and Mac exited the classroom. She did not wait for introductions. Instead, she approached with a smile and extended her hand. "Emma, Lester, it's such a pleasure to meet you. I'm Catherine. I caught your closing comments, Emma. You could have heard a pin drop in that room."

Mac agreed. "You're a persuasive speaker, Emma. It was an honest, informative debate."

"I'm convinced that's the only way." Emma leaned against her husband when he put his arm around her shoulders, then sighed wearily. "I'm beat."

Lester hugged her tightly. "Can I buy you a drink?"

The Four Seasons Hotel was minutes away. Mac valeted his vehicle, then the four of them settled at a window table in the lounge. The room had a sweeping view of Lady Bird Lake and the bridge over Congress Avenue. After drinks were ordered and served, Catherine asked Emma how long she had known Clay Borger.

"Actually, I just met him tonight. He seems like a fine man. The last years he was on the force, he worked cold cases." She turned to her husband. "He offered to review Jude's case."

Lester spoke directly to Catherine. "I'm not sure how much Mac has told you, but our son's conviction is under direct appeal. To get a new trial or to get the conviction overturned, we need to present new evidence, evidence that could have influenced the jury's decision."

Catherine nodded. "When new evidence is uncovered, it's often because someone investigated the case with fresh eyes."

"That's what we're praying for."

Mac was preparing to ask when they would be visiting Jude when he noticed a man walking toward their table. He looked familiar, but Mac could not put a name with the face. The guy's graying hair was carefully combed across his crown, an attempt to conceal his bald spot. Rimless glasses added to the middle-aged effect. Mac acknowledged him with a nod when he paused at their table.

"Good evening, Catherine, Mac."

Catherine looked up and smiled. "Hello, Luther." She shook the man's hand. "Meet our friends the Donovans." Catherine introduced Emma and Lester. "Luther works the political beat for the *Statesman*."

Pleasantries were exchanged, then Luther Pelton apologized for interrupting. "Just wanted to tell you that I heard the news."

Catherine frowned, clearly puzzled. "I'm not following you."

"The governor's race. I hear you're tossing your hat in the ring."

Catherine tried unsuccessfully to hide her surprise. She recovered quickly, waggling her hand in a gesture of denial. "Then you know more than I do."

"But you're considering it," the man pressed.

Catherine picked up a menu. "All I'm considering at the moment is which appetizer to order." Luther Pelton chuckled, wished them a pleasant evening, then sauntered away. Catherine placed the menu back on the table and turned to Mac. "So much for keeping that topic under wraps."

CHAPTER 11

Rebecca opened the door to the preparation room, then turned on the overhead lights. The room's walls were painted linen white, the vinyl flooring a dove gray. Cupboards of all sizes lined the rear wall. Some shelves stored items found in any residence: sheets and pillowcases, towels, razors and shave cream, nail files and clippers, shampoo and conditioner. Other cabinets, though, stored items most people had never seen and likely did not care to. Plastic drums held embalming powder and autopsy compound. Well-organized shelves were lined with bottles of arterial fluid, dye, cavity fluid, and disinfectant soaps and sprays. Drawers held boxes of gloves, masks, and shoe covers. Others contained mouth-formers, designed to substitute for missing dentures, and small plastic caps which, when placed over the eyeball, kept lids from opening.

At the moment, Rebecca needed nothing more than a pair of gloves. She pulled them on, then stood next to the cot bearing Zoe Hewlett's body. Gently, she removed and folded the cot cover, dark blue and embroidered. Baker & Grant. Zoe had lived fewer than twenty-four hours after the ventilator had been turned off and the tubes withdrawn. Her body, so tiny it could have been that of a child, was wrapped in a white sheet. Rebecca eased the cloth back from her face and groaned. Impossible that this was the body of a young woman in her early twenties. She was emaciated and jaundiced. Her blonde hair, dry and straw-like, had fallen out in patches. Dehydrated lips cracked and peeled. With her mouth sagging open, Zoe's teeth were exposed, discolored and chalk-like. Meth-mouth.

What a waste, Rebecca thought. What a tragic waste.

The door to the prep room opened. Jake Spencer walked in, his expression grim. "Dreadful, huh?"

Rebecca recalled the first time she had met Jake. Her father had introduced them after Jake's first and only job interview. "Rebecca, meet Jake Spencer. Our search for a senior funeral director is over. I offered him the position, and he accepted it."

As he had been that day, Jake was impeccably dressed. He wore a dark blue suit, crisp white shirt, and a patterned tie in shades of blue and gray. At six feet four, Jake was an impressive man with a graceful masculinity. But it was his utter warmth and disarming genuineness that set him apart, not only as a funeral director, but also as one of Rebecca's dearest and most trusted friends.

"Were Zoe's parents at the hospital?" she asked, gazing down at the pitiful form before her.

"They were. Both seemed at peace. Gerald gave me this." Jake removed a necklace from his pocket. "He wants it cremated with her."

The necklace was a silver cross on a chain. As Rebecca placed it around Zoe's thin neck, she thought of little Nina Jones and finding the locket in her collapsed casket. Nina's father had wept when Rebecca placed the locket in his hand. Then he had hugged Rebecca and thanked her. "This will be such a comfort to my wife."

In accordance with her wishes, Zoe would be cremated. "We don't want viewing," her mother had said. "Only a memorial service." Baker and Grant did not have a crematory, so Zoe would be transferred to a nearby cemetery which did. Until the cremation permits were secured, her body would be refrigerated. The three-body refrigeration unit was positioned in an alcove off the far side of the preparation room. While Rebecca rolled the cot next to it, Jake lowered the middle door, then pulled the stainless-steel tray toward him. Zoe was so light that Jake could easily have moved her with no help from Rebecca. Instead, without a word, the two lifted the limp, lifeless body off the cot and placed Zoe gently on the tray.

While Jake slid the tray back inside the unit, checked the temperature, then closed the door, Rebecca stripped the cot and pillow of linens. "Did you schedule the arrangement conference?" she asked, shoving the linens into the hamper, then removing her gloves.

"This afternoon." Jake removed his gloves, then retrieved fresh linens from a cabinet. "Two o'clock."

"Perfect." Together, they readied the cot, then Jake smoothed on the cover. Rebecca checked her watch. "It's almost noon. Want to get some lunch?"

"Sounds good." At the sink, washing their hands with disinfectant soap, they decided on the Highline Grill.

Half an hour later, they were saying hello to Addie. "Aren't you a handsome pair?" she said, clutching menus to her chest. "You look like you could be brother and sister." She escorted them to a table by the window, handed them menus, and took their drink orders.

After Addie was out of earshot, Jake said, "Be glad you didn't make the removal. Nichole and Jessica were both there."

"I thought they might be." Rebecca offered a guilty, little grin. "I'm guessing you weren't actually out of the building when Karen took the death call."

"In my office signing payroll checks," she confessed.

Jake chuckled indulgently, then opened the menu. It was a formality. He always ordered the same entrée. Green salad with grilled trout.

"So was Nichole wailing?" Rebecca asked, perusing the lunch specials.

"No. She was being stoic for Gerald and Susanna."

"And Jessica?"

"Clinging to her boyfriend as if she might collapse."

Addie returned with glasses of iced tea. "Have you decided what you want?" She looked at Jake. "Let me guess. Green salad with lemon vinaigrette and grilled trout."

"I'm getting way too set in my ways, Addie. The next time I come in, I want you to surprise me."

Addie laughed. "Let's do it. You won't be disappointed." She turned to Rebecca. "What are you having, hon?"

"I'll have the salad, but with grilled chicken."

"Good choice." Addie retrieved the menus, then stepped closer, leaning forward. "I heard Zoe Hewlett died this morning."

"Sadly, she did," Rebecca answered quietly. News flew fast in Sparrows Cove.

"Poor little thing. She just couldn't beat it." Addie sighed, clutched the menus to her chest again, then reclaimed her smile. "I'll have this right out."

Jake glanced behind him, noting that the table was still empty. He kept his voice low. "Rebecca, do you know who Jessica is involved with?"

"No clue. Why should I?"

"It's Seth Palmer."

Rebecca stared at Jake as if he were speaking a foreign language. Seth Palmer was one of the eyewitnesses the night of the convenience store robbery. "Seth Palmer and Jessica? You can't be serious. They met the night Callie was killed, and now they're dating?"

"Bizarre, isn't it? Eyewitnesses in a capital murder case. Now they're a couple."

"I'm stunned." Rebecca frowned and shook her head. "I suppose stranger things have happened."

"Nothing leaps to mind."

"Nichole hasn't even mentioned the guy since Jude Donovan's trial, certainly not that Seth and Jessica were involved." Rebecca squeezed lime into her tea, then pointed at the slice on Jake's glass. He nodded, and she plucked it off the rim. "The three of them were joined at the hip during the trial, but it never occurred to me that they'd kept in touch."

"If the trial were going on now, the prosecutor would think twice about putting Jessica on the stand." Jake unfurled his paper napkin and positioned his silverware. "It's obvious she's on drugs. Probably meth. All the signs are there. What's the deal with methamphetamines around here anyway?"

"No idea. What about Nichole? Do you think she does drugs?"

"I don't see her often enough to speculate. What do you think?"

"I try not to think about her at all."

Jake took a drink of tea. "I ran into Russell at the pharmacy yesterday. He was picking up prescriptions. Poor guy. He didn't look well at all."

"He's really struggling." Rebecca recalled how vulnerable Russell had looked the day she and Liam entered his apartment. "He knows Jude Donovan's appeals could drag on for years. Russ is afraid that during that time Texas will declare a moratorium on executions. A group called the Texas Innocence Initiative is pressing for it. Russ has written letters to the Board of Pardons and Paroles and the governor's office, maybe others. He includes a picture of Callie and Derek Jaxson."

"Maybe that's a good thing, Rebecca. He's being proactive. Maybe that will help with his depression."

"I hope so," she said, speaking softly. Patrons had begun to fill the tables near them.

Rebecca inquired about Jake's family who lived in Dallas, as well as his close friend Keri. Jake claimed theirs was a platonic friendship, and Rebecca desperately hoped it was. If Jake moved back to Dallas, she would never be able to replace him, not as a funeral director or as one of her closest friends.

Grinning, Rebecca watched Jake slide a basket of crackers in front of him, then paw through the packets. "You do that every time."

"What?"

"You explore the cracker basket, but you always choose the same thing. Saltines."

"I choose these club crackers sometime," he argued with a noticeable lack of conviction.

"I've never seen it."

"Well, I'm sure I must have." He smiled sheepishly. "I'm so set in my ways. I need a life outside the funeral home. So do you."

Their salads arrived. Both looked delicious. Addie set a tiny pitcher on the table. "Here's some extra dressing. Enjoy."

Rebecca ground pepper onto her salad, then handed the mill to Jake. They ate in companionable silence, but only briefly. "Rebecca, if there's anything I can do to support Russell, let me know."

"I will," she answered, recalling the image of Russell slumping forward in his recliner and running his hands through his messy hair. This picture is in my head. Callie lying on that filthy floor. Scared. Bleeding. Dying. Tears had streamed down his face. He had wiped them away with angry swipes.

Russell's pistol was still locked in the safe at the funeral home. Knowing it was there and not in his nightstand offered little comfort. Becca, you don't think that's the only Glock I own, do you?

CHAPTER 12

Mac parked his Tahoe in the garage, turned off the engine, then massaged the knotted muscles in his neck. It was nine o'clock. He had just driven in from San Antonio. He was hungry and dead tired. He had not spoken with Catherine since early that morning. He found her in the family room reading a Daniel Silva novel. She was dressed for bed in a silky gown and matching robe. Her face was free of makeup, and her glossy, brown hair was curly and damp. She set the book aside when he entered and gave him a warm smile.

"Welcome home. You've had a long day." They kissed, then Mac immediately yawned. "Did you have dinner?"

"A Coke and some unsalted peanuts."

"Who sprang for that?" Catherine's silky, brown eyebrows rose a tad. "The title company?"

"Came out of my commission." Mac yawned again, yanking out his shirttail. "I need a shower."

"And then a cold beer and a hot roast beef sandwich?"

"Sounds great. Have we got any kettle chips?"

"Sea salt and vinegar?"

Mac gave the option a thumbs up. "Meet you in the kitchen. I want to hear about your day."

A short fifteen minutes later, he was not just hungry and tired, but also sleepy. He entered the kitchen to the sound of a spatula scraping across the griddle. Catherine was giving his sandwich a quick toast. He pulled back a stool at the island and sat.

"I thought you'd be home earlier." She took a beer from its temporary location in the freezer, popped the tab, and handed it to him. "Problem at the closing?"

"The closing agent. The guy must have thought he was getting paid by the word." Mac took a long swig from the chilled can as Catherine cut his sandwich in half. She arranged the triangles on the plate by a pile of kettle chips, then set it in front of him. "Michaela calls these chips seesaw and vinegar."

Catherine grinned. "She missed you tonight."

"I'll have breakfast with her in the morning."

The sandwich was thick with slices of roast beef, a perfect medium rare. Mac hadn't asked for cheese, but a slice of sharp cheddar melted over the edge onto the crust. Perfect. His weariness lifted with each bite. "Tell me about your day."

Catherine tightened the lid to the mustard jar and put it in the refrigerator. "I met with Phil again. He and Lillian Tate came by the office."

Mac took another drink of beer, then popped some chips in his mouth. "Who is Lillian Tate?"

"She's a recent notable in the Republican party. She moved here from Fort Worth. A very productive fundraiser."

"Let me guess. Phil was singing your praises, applying pressure with kid gloves."

"That pretty much describes it." Catherine filled the sink with water, then washed dishes while Mac enjoyed his sandwich. When he was done, she rounded the island and stood at his side. "So where are you in all this? I can't get a read on you."

Mac pushed aside the empty plate, then swiveled toward her on the stool. Putting his hands on his wife's waist, he pulled her close. "I'm not on board, but that doesn't mean I can't be."

"Fair enough."

They talked for another half hour. Finally, Catherine said, "Let's table this for now." When Mac agreed, she asked, "Would you do something for me?"

"Name it."

"Don't go in your study and start checking your email. You need some rest."

He slept for eight hours straight. The bed was empty when he woke, the shutters still closed. Mac shut his eyes. He had another long day ahead of him. Catherine had probably already left for work. He heard a gentle tap-tap on the door and opened his eyes again. It was Michaela's personal signal. "Come in."

Easing the door open, the child peeked around the edge and grinned. "Good morning." She held a glass of orange juice in her little hand and almost made it across the room before sloshing some on the floor. "Oops. Sorry."

Mac swung his legs off the side of the bed and stretched. He took the glass from Michaela's sticky hand. "Thank you, sweetie." Her hair was in a messy ponytail, and she was wearing mismatched shorts and a tee shirt. It was not her summer camp uniform which was khaki shorts and a color-of-the-day knit top. "No camp today?"

"Counselor conferences."

"What are they conferring about?" Mac asked, just to hear what she would say.

"No clue." Michaela nudged her granddad's slippers next to his feet. "Catherine said you're looking at a ranch today. Could I go with you?"

Recently, Michaela had stopped calling her grandmother Gran. Sierra had decided that it was best to ignore the change, so Mac was falling in line. "I'd sure enjoy your company. You need to change clothes though."

Michaela looked down at her outfit, as if she had forgotten what she was wearing. "I'll put on my boots and jeans and my company shirt."

Mac stifled a laugh. After their first trip together, Michaela had told Sierra that she needed a company shirt, a red polo with the LSL&R logo. "Think we should invite your mom to go with us?"

"No," she answered pleasantly. "This is really a business trip."

That child, Mac thought, amused. He could never predict what she would say. She was such a happy little thing, rarely out of sorts. He wished he could freeze her at the age she was now. The older he got, the faster life flew.

Now seemed like a good time to talk to her about what happened at the club, and to give Michaela the watch. Mac finished his juice, then went into the bathroom to brush his teeth and wash the stickiness from his hands. Pulling on his robe, he returned to the bedroom, then settled into an upholstered chair by a window.

"Let's chat a minute." Michaela climbed onto his lap and got comfortable. "We haven't had a chance to talk since the day your dad surprised you at the club. I know you're not fond of last-minute schedule changes. Neither am I. At first, I thought a change of plans was what upset you, but then when we talked in the café, you let me know it was more than that." Mac picked up her hand. "Remember what you told me?"

Michaela nodded, a tiny little movement of her head. "That I was afraid."

"Afraid of what?"

"Another vacation."

"That's right." Mac squeezed her hand. "Knowing you feel afraid hurts my heart, sweetie. You know why?"

"You love me with your whole heart."

"I sure do." Mac kissed her forehead. "One of my responsibilities as your granddad is to be sure you feel safe and protected. I let you down before, but you forgave me, didn't you?"

"Yes. You didn't mean to."

"No, but I should have been paying closer attention." Mac took the child's chin in his palm. "You did the right thing by telling me you're afraid of another vacation. And I promise you, sweetheart, I will do everything in my power to be certain that doesn't happen. Deal?"

"Deal."

"Give me a hug, then I have a surprise for you."

"The good kind?"

"Yes, the good kind." Mac chuckled as they hugged, but tears gathered in his eyes at the feel of Michaela's little hand patting his back. "Your surprise is in my dresser. Top drawer on the right."

"Which is the right?"

"You tell me." Mac watched as the child studied her hands, mouthing the words ring and right. She raised the hand on which she wore a little silver ring. "Correct."

Michaela padded across the room, opened the drawer, then withdrew the velvet bag. "Ooh. Is this it?"

"That's it."

"What's in it?" she asked, closing the drawer with her shoulder.

"Bring it over here. We'll look at it together."

Walking across the room, Michaela pulled both ends of the drawstring, untying the bow. At Mac's chair, she opened the top, stuck her hand inside, and wiggled the watch free. "Granddad. A watch. A big girl watch." Immediately she began unbuckling the band. "Turquoise. It's my favorite." With ease, she placed the band around her left wrist, pressed it against her abdomen, and buckled it in place. It was a perfect, snug fit. "It's so beautiful." She hugged Mac again, kissing his cheek. "Thank you, Granddad."

"You're welcome. I chose this watch because it has numerals around the face. It's important that you learn how to tell time."

"I will. I can do it."

"This is a very special watch, Michaela." Mac took both the child's hands in his. "And it would bring me lots of happiness if you'd wear it all the time. Just like you do the ring your mom gave you for your birthday. Would you do that for me?"

"I promise. And I promise I won't lose it."

"I know you'll do your best." Mac imagined the tracking device inside it. "But if you should ever misplace it, just let me know. I'll be able to find it."

♦ ♦ ♦

MAC HAD TOLD HIS PILOT they needed to be wheels up at ten o'clock, and they were. The flight to Junction would take less than an hour. Michaela was a great little passenger, and she loved to fly. She was observant and curious, but an easy child to be around. He could not imagine his life without her. Graham would be in town that weekend for his scheduled visitation. Mac hated the thought of it, but he was not worried that the guy would try to leave town with her. Travis Wheeler would be on the job, tracking their every movement.

Gazing out the window with Michaela sitting quietly at his side, Mac thought about Catherine. If Phil could be believed, she had a good chance of becoming governor. Politics could be a tough business, though, and Mac loathed the idea of his wife being attacked or smeared. And he was definitely concerned about people prying into his family's private life.

"Granddad." Michaela tore open a bag of peanuts and spilled some in her lap. "Nice day for flying, huh?"

Mac leaned over and kissed her on the head, just above her ponytail. "Sure is, sweetie. Thanks for coming with me."

CHAPTER 13

The chapel at Baker and Grant Funeral Home seated two hundred people. At the memorial service for Zoe Hewlett, half of the sturdy oak pews were empty. Most of those in attendance were either family or friends of her parents. Typically, the service for a young person was an overflow crowd. The absence of contemporaries was not uncommon, though, when the service was for a person isolated by drug abuse.

The focal point of the chapel was an oak-trimmed proscenium. On the rear wall beyond it hung a drapery in warm, soothing earth tones. Normally, a casket stood in front of the drapery, but for Zoe's memorial service, Rebecca had placed a narrow, linen-draped table there. On it, she had positioned a simple arrangement of stargazer lilies.

Standing in the rear of the chapel, Rebecca glanced at her watch. Ten minutes until service time. Jake would seat the officiant, a pleasant man who was Susanna Hewlett's brother. The musician, Zoe's cousin, was seated on a stool, strumming his guitar. The gifted young man had selected a pleasing medley of songs for the prelude.

Although hoping to avoid them, Rebecca assumed that Nichole and Jessica would attend the service, but they had not yet arrived. When the minister was seated, Rebecca left the chapel, closing the doors quietly behind her. Nichole and Jessica were standing in the foyer. Nichole was tastefully dressed in a simple black dress and ballet flats. Jessica, too, was in black, but the color rendered her skin tone a pasty white. She was as thin as a wafer. Her cosmetics were overdone, and Rebecca understood why as she neared. The makeup was meant to conceal active blemishes and scars from those that had cleared.

Susanna Hewlett could be right, Rebecca thought. Like Zoe, Jessica was probably doing meth.

Rebecca greeted the two with detached courtesy. "Hello, Nichole, Jessica. The service is just beginning. The memorial book is inside the chapel, if you'd like to leave your names."

"Thank you. We will." Nichole's courteous response sounded artificial and dismissive. "We're waiting for someone."

The front door opened. A young man entered, removing his sunglasses as he scanned the foyer. He was nicely dressed in a black shirt and black jeans. His dark hair was streaked with blonde and spiked straight up. It took Rebecca a moment to realize that the young man was Seth Palmer. Tucking his sunglasses in his pocket, he approached Rebecca and extended his hand.

"Hello, Rebecca. Seth Palmer. It's good to see you again. I wish it was under different circumstances. How are you?"

"I'm well." Rebecca took his hand, but quickly released it. "I'm surprised to see you. I didn't realize the three of you had kept in touch."

"We've tried to be there for each other." Seth stepped between Nichole and Jessica, drawing them near with his arms around their shoulders. "No one else understands what we've been through."

A wave of resentment passed over Rebecca. "I suppose that's true."

"It was the worst night of our lives," he added, stroking both women's upper arms. "One we'll never forget."

Jessica gazed up at Seth, her eyes flooding with sudden tears. "First Callie and now Zoe."

He kissed her forehead and whispered, "I know, Jess."

Rebecca seethed. She could feel her face reddening. The worst night of their lives? At least they have lives. What about Callie? Jessica has never been the same since Callie's death. Did they ever even think about Callie? Rebecca's pulse was racing. If she didn't get away from these people, she thought she would scream. She stepped aside, motioning to the chapel doors.

Holding hands, Nichole and Jessica walked away, but Seth hung back. "Rebecca, Nichole feels horrible about what happened to Callie. She thinks you still blame her."

Rebecca glared at him, unblinking. "I don't care to discuss this."

"I understand," he persisted, his tone placating. "But your daughter is dead because of Canon and Donovan. Not Nichole. Remember, she helped get Jude Donovan convicted."

Rebecca's temper was at a flash point. The last obstacles of restraint were falling away when Jake emerged from the visitation area. Exchanging looks with Rebecca, he quickly strode across the foyer. "I'm sorry to interrupt, Rebecca, but you have a call holding."

Rebecca turned away from Seth without another word, Jake at her side. "That guy's got a lot of nerve," she muttered through clenched teeth. "How dare he lecture me about who's responsible for my daughter's death?"

Jake followed Rebecca into her office. "What did he say to you?"

Rebecca paced, mimicking Seth in exaggerated tones. "We've tried to be there for each other. No one else understands what we've been through. It was the worst night of our lives. One we'll never forget."

"That guy's a real piece of work. What a phony. I'm so sorry, Rebecca."

"I shouldn't have let him get under my skin." She turned her desk phone toward her with a snap. No lights were blinking. "Whoever was holding hung up. Did Karen say who it was?"

"Oh, you didn't have a call. It was the look on your face. I knew you needed to get away from that guy." His grin was good-natured and mischievous. "Anything else I can do for you?"

Rebecca returned his smile. "As a matter of fact, there is." She explained that her car was being serviced and would not be ready until tomorrow. Jake agreed to take her to her parents' home so that she could get her mother's car.

When the service for Zoe Hewlett was over, Rebecca returned to the chapel. She spoke briefly with Gerald and Susanna, then dismissed the guests. Some came forward to offer condolences to the family, others made their way to the exits. Seth, Nichole, and Jessica left together, walking side by side down the aisle. Seth had his arm around Jessica's waist, supporting her as if she might collapse. Nichole walked next to him. They were almost at the door when Seth reached behind Nichole and stroked her back. She crooked one arm behind her, and they left the chapel holding onto each other's hand.

◆ ◆ ◆

HER MOTHER'S INFINITI was low on fuel. Normally, Rebecca bought gas at a Texaco station in her neighborhood, but today she needed to go to the post office and there was a convenience store nearby. The maddening encounter with Seth Palmer had left her with lingering anger and resentment that she had not yet cast off. The guy was smug, overtly arrogant, and his attentiveness toward Jessica seemed spurious. "Not that I care," Rebecca muttered. "The three of them deserve each other."

Turning right at the 7-Eleven, Rebecca parked next to the pumps. Her mother's car was ding-free, so she was careful to leave ample room to open the door without banging it against the iron post guarding the pumps. Credit card in hand, she stood at the rear fender of the Infiniti and stared blankly. "Well, hell," she blurted. The fuel door was on the passenger side. Grumbling, she got back into the car, then repositioned it to the street side of the island.

With the nozzle inserted and the pump clicking, Rebecca leaned against the rear fender, frowning toward the store. For months after Callie's death, the simple act of fueling her car had evoked an avalanche of haunting images. Entering a convenience store had been unthinkable. But slowly, over time, life had seeped through her grief.

Almost against her will, Rebecca recalled the day she and her father had driven to the outskirts of Houston to see where Callie died. "We'll take your mother's car," her father had said. "It's a little more comfortable than my truck." The night before the trip, her father had met with Nichole. With the help of Google Earth, the two had generated a sketch of the convenience store and its surroundings. Rebecca's father had taken detailed notes of Nichole's account of what had happened.

Rebecca had always felt protected in her father's presence, but never more than that dreadful day. Her nerves had been strung so tight, her mind so cluttered, that focusing on her father's words had almost overwhelmed her.

"NICHOLE WAS DRIVING WEST ON the frontage road of Interstate 10," Nelson Grant explained to his daughter. "That's where we are now. The convenience store is up ahead." He reached across the console and took Rebecca's hand. "Are you sure you want to do this?"

"I'm sure." When the store was fully in sight, Rebecca tightened her grip on her father's hand. It was a shabby place, not at all what she had expected. "Of all places to stop. Why here?"

"Nichole said she was running low on fuel. In her defense, it probably looked better at night." Nelson Grant activated the turn signal, slowing the Infiniti to a crawl. "Nichole said she entered here." He turned right at the first curb cut. The fueling island, positioned parallel to the frontage road, had only two pumps. "There was a Mercedes-Benz parked at the pumps. The customer would have been at pump one. Yes, pump one. That makes sense."

"How do you know that?" Rebecca asked, trying hard to focus. For some reason, she was not sure why, she had to know exactly what happened that night.

"The fuel door of a Mercedes-Benz is on the passenger side. Nichole said she parked behind it, so the Mercedes had to have been parked at pump one." Nelson Grant eased the Infiniti next to pump two, also on the street side of the island. "She would have parked her Mazda about here. It was hot that evening, so Nichole lowered the windows." He put the car in park, lowered the windows of the Infiniti, and turned off the engine. "The other customer, Seth Palmer, was standing between his Mercedes and the pump, looking down at his wallet. At some point, Nichole noticed a black Honda parked in front of the store. She thinks it was parked over there." He pointed to the area far to the left of the door. "There was a man in the driver's seat. That would have been Jude Donovan. And there was a man outside the Honda. Nichole doesn't recall exactly where he was standing, but definitely on the passenger side. That would have been Calvin Canon."

Rebecca stared past a trash bin between the pumps, toward the west end of the building. Calvin Canon had been standing right there, a handgun probably hidden in the waist band of his shorts or jeans. Armed robbery was no big deal to him. Minutes later, he had murdered two innocent people. "Did Nichole watch him go inside the store?"

"She has no specific recollection of that, but who knows? She might not admit it." Nelson Grant drew in a deep breath, then continued. "Jessica was in the front passenger seat of the Mazda, and Callie was in the back. Nichole got some cash out of her purse, then sent Callie inside to get them some water. Nichole dug out her credit card, then walked around to the pumps." Nelson Grant exited the Infiniti, walked around the rear, and stood in the space between the vehicle and the pump. "While the pump was running, Nichole was standing by the window of her Mazda talking to Jessica. Callie was still in the store." He paused, gathering himself. "Then they heard gunfire." His voice cracked. "Nichole and Jessica started screaming. The other customer, the driver of the Mercedes, yelled for them to get down. Jessica took cover inside the Mazda, and Nichole ducked down behind the pump, somewhere around here." Nelson Grant crouched, demonstrating what Nichole had described. "That's when Nichole heard a car engine fire up and tires squealing. She peeked around the pump and saw the black Honda racing off the parking lot."

Rebecca recalled something Russell had said. "Thank God Nichole had the presence of mind to get a look at the license plate. Without those three letters, the cops might never have tracked down Jude Donovan."

Nelson Grant stood. "Then everything went quiet. Seth Palmer rushed over to Nichole. They both crouch behind the pump. Nichole panics. Oh, God. My sister's in there. Then in less than a minute maybe, Seth stood slowly and looked over the top of the pump toward the store. Calvin Canon was lying on the sidewalk, blood oozing from his head. Seth Palmer told Nichole to stay put, and he ran to the convenience store to get Callie." Nelson Grant moved next to the open window, then leaned toward his daughter. "Are you sure you want to do this?"

Hand in hand, Rebecca and her father made their way across the grimy driveway to the spot where Calvin Canon had collapsed and bled out. They stepped onto the raised sidewalk, moving aside when a customer exited the store. "Canon had threatened the clerk with a gun once before," Nelson Grant explained, still holding his daughter's hand. "That night, though, Derek Jaxson was determined to defend himself. The store camera video, inferior though it was, shows Calvin Canon brandishing a gun. Derek grabs a bat and starts swinging, striking Canon multiple times in the head. It also showed Callie scrambling toward the exit."

Holding tight to her father's hand, Rebecca turned toward the door. Looking through the grimy glass, she said, "Did he aim at her?"

"No, honey. Canon was high on meth, struggling with the clerk, firing his gun. Two rounds struck Callie."

"One in her neck," Rebecca whispered, her voice weak and raspy. "One in her temple."

Nelson Grant drew his daughter close and whispered, "Our brave little Callie almost made it to the door."

THE FUEL PUMP CLICKED OFF, startling Rebecca. She took deep, calming breaths, then blinked away tears that had gathered in her eyes. With the transaction finalized and receipt in hand, she got inside the Infiniti and rested her forehead momentarily on the steering wheel. "Oh, Callie. I'm so sorry. You must have been so scared."

On the drive home, Rebecca's thoughts returned to the long, mostly silent drive back to Sparrows Cove from Houston. Her father was an alert, conscientious driver, but he had seemed unusually vigilant, scrutinizing passing vehicles. Finally, Rebecca had offered to drive.

"I DON'T MIND," Rebecca assured her father. "You've been driving for hours. You seem a little edgy."

"I'm fine," her father insisted, his brow furrowed. "I'm just having trouble reconciling something."

"What do you mean?"

"On every Mazda I've seen today, the fuel door is on the driver's side. I'm sure Nichole said she parked behind the Mercedes." He asked Rebecca to retrieve the sketch from the glove box. "Let me look at that." He pinned the paper against the steering wheel with his thumbs. "Yes. The Mercedes is at pump one. The Mazda is at pump two. Both on the street side of the fueling island."

"I'm sorry, Dad," Rebecca responded, aware of a niggling sense of guilt. "I'm not following you."

"She wouldn't have backed up to the pump," he said, speaking to himself, ignoring his daughter. "That doesn't make any sense."

Rebecca was so tired, so mentally drained, that she had no energy to respond. Callie died inside the store. Derek Jaxson lost his life trying to fight off a gun-wielding meth addict. What difference did it make where Nichole parked her car? "I'm sorry, Dad. Could we discuss that later?"

"Never mind, honey." Nelson Grant laid the unfolded sketch in his lap. "It was a horrible night for Nichole. I guess she's just telling it the way she remembers it."

CHAPTER 14

The helicopter was in use, so Mac McKeon had no choice but to drive to Kerrville to show the Donovan ranch. Time on the road, though, had given him time to think. For now, he would not tell Sierra or Catherine that Michaela's new watch had a tracking device in it, or that he had hired Travis Wheeler and Caleb Baker. His wife and daughter needed to know, though, that Michaela worried about Graham taking her away again, that the child was fearful. Then Mac would insist that the custody agreement, which Graham still had not signed, be changed. Someone needed to be with Michaela when she was with that man. It was the only way she would be safe, the only way she would feel safe. Mac knew that modifying the custody agreement would be kicking a hornet's nest, but so be it. He would not hand his granddaughter over to that man every other weekend knowing how she felt.

A week had passed since Catherine had been asked to run for governor. Word was clearly getting out. The Statesman reporter had made that clear the night they had had dinner with Emma and Lester. With each passing day, Mac grew more opposed. A political campaign would put their family in the spotlight. It would disrupt their lives. And he worried about Catherine's safety. Political races could get heated, and sometime crazies came out of the woodwork. No. He did not want her to run. But for now, he would keep his opinion to himself and give

Catherine space. There was no doubt that she would eagerly serve as governor, that being the first female Republican ever to hold the office would be a phenomenal, history making honor.

Catherine had not always put family before her profession. What driven parent had? Mac could only trust that she would this time. He loved his wife, and the last thing he wanted to do was say, "I'm sorry, honey, but I'm asking you not to do it."

Mac arrived at the Donovan ranch just before noon. Late July was not an ideal time of year to show central Texas ranch land, but fortunately higher than normal spring and summer rains had replenished aquifers, fed rivers and creeks, and raised lake levels to their highest in years.

Emma greeted Mac at the door. She did not look well at all. Her face was pale, and her eyes were bloodshot, as if she had been crying or had not slept well. They joined Lester on the back porch where they settled at a round, oak table.

"Tell us about the prospective buyer," Emma said, pouring Mac a glass of iced tea and setting it before him.

"His name is Ben Morrow," Mac explained, squeezing lemon. "He's from Dalhart. Made his money in oil and natural gas and wants a ranch in the hill country. He's not just kicking tires, Emma. If Ben finds what he wants, he's ready to make an offer."

Emma received a text message and responded to it. Mac noticed that her fingers trembled when she tapped her phone. "That was Clay," she said to Lester. "He's almost here." Emma explained to Mac that they had hired the retired detective to work on Jude's case. "He's already gotten started." She fiddled nervously with the rubber edge of her cell phone case. "We have to get Jude out of that place."

"How was Jude when you visited him?"

"We didn't get to see him," Lester answered. "The morning we were supposed to leave, we received a phone call from the chaplain that counsels Jude. He said Jude didn't want us to come, that seeing us and having to say goodbye was too much right now. Jude suffers from depression. He claims that he's getting his medication, but there's no way to know if he's taking it." Lester gazed toward the hills, his eyes blinking slowly as if he were conserving energy. "The chaplain seems to genuinely care about our son. He thinks he'll come around, that he will improve. But until then, we won't be seeing him at all."

Mac remained silent. What was there to say? Worthless words of encouragement? Empty platitudes? How did these good people bear up under such agony? When would it end? Or would it?

Knowing Clay Borger was on the way, Mac suggested that he show Morrow the ranch first, and the house last. "If you would, Emma, send me a text when you're wrapping things up. I don't want to interrupt."

When Clay Borger arrived, Mac offered to excuse himself, but Lester said he was welcome to stay. Clay was a pleasant fellow with a firm handshake and friendly smile. His salt-and-pepper hair was neat, his face clean shaven. As the four drank iced tea and chatted, Mac understood why the Donovans had taken a liking to the man.

Lester asked Clay to bring them up to speed. "I'm assuming Jude's attorney was cooperative."

"He was. I reviewed the case file, as well as the trial transcript. As you know, it was primarily a circumstantial case, but then many cases are. The prosecutor's closing argument was well done. Orderly. Passionate. And obviously persuasive. I'm no expert, but I think Jude's attorneys were out-lawyered."

Lester looked at Emma, raising his eyebrows. "So we're not the only ones who think that."

Clay opened his worn leather briefcase, then removed a stack of papers. "My focus was on what evidence presented at trial could have persuaded the jury to convict Jude. The prosecutor basically argued four points." He referred to his notes. "The first three addressed Jude's conduct. He admitted to being parked in front of the convenience store, possibly for three minutes, but insisted that he had not gone inside. Although that sounds like a good thing, the prosecutor used it against Jude, asking the jury to use their common sense. Why would Jude Donovan drive to a convenience store, stay in the car for at least three minutes, then speed away when he heard gunfire? Why? Because he didn't want to get caught there."

"He intended to go inside," Emma argued. "He was digging change out of his console."

"The defense attorney argued that, but not very effectively. And then there's the fact that by the time law enforcement searched the Honda, there was no change in the console." Clay referred to his notes again. "The other piece of circumstantial evidence is that Jude fled the scene. The prosecutor conceded that fleeing was not an unreasonable reaction, but that a good citizen with nothing to hide would have called 911. A good citizen with nothing to hide would have come forward to see if he could help law enforcement, but Jude did neither."

"He should have reported the shooting," Lester admitted. "He knows that. But he didn't want to get involved. I know that sounds bad, but he had good reason to be fearful of the police.

And as far as coming forward with information, he didn't have any information to offer, Clay. Nothing."

"I hear you, Lester," Clay answered, then continued. "I think the most damning piece of circumstantial evidence is that Jude detailed his car early the next day. Why? According to the prosecutor, he did it for one reason only. To get rid of Calvin Canon's fingerprints."

Lester grimaced. "That was a terrible moment in the trial. When the detective was being cross-examined, Jude's attorney asked him what reason Jude had given for detailing his car. One of the jurors chuckled when the detective said that Jude drove for Uber. He needed an immaculate car for work that night."

"That's never good when a juror scoffs at testimony."

"People in the courtroom laughed too," Emma added. "The judge halfheartedly used his gavel to silence them. Lester's right. It was a terrible moment."

Clay acknowledged Emma with a slow nod, then continued. "Now to the three eyewitnesses. Jessica Hart must have pulled a bag over her head when they reached the convenience store. She saw nothing, according to her testimony. She didn't notice Jude's Honda or Calvin Canon. Maybe she was in shock when she gave her statement, but she only had a vague recollection of there being another car at the pumps. Nichole Shane, on the other hand, testified that when she pulled onto the parking lot, she saw Canon in the vicinity of the Honda, near the passenger door. Seth Palmer, who had arrived shortly before Nichole Shane, testified that he saw Canon exit Jude's car from the passenger side, then go inside the store."

"Seth Palmer is lying," Emma demanded. "Canon was never in Jude's car. Never."

"Jude's lawyer pounded that home in his closing argument, but the prosecutor reminded the jury to use their common sense. Jude drove to the convenience store, but never got out of the car. Calvin Canon lived five miles away. He was overweight. Five-nine. Two hundred pounds. Use your common sense, the prosecutor said. The man did not walk to the convenience store."

"And there was no Uber app on his cell phone," Emma muttered angrily. "That's what the prosecutor said to the jury. Sarcastic jerk."

Clay concurred. "The man could be snide, all right. No argument there." He straightened his papers in finality. "So that's basically the prosecutor's case. Jude drove Calvin Canon to the convenience store. He knew the guy was high on meth, and that he planned to rob the place. When things went haywire, and he heard gunfire, Jude fled. That night he parked his car at his apartment complex in an area not visible from the street in case the cops were looking for a black Honda. The next day, he detailed his car, wiping it clean of fingerprints."

Mac wondered how police had zeroed in on Jude. There must have been thousands of black Hondas in the Houston area. Emma answered the question for him.

"Poor Jude. If Nichole Shane hadn't provided the partial license plate number, he wouldn't have been brought in for questioning. None of this would have happened."

Lester remarked that Jude had never strayed from his initial statement to the police. "And there's a reason for that, Clay. Jude was telling the truth."

Mac expected Clay to agree with Lester, but he held back. Clearly, Clay was not convinced of Jude's innocence. But, Mac acknowledged, maybe his opinion was irrelevant. His job was to uncover new evidence if, in fact, there was any.

"Of course, this is hindsight," Clay commented, "but your son should have had an attorney with him. By the time he asked for one, the detectives had already decided they had Canon's getaway driver."

Lester stared out toward the barn, the lines in his face deepening. "I will never understand why the prosecutor went for the death penalty. Even if Jude had driven Canon there, which he did not, how was he to know he would rob the place? How was he to know that Canon had a gun? How was he to know that two innocent people would end up dead?"

"Capital murder can be a complex issue, Lester. No doubt about it. In this case, the prosecutor went for the death penalty to send a message to the public. Harris County is tough on crime." Clay picked up a napkin, then wiped a water ring from the tabletop. "And then there are the victims and their families. The store clerk, Derek Jaxson, was a fine young man. He worked full time at Home Depot. The convenience store was a second job so that his wife could stay at home with their children and finish her degree online. And Callie Shane. That girl was only seventeen. Innocent as the day is long. All she was trying to do was buy a couple of bottles of water and get back to her family in Sparrows Cove."

Mac sat silently. Two innocent young people. Dead. Families devastated. Not just Derek Jaxson and Callie Shane's. But Lester and Emma's. And, the thought occurred to him, Calvin Canon's family. An avalanche of misery had been set off by one man's choice, most likely a decision influenced by methamphetamines.

"Where do we go from here, Clay?" Lester asked, wearily.

"I'm going to Sparrows Cove," Clay answered, returning the papers to his briefcase. "I want to speak to Jessica Hart and Nichole Shane."

"What are the chances they will talk to you?" Emma asked.

"Pretty good, I'd say." Clay grinned slyly. "Depends on who they think I'm working for. I want to know what was said before the cops arrived."

"Why is that significant?"

"Witnesses in a stressful situation are susceptible to suggestion. They soak up information like a sponge. That's why investigators separate witnesses as quickly as they can, so that they don't contaminate each other's recollection. But the cops didn't get to the scene right away. It was eleven minutes. I guarantee you there were some frantic, disjointed conversations going on in the interim." Clay shook his head, raising a single hand. "Don't get me wrong. I'm not suggesting Seth Palmer and Nichole Shane were getting their stories straight. As far as I know, they had no reason to. But it's a fact that eyewitnesses are influenced by what another eyewitness has to say. Seth Palmer and Nichole Shane's statements placed Jude in the investigators' crosshairs. Looks to me like that's where your son stayed."

Mac's cell phone vibrated. He fished it from his pocket, then read a text from Ben Morrow. Just landed. ETA 20 min. Mac responded. Eager for you to see this place. Think it's what you're looking for. He returned his cell phone to his pocket. "Ben Morrow is on his way."

Emma's stoic determination to be strong melted away. Covering her quivering lips with her fingertips, she apologized, then rushed inside the house.

"It's been a tough few days," Lester explained, standing. "And she loves this place. Selling it is breaking her heart, but she would give up her life to save Jude."

As Lester walked away, Mac's thoughts returned to his own family. He submerged himself into memory, reliving the desperate panic he had endured when Graham abducted Michaela. *Dad said my mom needed some time to herself. What did I do wrong, Granddad?*

Like a grassfire sparked by lightning, anger ignited deep inside Mac. There was nothing, nothing he would not sacrifice to keep Sierra and Michaela safe.

CHAPTER 15

Rebecca wiggled her feet into padded slippers, then tilted the slats of the shutters. The view from her second-floor bedroom was directly over the lake. Rays from the early morning sun glinted on the rippling water. Treetops stirred with the whisper of a breeze. Gazing through the wooden slats, she resisted recalling how much Callie had loved their cove.

In the kitchen, she poured coffee, strong and black. At two in the morning, she had taken a sleeping pill, kept awake since midnight by the fruitless "if onlys." If only she had not let Callie go to Galveston. If only the girls had left the island when they were supposed to. If only Nichole had bought gasoline somewhere else, anywhere else. When the "if onlys" had not stopped running through her head, she had reached for the sleeping pill. Before it had taken effect, she had pictured herself pumping gas at the 7-Eleven and reliving the trip to Houston and back. Before falling asleep, she had been actively longing to speak to her father.

With no appetite for even a toasted English muffin, Rebecca took her coffee to the breakfast table. Today was a much-needed day off. She was always reachable, but hopefully she would not be needed. The oven clock read eight-fifteen. Her parents were early risers. Even taking into consideration the time zone difference, they would be awake by now. Eager for answers, she placed the call. "Good morning, Dad. How is Big Sky Country?"

"I don't know, honey. We're in Wyoming."

"Oh, right. Montana has the big sky."

Her father's chuckle was a balm to Rebecca's unsettled nerves. "We're having a great time," he assured her. "The lodge is right down our alley. Spacious accommodations. Excellent restaurants here and nearby. Your mother and I took a long hike yesterday. Beautiful country. We've already decided to come back in the winter and explore more of the valley."

They continued chatting pleasantly. When the conversation slowed, Rebecca reluctantly said, "Dad, I'm sorry to bring up a painful subject, but I need to ask you something."

"Sure, honey. What's on your mind?"

"It's about a conversation you and I had on the way back from the convenience store in Houston." She paused, allowing her father to gather his thoughts. "You were troubling over where Nichole parked her Mazda the night of the incident."

Without hesitation, he said, "I remember very well. What brought that to mind?"

"I borrowed Mom's car while mine is being serviced. The Infiniti was low on gas, so I went to the 7-Eleven to fill it."

"Why not your Texaco? You never go to a convenience store."

If only I hadn't, Rebecca thought. "I had an errand to run. The 7-Eleven was on the way. Anyway, Dad, I wasn't paying attention when I pulled up to the pump, and I parked Mom's car on the wrong side."

"I see. Just like Nichole did that night."

"That's what I wanted to ask you about," Rebecca replied, noting how quickly her father had connected the two events. "It caused me to wonder if you ever made sense of what was troubling you."

"I suppose you could say that." Her father's response was half-hearted. "After you and I got home that evening, I showed the sketch to Nichole again. I asked her if everything was accurate. She assured me that it was. But when I pointed out that the fuel door on her Mazda was on the driver's side, not the passenger side, she got flustered and agitated. Then she turned on the waterworks and said she didn't know what I was talking about, that I was confusing her. I apologized for upsetting her and said that I must have misunderstood, although I knew I hadn't. Finally, she dialed back the tears, then acted as if a light had come on in her head. You're right, Granddad. I was parked on the wrong side of the pump. I totally forgot that."

"Are you telling me that Nichole was not fueling her car when the gunfire started?"

"If you believe Nichole, she was standing by the passenger window talking to Jessica when the shots rang out. She hadn't noticed that she was parked on the wrong side of the pump."

"That's ridiculous," Rebecca insisted, her voice shrill. "Even for Nichole. She was in her own car, and she forgot which side the fuel door is on?"

"Apparently so. She said she was in a big, nervous rush because they were running late and wasn't paying attention."

Rebecca sat silently, processing. "The one and only time I sat down with Nichole for an account of what happened that night, she was very detailed. She parked behind the Mercedes and lowered the windows. She gave Callie five dollars for water, then watched her go inside the store. She saw the Honda with the driver inside and another man standing nearby. The gunfire. The panic. The Honda speeding away." Rebecca stopped, unable to go any further. "But she failed to mention to me that she never had the chance to buy gas."

"I don't know what she said to you, but she didn't disclose that detail to me until you and I returned from Houston, and I brought up the issue about the fuel door."

Rebecca fell into a thought-filled silence, then conceded that the omission might have been an honest oversight. "That was only two weeks after the incident. Think what you will about Nichole, but that was a traumatic experience." A question took shape in Rebecca's mind. "Dad, why have you never mentioned this to me?"

"What good would it have done? What was I supposed to say? Oh, by the way, Nichole and Jessica were outside yacking away about who-knows-what while Callie was trapped inside a store with a meth-crazed criminal with a handgun."

♦ ♦ ♦

REBECCA AND MYRA PERRIMAN were as different as night is from day. Rebecca carefully measured her words, conscious of how she presented herself, and how others perceived her. Myra spoke her mind freely and could not care less what others thought of her opinions. Even when Rebecca and Russell had been married, Myra had not minced words about her view of Rebecca's stepdaughter. Her son had dated Nichole for a short time, and Myra had voiced her disapproval at every turn. Early on in the relationship, her son had said, "Mom, can you say one positive thing about Nichole?" Myra had shot back, "I'm positive she's wrong for you. You'll realize it, too, when you catch her in a blatant lie."

Myra arrived at five-thirty, eager for a vodka tonic and "time with my best friend." Tan and fit, she was dressed in navy capris, a crisp white blouse, and metallic silver flats. Rebecca had set up a makeshift bar on the deck and immediately mixed their drinks. With a cheese tray and a basket of crackers on a table between them, they stretched out on chaises and started catching up.

In short order, Myra raised one of her favorite topics. Politics. She was actively involved in the Republican Party at the local and state level. "Rumor is that Catherine McKeon is considering a run for governor. I know she's been approached. She's the editor of Texas Times Monthly. Actually, I think she's president now. She'd be a great candidate and a phenomenal governor. And the first female Republican to hold the office."

A cabin cruiser slowed, then eased through the mouth of the cove. Silver Star. As if the silver-haired captain could hear her, Myra called out. "Hi, Dad." Her father briefly sounded the horn. His granddaughters, sunning on the forward deck, squealed and covered their ears. Laughing, Myra waved at her nieces, both in their teens, and Rebecca followed suit. The elegant boat cruised the cove gracefully, then headed back toward open water. Rebecca and Myra watched it until it disappeared.

"It's been almost two years …" Myra's voice trailed off, but then continued. "You've shown so much courage, my friend."

"I wouldn't be where I am now without you."

Myra picked up her drink and took a satisfying sip. Rebecca noticed a snap in her eyes. "Who was that guy Jessica was hanging all over at Zoe Hewlett's memorial service?"

"Seth Palmer."

"That's what I thought. How did Seth Palmer know Zoe Hewlett?"

"Through Jessica. Seth and Jessica are involved."

"In what? The drug trade?"

Rebecca laughed.

"It was a logical conclusion," Myra retorted. "One look at Jessica and you know she does drugs. She looks horrible, particularly her complexion. And you didn't know they were involved?"

"No idea. When Nichole deigned to speak to me, she jabbered on and on about every little detail of her life, but she never mentioned that Seth Palmer is dating her best friend. The three of them were tight, though, at the trial. Maybe it's not that odd that they would keep in touch."

"It's definitely odd that Nichole would keep her mouth shut about it."

Rebecca plucked a lime wedge from her drink and gave it another squeeze. "Seth provided me a heartfelt lecture on why I shouldn't blame Nichole for Callie's death."

Myra smirked as she layered cheese on a cracker. "I don't like that guy. He was so smug and cocky at the trial, especially when he was on the stand. It's sickening to me to think that Callie was with the likes of them the last moments of her life."

The last moments of her life.

"I guess I'll never know what actually happened that night," Rebecca said, her tone more resentful than resigned. "To make matters worse, I found out today that Dad withheld some information that I clearly deserved to know." She skimmed over the conversation she had had that morning with her father, ending with, "It wasn't until we were on our way back from

Houston that Dad realized that the fuel door of a Mazda is on the driver's side."

"Let me get this straight." Myra walked to the makeshift bar to freshen her drink. Frowning and stirring the mixture with her index finger, she returned to the chaise and sat on its edge, facing Rebecca. "Nichole didn't mention that she hadn't bought gas that night until Nelson caught her in a lie."

"I don't know that she was lying."

Myra threw up a hand in exasperation. "Were her lips moving?"

Rebecca chuckled, infinitely grateful for her friend's unfiltered reaction.

"I don't buy it," Myra said adamantly. "Nichole didn't forget to tell Nelson about that."

"But why not mention it?"

"Oh, I don't know, Rebecca." Her voice shrilled with frustration. "Because they weren't at the convenience store to buy gas. Because they were there to meet up with Seth Palmer. Because Nichole's decision cost Callie her life." She swiveled on the chaise, staring toward the water. Her frown of concentration signaled that she was not done with the subject. "Knowing why they were there that night doesn't change anything. I get that. But that girl owes you the truth. You are Callie's mother."

"That's never going to happen."

Myra ignored her. "Too bad you don't have access to Nichole's credit card statements. If she bought gas before leaving the island, then that proves that she lied about why she stopped at that particular convenience store."

"She didn't have a credit card back then," Rebecca said absently, then sipped her drink. "Russell was paying her expenses because Nichole was taking classes. She would have used his card."

"Did he receive paper or electronic statements?"

"I don't remember. Paper, I think."

Myra was like a dog with a bone. "We need to find out if Nichole bought gas before she left Galveston. If she did, then they stopped at the convenience store for some other reason, and it wasn't because she wanted a bottle of water." Myra looked at Rebecca and raised a silencing hand. "And don't say, What difference does it make? You deserve to know the truth, and Nichole cannot be allowed to get away with a lie of this magnitude."

Myra's determination was contagious. I do deserve to know, Rebecca thought. Callie was my child. I have a right to know. "The household bills are in the attic."

"How many years do you keep them?"

"Until I feel like shredding."

"I use the same system." Myra grinned, then took a long swallow of her drink. Never one to let grass grow under her feet, she said, "Let's go see what we can find."

Access to the attic was through a narrow door on the rear wall of an upstairs storage room. Rebecca opened it, reached inside, and switched on the overhead lights. The space was excruciatingly hot and stuffy. A three-shelf metal stand near the door was loaded with neatly marked cartons and bankers boxes. One box, though, had been hastily labeled, the scrawling print hardly legible.

"Just look at that," Rebecca muttered. "Even my handwriting was a mess." She lifted the lid and peeked in. "Yes. These are from the year Callie died."

Myra pulled the heavy, dusty box off the shelf, then locked her arms around it. With the attic lights off and the door closed, they made their way downstairs and outside to the deck. Groaning, Myra set the bulky box on the foot of a chaise. "Would Russell have noticed where Nichole bought gas when he was paying the bill?" She did not wait for an answer. "No. He was such a mess after Callie died. He wouldn't have scrutinized the charges on his statement. Furthermore, he may have known the truth by then."

Unable to keep up with Myra's unilateral conversation, Rebecca sat next to the box and removed the lid. The bills were grouped with thick rubber bands. She lifted the bundles out one at a time, setting them aside. "Electric. Propane. Miscellaneous. Cable. Master Card." She tensed and looked at the name. "No, these are mine." She continued pawing through the box. "Security. Yard Service. Wait. Here they are. Master Card. Russell Shane." She stripped off the rubber band and began thumbing through the statements. When she located the one paid in August, she slid it from the stack and folded back the first of the stapled pages, squinting at the lengthy list of itemized charges. "I can't read this without my glasses." She held out the papers to Myra. "The incident was July thirty-first."

"I know that." Myra wiped her dirty hands on her pants and took the papers.

"Sorry. Of course, you do."

Frowning over the document, Myra scanned the first page. "Nothing there." She folded it back and examined the following page, staring at the entries with intense concentration. Gasping suddenly, she jabbed the paper with her finger. "There it is." Myra popped up, then squeezed onto the chaise next to Rebecca.

"Right there." She jabbed the entry again. "July thirty-first. Texaco. Galveston. Thirty-two dollars and twenty-five cents." Words spilled from Myra's mouth. "That little liar. She didn't stop at that convenience store to buy gas. They were meeting Seth Palmer. Those three were thick as thieves during the trial because they already knew each other."

Rebecca took the papers from Myra. She stared at the blurry entry. July 31. Texaco. Galveston. $32.25. Her pulse was racing, but her thoughts were lagging. "Nichole stopped there just so Jessica could see her boyfriend?"

"No way," Myra protested, her eyes blazing. "That was a drug buy. Nichole pulled in directly behind Seth's car. She didn't care which side of the pump she parked on. They were there to buy drugs." Myra jabbed the air with her index finger, as if Nichole were standing in front of her. "And that's why she sent Callie inside that damn store. To get rid of her."

CHAPTER 16

The house was quiet when Mac McKeon got home from work. Catherine had flown to Amarillo early that morning to speak to a journalism class at a college there. Bryant had arranged for the jet to pick her up when it was repositioning from Colorado Springs back to Austin. Mac had texted her earlier but had not received a response. Hopefully she was en route home.

It was Michaela's bedtime. Sierra was probably reading her a story, as was their routine. Last night, Catherine had said that their daughter was weary. "It's fear. She lives under the fear that Graham might abduct Michaela again."

Mac went straight to his study and emptied his briefcase. He did a quick scan of his emails, but there was nothing that could not wait until morning. Next to the base of his desk lamp lay an envelope addressed to Catherine. It was marked PERSONAL. On a Post-it note, she had written PLZ READ. The sender was Russell Shane at an address in Sparrows Cove. The name was instantly familiar. "Sparrows Cove. Shane." Was this man related to Callie Shane? He had to be, but why was he writing to Catherine?

Intensely curious, Mac removed the letter and unfolded it. Two photographs slipped out. The first was a portrait of a young Black family, the type of picture that might be taken for a church directory. Father and son wore dark suits, blue shirts, and similar ties. The little boy, maybe three or four, was sitting on his father's knee. The mother, smiling proudly, held her daughter in her lap, both wearing what looked like Easter dresses. Mac turned the picture over. Derek Jaxson, his wife, and children. A wave of sadness washed over Mac. Derek Jaxson. The clerk at the convenience store. Calvin Canon had shot and killed this fine young family man.

The second picture was a snapshot of a lovely teenage girl leaning against the trunk of a tree. Her long, wavy hair had been gathered and pulled forward over her shoulder. She was smiling into the camera, her eyes dark as raisins, her face the image of innocence. Mac turned over the picture. Callie Mae Shane. Age 17. He cringed. This beautiful girl was dead.

Mac set the pictures aside, but for a moment he could not look away. "That monster shot these innocent people." And a jury had been convinced that Jude Donovan was his accomplice. His fingertips lingered on the pictures, but then he picked up the letter and unfolded it.

Ms. McKeon:

I have mailed this letter to your home to be certain that it reaches your hands. I have included photos of my daughter Callie Mae Shane and Derek Jaxson with his family. They were murdered in a convenience store near Katy. Callie was seventeen. Derek was twenty-six. Justice was served to one of their killers, Calvin Canon, but his accomplice, Jude Donovan, still sits on death row.

You attended a death penalty discussion at St. Edward's University. The Texas Innocence Initiative was represented by Jude Donovan's mother, a fact that she probably withheld because disclosing it would have tanked her credibility. I have sympathy for Emma Donovan. Not only is her son an accomplice in a double murder, but also she is being exploited by the Innocence Initiative.

Historically your magazine has been against the death penalty and sympathetic toward death row inmates. Your presence at the panel discussion suggests that readers can expect another slanted and biased look at the topic, including interviews from do-gooders at the Innocence Initiative. If so, I hope that you will at least be honest with your readers.

The mission of the Initiative is to spare the lives of the worst of the worst. Murderers currently on death row. Those offenders were sent there by jurors who actually heard the evidence presented at trial. If the Innocence Initiative genuinely cared about the innocent, they would not be trying to delay or stop executions of death row inmates.

The innocents, Ms. McKeon, are people like my daughter Callie and Derek Jaxson. If a member of your family had been murdered by the likes of Calvin Canon and Jude Donovan, I'm sure that your magazine would tackle the Innocence Initiative head on. You would advocate for the victims and their families, not the killers.

You have a chance to do the right thing, Ms. McKeon. I certainly hope that you do it.
Sincerely,
Russell Shane

Mac read through the letter a second time. Had Russell Shane been at Saint Edward's that day? Surely not. Emma and Lester would have noticed him. Also, had he been in attendance,

Russell Shane would have known that Catherine did not arrive until the event was almost over. So how had he known she was there? Mac had deep sympathy for Russell Shane, but the tone of the letter sent up red flags. Somehow the man had secured their home address and mailed the letter there. Catherine was not unaccustomed to hostile letters and ignored most of them. But Russell Shane deserved a response. Catherine needed to be cautious, though, in how she responded.

"Poor man," Mac thought, looking down at the picture of his beautiful, young daughter. He was right about one thing. If Mac were in his position, God forbid, he would want his daughter's killer executed too.

Mac sighed loudly, then put the letter back in the envelope. He took another look at the pictures and put them inside too. What a tragedy.

Tired and hungry, Mac walked down the hall to Michaela's room. Quietly, he nudged the door open and peeked in. The child was sound asleep. On the bedside table was her "bluebonnet bowl," a lopsided piece of pottery she had made in an art class at a local children's museum. The hand-painted bluebonnets looked more like Q-tips on stems than wildflowers, but the child treasured the piece. She and Mac had agreed that the bluebonnet bowl was the perfect place for her new watch. "When you go to bed at night, put it in your bowl. Then when you get dressed in the morning, put it on again. Never leave the house without your watch, just like your ring."

Mac had used the iPhone app multiple times already, tracking her from the house to the club and back home again. It worked seamlessly. Knowing his granddaughter's location at all times was reassuring to Mac, but it did nothing to reassure Michaela.

Today, though, he had spoken with a friend of his who was a family law attorney. Mac had a plan now. One way or another, Graham Hollister was going to agree to it.

Mac left the door ajar, then made his way to the kitchen. He found Sierra washing dishes. Looking at her now, Mac acknowledged that what Catherine said was true. His daughter was struggling. She was far too thin. Dark crescents marked her lower lids. She smiled when people were around, but looked lonely, almost frightened, when she thought no one was watching. Like now, Mac thought, as he entered the room.

"Oh, hi, Dad." Sierra smiled broadly as she dried a pot that was almost too heavy for her to handle. She was wearing a sleeveless blouse. Her arms had lost muscle mass. "I didn't know you were home. How was your day?"

"Long."

"Are you hungry?"

"I'll get something in a minute. Need to chat with you first."

"Sure." Sierra put the pot away. "I'm all done here." She rounded the bar, and they sat side by side. "What's on your mind?"

Mac regretted having to broach a painful subject, but he had no choice. Sierra had to know what Michaela was going through. "Has Michaela said anything to you about being afraid?"

"Afraid? No."

"She's afraid that Graham will take off with her again."

A look of intense regret claimed Sierra's face and swept into her eyes. "She said that?"

"The day he showed up at the club."

When her hands began to quiver, Sierra tried to hide them in her lap. "I had no idea."

"We can't allow that."

"No, we can't. I'll talk to her."

"Talk isn't going to get it." Mac's tone was abrupt. "But I've got a solution, and I expect you to go along with it."

"What do you mean?"

"I talked to an attorney today. Not yours. A friend of mine. He recommended that Graham have supervised visitation."

"Supervised visitation? Dad, Graham will never agree to that."

"Then take him to court," Mac demanded, instantly annoyed.

"Dad, if I—"

"I don't want to hear it, Sierra Catherine." Mac's frustration was spiking, but he ignored it. "Stand up for your daughter. She's afraid. Michaela deserves better than this mess."

Sierra nodded, her face crumpling. "Yes, she does." Her voice broke. "I'm sorry, Dad." Tears flooded her eyes as she pushed back the stool and stood. "I'll talk to my lawyer. I promise. Goodnight."

Mac stubbornly said nothing to Sierra as she left the room. He was fed up with his wife and daughter tiptoeing around Graham Hollister. Couldn't they see that he was bullying them? "No more of this." He would not let the man keep pushing his family around.

Wearily, Mac walked to the refrigerator and opened the door. He got a can of beer from the top shelf, popped the tab, and took a long swallow. He was hungry, but the last thing he wanted was fresh fruit or a cold sandwich. He shoved the door shut and started toward the pantry. It was then he noticed a note on the countertop anchored down by a pepper mill.

Dad, I made your favorite. Pot roast and garlic bread. It's in the warming oven. Use the mitt. (Smiles.) Enjoy! Rest well. See you in the morning.

Mac felt a painful twinge in the pit of his stomach. "Damn you, Graham Hollister."

CHAPTER 17

B ut for the red lights on Liam Montoya's patrol car flashing up ahead, Rebecca and Jake would have driven past the unlit, unpaved lane leading to the Pattons' lake house. The death call had come in at three in the morning. In a county with no medical examiner, the death had been reported first to the sheriff's office, then to the Justice of the Peace. After a brief, unobtrusive investigation to determine the cause of Alvin Patton's death, the judge had released the ninety-year-old man's body to the funeral home.

The old lake house, two-story with a wraparound wooden deck, was perched at the water's edge a quarter mile off the main road. Jake and the Pattons were acquaintances and members of the same church, so Rebecca was there to assist, not to take the lead. Jake pulled the first-call car to a stop behind the patrol unit.

On the sidewalk, the two exchanged quiet greetings with Liam who explained that Alvin Patton had died in an upstairs bedroom. "The staircase is really narrow and makes a ninety-degree turn about halfway up. I don't know how in the world you'll get a gurney up there."

Residence calls were fraught with possible hurdles, so when Rebecca had taken the death call, she had asked pertinent questions of the Pattons' granddaughter. "Mandy mentioned the stairs, so we brought a specialized cot for the transfer," she explained.

"Need my help?" Liam offered. "Alvin's not a small man."

Rebecca accepted, and they made their way to the house where lanterns mounted on both sides of the front door glowed pleasantly. The door opened and Mandy Patton appeared, dressed in black crop pants, a knit tunic, and flip flops. Jake joined her inside, but Liam and Rebecca waited on the porch. She thanked him for the escort from the main road, then the two made small talk in the glow of the lanterns. Liam asked about Russell.

"I haven't seen him," Rebecca confessed, "since that day at his apartment. Have you?"

"No. I figured I'd run into him today at the bank, but he wasn't there." Liam's thick, black brows tightened in a frown. "Did you know Russell took a leave of absence?"

It was an instantly unsettling question. "I had no idea."

"I got the impression it wasn't completely voluntary."

The door opened, and Jake reappeared. "Mandy and her grandmother will wait in the living room while we make the removal." He strode along the shadowy, stone sidewalk, then opened the rear door of the first-call car. Grasping a bar on the end of the cot, he pulled it toward him, allowing wheeled supports to drop and then lock into place. Smoothing the blue velvet cover, Jake then maneuvered the cot to the porch. Activating a series of levers, he easily converted the cot into a straight-back chair, which he rolled through the door and into the small, cramped foyer. He and Liam easily carried it up the narrow staircase, Rebecca following behind.

In the bedroom, a painted iron bed had been positioned on the east wall, providing a full-on view of the lake glistening in the moonlight. A thin, white sheet had been smoothed over

Alvin Patton's long, broad-shouldered body. Bloodless lids rested like shriveled petals over his eyes. Wisps of silver hair had been neatly combed, no doubt by his wife or granddaughter making sure he was presentable when outsiders arrived.

Minutes later, with Alvin Patton's sheet-draped body strapped securely to the chair, the men made their way down the stairs, then out the front door to the sidewalk where they converted the chair to a cot again.

"I'll get the family," Jake said. "They want to say goodbye before we leave."

"We'll wait by the car," Rebecca said, and led the way.

With the removal complete, Jake and Rebecca returned to the funeral home, arriving at five in the morning. With Alvin Patton's body placed safely on the embalming table, they agreed that the procedure could wait a few hours and said goodbye at their cars.

On her drive home, Rebecca's thoughts returned to Russell, and she felt guilty. She should have been more supportive, kept in closer touch. Was his job in jeopardy? He had been a loan officer at the bank for ten years. She would phone him later today. As exasperating as the man could be, he was Callie's father.

But at noon, when she phoned Russell, he did not answer. Her calls went to voicemail the subsequent two attempts as well. Russell did, however, answer the door when, out of worry and exasperation, Rebecca drove to his apartment to check on him.

"Did you forget where I hide the key?" he asked, hip cocked and shoulders slumped.

"May I come in?" When he nodded and stepped aside, Rebecca entered. The room was cool and tidier than before, but a half-empty bottle of Absolut sat next to a tumbler on the chairside table. "I wish you would return my calls, Russ. I know I've been harsh with you recently, but I worry when you don't answer the phone."

Russell dropped into his recliner. "I don't mean to worry you." He appeared even thinner than a week ago, but his eyes were red and puffy. "Sometimes I don't feel like talking."

"I understand. But maybe you could just send me a quick text." Rebecca sat on the sofa, looking across the room at the cluttered desk and a stack of bills. "You're not at work. Are you not feeling well?"

"I'm taking a couple of weeks off."

"Are you going out of town?"

"Not anytime soon." The air conditioner kicked on, and Russell's hand jerked. His nerves were clearly on edge. "I should go see Dad, but I wouldn't be very good company."

"You two haven't been fishing in a long time."

"I'll try to get up there, but I have a meeting in Austin tomorrow night."

"What kind of meeting?" Rebecca felt momentarily hopeful. Had he finally located a support group of some kind? Austin was an hour drive away, but anonymity might appeal to Russell's private nature.

"A guy from Houston is giving a speech against the push to end the death penalty."

No, Russ, Rebecca thought grimly, her heart sinking.

"I'm really worried, Becca. Jude Donovan got a fair trial. The jury found him guilty and sentenced him to death. Now the Texas Innocence Initiative and others of that ilk are determined to interfere with justice. It's not right." He looked at Rebecca with something close to desperation in his eyes. "And now they have that Catherine McKeon in their corner. I saw her on the news when she showed up at one of their events. You can be sure that two-bit, liberal rag she runs will be railing against the death penalty."

Russell had to stop torturing himself, but what good would it do to tell him so? Rebecca cringed to think how he would react if he knew Catherine McKeon had been asked to run for governor.

"Becca, I don't mean to rush you, but Nichole and a friend are on the way over. I need to take a quick shower."

"Of course." Rebecca stood, speaking to Russell as she picked up her purse. "Give my best to your dad. And, please, answer your phone or send me a text."

Nichole's friend, Rebecca discovered when she stepped out the door, was Seth Palmer. The two were standing in each other's arms next to his Mercedes.

♦ ♦ ♦

MYRA'S CAR WAS PARKED in front of Rebecca's house when she returned home. She had used her key to deliver a container of freshly made salsa and a bag of Rebecca's favorite chips. They agreed that a perfect accompaniment was Grey Goose and tonic, and that there was no time like the present. Myra navigated the kitchen as if it were her own, while Rebecca sliced a lime and mixed their drinks. They had just settled in for a chat in the family room when the doorbell rang. Rebecca grumbled, walked to the front window, and peeked out. She did not recognize the man on the porch who had stepped back from the door and seemed to be sizing up the neighborhood. He wore neatly pressed jeans, black boots, and a button-down white shirt, the sleeves of which had been neatly folded back. His salt-and-pepper hair was well styled, short, and neat.

"Let me see what this guy wants," Rebecca said, then opened the door.

"Good afternoon," the stranger said pleasantly.

"Good afternoon. Can I help you?"

"I'm hoping to catch Nichole at home."

"Nichole? She's not here."

"Do you know when to expect her?"

"I'm not sure," Rebecca answered, curious as to who the man was. Nichole had not lived at that address for more than two years, although she and Russell both still received mail there occasionally.

"Nichole does live here, right?" The man removed a business card from his pocket but kept it in his hand. "I was given this address."

Rebecca glanced over her shoulder at Myra who was walking toward her, drink in hand. "He's here to see Nichole."

"What's she done now?" Myra muttered.

Rebecca reached for the man's card and read it. "Clay Borger. You're a private investigator?"

"Who are you investigating?" Myra asked bluntly.

"Do you mind if I come in? Or we could talk out here on the porch."

Cautious, Rebecca chose the porch, stiflingly hot though it was. Myra set her drink on a chairside table. "Care for a vodka tonic?" When Clay Borger accepted, she said, "Don't start talking without me." She returned in record time, then sat next to Rebecca who had done no more than give the man her name. "I'm a friend of Rebecca. Myra Perriman."

"Nice to meet you." Clay Borger sipped his drink. "Excellent. Thank you, Myra."

"What do you need to talk to Nichole about?" Rebecca inquired.

"It's regarding … I'm sorry. Rebecca Grant. You're Nichole's stepmother. I have your name as Rebecca Shane."

"Then you have it wrong."

"I didn't make the connection. You're Callie's mother."

Rebecca flinched at the sound of her daughter's name, resenting somehow the man's familiar tone. "How do you know about Callie?"

"Who are you working for?" Myra demanded testily.

"Jude Donovan's parents."

"And you have the nerve to show up here?" Rebecca snapped.

"I apologize. This is the address of record for Nichole." The man leaned forward, resting both elbows on his knees, his posture earnest. "The Donovans are trying to save their son. They believe in his innocence."

"The jury didn't," Rebecca said curtly.

"You're right. They didn't. My job is to be sure that the jury heard the whole truth."

"And you don't think Nichole told the truth?" Myra questioned.

"I'm not saying that. I'd just like to talk to her, and to Jessica Hart."

"What about Seth Palmer?" Myra pressed. "His testimony was the most damaging." Before the man could respond, she touched Rebecca's hand, then asked Clay Borger to excuse them. Inside the house and out of earshot, Myra said, "Are you going to tell him?"

"Where to find Nichole?"

"No. Are you going to tell him that Nichole lied about why they were at the convenience store that night?"

"Of course not." Rebecca's voice rose in pitch with disbelief. "Why should I?"

"Because it's the right thing to do," Myra insisted. "You have to."

"No, I don't." Rebecca felt her pulse begin to race. What could Myra possibly be thinking? "Why the girls were there is irrelevant."

"You don't know that." Myra's intensity escalated. "But you do know Nichole lied. Maybe she also lied about what she saw. Maybe Seth Palmer lied about what he saw."

"And maybe you want to cause trouble for Nichole."

A flash of anger sparked in Myra's eyes. Rebecca had seen it before and braced herself. Moments of silence ticked, then Myra grasped Rebecca's hands. "I'm sorry. You're right. You don't have to say a thing to that man right now."

"And neither do you. Not a word. I need time to think." They agreed with nods of understanding, exchanged quick hugs, and returned to the porch.

Beads of perspiration had collected on Clay Borger's forehead. He wiped them away with a handkerchief. "I apologize for upsetting you, Rebecca. I didn't know this was your home."

Rebecca and Myra sat, ignoring the man's apology. "What do you hope to accomplish by talking to Nichole and Jessica? They told the police what they saw, and you've surely read their trial testimony."

"Jessica claims not to have seen anything, which I find odd. Nichole said she saw Canon standing by the passenger side of Jude's car. Seth Palmer, on the other hand, testified that Canon got out of the Honda, which Jude vehemently denies. I'm just wondering what was said before the police arrived. Don't get me wrong. I'm not suggesting that Nichole was untruthful. But there is the possibility that her recollection was influenced by Seth Palmer's certainty. He swore that Calvin Canon and Jude Donovan were together that night, but Jude swears they were not."

"Well, of course, he does," Rebecca snapped. "What do you expect?"

"I get your point, but even as Jude was facing a capital murder charge, he maintained his innocence. And when the district attorney offered to take the death penalty off the table, Jude refused to plead guilty."

"Why would Seth Palmer lie?"

"I don't know the answer to that." Clay Borger looked Rebecca straight in the eyes. "But this I do know. Someone is lying, and Jude Donovan's parents are convinced that their son is telling the truth."

CHAPTER 18

Sierra had assembled a peach pie and put it in the oven before she and Michaela left for the mall. The aroma of cinnamon, ginger, and brown sugar filled the kitchen as the timer ticked down. Catherine had asked Mac to take the pie out of the oven while she freshened up. Phil Kuykendall was stopping by for dessert again. "I'm not expecting an answer," he had assured her, "unless you're prepared to say yes."

Catherine had by no means reached a decision, but Mac worried that the prospect of running for governor was taking root. Traveling statewide, connecting with voters would be exhilarating to his wife. "I have a lot of questions for Phil," she had said over dinner, "starting with what my role would be in the campaign organization itself." Mac knew what Phil would say. "Trust me, Catherine. The infrastructure is already in place and the money will be. You'll have the best possible staff to run your campaign."

Generally, Mac and Sierra shared the same viewpoint on everything, but not this time. It was Sierra and Bryant who had formed a united front, immediately making their opinions known and clear. "What an honor, Mom. You would be a great governor." "Sierra's right, Catherine. How could you possibly say no? And you would be the first female Republican governor in the state of Texas." Brooke's reaction dovetailed with Mac's. "Mom, you're nearly sixty years old. Why in the world would you want to subject yourself to the grind of a political campaign?"

Mac checked the oven timer. Three more minutes. He retrieved his iPhone and opened the tracker app. Following the prompts, he downloaded a Google Map. On it, a flashing M indicated that Sierra and Michaela were in the parking lot at Barton Creek Mall. If he zoomed in closer, he could get a precise location if he ever needed to alert the police. If Graham Hollister did not bow up like the jerk that he consistently was, Mac would never have to use that feature, and neither would Travis Wheeler.

Phil Kuykendall arrived promptly at eight o'clock. Catherine hardly had time to serve him a slice of peach pie and coffee before the man jumped right in. "Well, Catherine, you've had a while to think. What can I do to make sure your answer is what I want to hear? Yes, Phil, I will run for governor."

Catherine laughed. "And to think, I was worried that you were coming here to withdraw the offer." She handed Mac a cup of coffee, then sat next to him on the sofa. "Seriously, Phil, I want you to know that being asked to run for governor is an enormous honor. And it's very humbling. I must admit, though, that the prospect is a little overwhelming. After all, I've never even run for elected office. But it's also very exciting. An enormous opportunity. Obviously, Mac and I are giving it serious thought."

Phil raised his cup, toasting. "Exactly what I wanted to hear."

"That being said, running for a statewide office is a massive undertaking. The question is: Do I have the drive? I'm not sure that I do."

Phil shrugged. "I hear that a lot." He cut a generous section of pie off the triangle, then chewed it vigorously. "That's delicious. You bake this, Mac?"

"Yeah. Like my lattice strips?"

Grinning, Phil pierced a peach and popped it into his mouth. "Catherine, I've known successful candidates who had no interest in campaigning at all. Hated it, to tell you the truth. But they did what the process requires. On the other hand, I've known candidates who were fired up from the get-go, couldn't wait to hit the campaign trail. They all turned out to be winners."

"So I shouldn't let my lack of fire at this moment carry too much weight?"

"Exactly. Focus on what it will be like to serve as governor, not on what it will be like to run. Think about critical issues, and how you will be able to lead and solve problems. I've heard you speak many times, Catherine. You are very effective when you talk about the Texas economy, keeping it strong and vital and growing. You realize the importance of maintaining a business-friendly environment, particularly for small businesses. You've addressed the critical matter of water usage, conservation, and how those issues sometime conflict with private property rights." He wiped his mouth haphazardly with a napkin. "Before I forget. I saw that you two attended an event at Saint Edward's recently. A panel discussion about the death penalty."

"How did you know?" Mac asked.

"Local news. Video footage showed you talking to one of the speakers." Phil paused to drink his coffee. "Any particular reason you attended the event?"

"One of the panelists is a friend of ours," Mac explained, his thoughts immediately straying. News coverage. That was how

Russell Shane had connected Catherine with the event. "Her name is Emma Donovan. She represented the Texas Innocence Initiative."

"They do important work. Criminal justice reform is gaining traction. Your friend is Emma Donovan?" He directed the question to Catherine. "What's her interest in the Innocence Initiative?"

When Catherine paused, reluctant to answer the question, Mac stepped in. "Emma's son is in prison. According to her and her husband, Jude was wrongfully convicted of capital murder. They're hoping the Innocence Initiative can bring about a moratorium on executions while they try to prove his innocence. Their son is on death row."

"Damn." Phil drew in a deep breath, then exhaled slowly. "Trying to prove your child's innocence. Can't imagine anything worse." When he spoke, his tone lacked its usual spiritedness. "Has an execution date been set?"

"Not yet," Mac answered. "The appeals process is underway."

Phil sat quietly, gazing down at the cup of coffee in his hand. Mac glanced at Catherine, wondering if she was thinking the same thing he was. Was Phil Kuykendall actually at a loss for words? Was he weighing what it was like for the family of a death row inmate?

Their conversation was cut short when Sierra and Michaela rounded the corner from the kitchen. "Are we interrupting?" Michaela asked, obviously prepped.

"Not at all. Come join us." When Michaela came to stand at his side, Mac whispered, "Good job." They exchanged hugs. "Say hello to—"

"I know. I know." The child smiled, looking directly at their guest. "Hi, Mr. K."

"How are you, Michaela?"

"Great. We went to the mall, then had ice cream. Tomorrow I'm taking an art lesson at Lajuna Gloria."

"Laguna Gloria," Sierra corrected, taking the chair next to Phil.

"Whatever." Michaela shrugged.

"I didn't know you were an artist." Phil set aside the now empty plate and cup.

"I painted a cow one time, but my friend thought it was a horse. A horse's tail is not like a cow's tail at all."

"Of course not. Ridiculous." Phil leaned toward Michaela, then spoke in a tone reserved for the outrageous. "Want to hear something else ridiculous? I have a friend who owns a big black horse. She enters him in jumping competitions. The horses are supposed to be well groomed and beautiful, but her horse's tail looked faded. Maybe it had been out in the sun too much. Guess what she did?"

"What?" Michaela inched closer, like filings to a magnet.

"She bought some hair dye and put it all over her horse's tail." Phil mimicked the messy process with his hands. "Problem is, every time he swished his tail the dye got all over the place, including his behind."

Michaela's fingers flew to her lips like little birds. "Oh, no!" Her eyes grew big and round. "What a mess!"

"Know what she did? She covered the horse's behind with a big plastic bag. Then she went right on dying the tail. Problem was, it was supposed to be black, but for some reason it turned out sort of blue."

"Oh, no. A black horse with a blue tail." Phil's audience erupted in laughter, Michaela taking the lead. "That's uh-larius."

"It was not a good look."

When the laughter died down, Sierra stood. "Michaela, it's time for bed."

Michaela told Phil that he was a great storyteller, said goodnight, then took her mother's hand. As they walked away, Sierra asked Michaela if she believed Mr. K's tale of the blue-tail horse, timing it so Phil would hear her answer. The child snickered. "Tale of the blue-tail horse. That's a good one, Mom."

For another half hour, Catherine peppered Phil with questions, while Mac primarily listened. It was clear that Catherine was moving closer to a decision. Generally, Mac could read his wife, but on this issue the pages were blurred. Phil suggested they talk again soon.

"I'm not pressing for a decision, but word that you're considering a run is already spreading. It's important that you have your response ready for media inquiries." He stood. "I need to be on my way. Thanks for the pie. Delicious." Escorted to the front door, Phil paused. "So, Mac, are you on board if your wife decides to run?"

Mac evaded the question. "The filing period is a while off. We've got time to chat about all this."

"Filing period, huh? He's done his homework, Catherine. That's a good sign." Phil grasped the door handle but didn't press the latch. "I'm sorry about your friends—"

"Lester and Emma," Catherine said.

"One thing is sure," he said emphatically. "When you're elected governor, you can give desperate people like them a much louder voice than they have now."

CHAPTER 19

A thunderstorm was moving through Jackson Hole, Wyoming. Rebecca had managed to get through to her father, but the cell phone connection was poor, and the call had dropped twice. She needed her parents' advice, though, so she tried again. Was Myra right? Was Rebecca morally obligated to tell Clay Borger that Nichole had not been at the convenience store to buy gas, and that two weeks after the murders she had lied? "We don't know that she lied to Dad," Rebecca had argued, but even to her own ears the words rang hollow.

When the call was restored, Rebecca asked her father to put her on speaker and apologized again for intruding on their trip. "I'm really at a loss though."

Even from two-thousand miles away, the sound of her mother's voice was reassuring. "We're listening. What were you saying about a private investigator?"

"He came to my house looking for Nichole," Rebecca explained, pacing her office. "He's working on Jude Donovan's case." Her parents exchanged words, but she could not distinguish them. As succinctly as possible, she recapped her encounter with Clay Borger, ending with his assertion that one fact was undeniable. Someone was lying. "And Myra thinks that it's Seth and Nichole."

"Did you say Myra?"

"Yes, Dad. I told Myra about Nichole backtracking on her story after you and I returned from Houston. She thinks you caught Nichole in a lie." In as few words as possible, Rebecca told her parents about locating Russell's credit card statement, then finding the fuel charge at a Texaco in Galveston. "Nichole hadn't driven but seventy miles or so. It makes no sense that they stopped at the convenience store to buy gas. Myra suspects they were meeting Seth Palmer, probably to buy drugs. Seth and Jessica are involved, who knows for how long." Her father's comment was muffled, but Rebecca distinguished the word methamphetamine. "Here's where I need your advice. Myra insists that I should disclose all this to Clay Borger." Silence followed. "Can you hear me?"

"We hear you," her father answered, sounding as if he were standing near a popcorn machine. "Can you hear me okay?"

"I can. Yes. What should I do?"

"Nothing." Even with the poor connection, his tone was emphatic. "JoAnn and I need to talk about this. I'll call you when we return to the hotel. But let me be sure I understood. You have proof that Nichole fueled her car before they left Galveston on Sunday."

"Yes. The charge is on Russell's statement." Again, her father's response was mangled. All she heard before the connection was lost were the words why she parked on the wrong side of the pump.

Rebecca set her phone aside, but continued prowling her office, arguing with Myra although she was nowhere around. "It's not my responsibility to tell Clay Borger anything. So Nichole lied. She and Jessica were there to buy drugs. Seth Palmer arranged the buy. Jude Donovan and Calvin Canon were dealers." None of that changed the fact that Calvin Canon murdered two innocent people, and that under Texas law, Jude Donovan was charged with capital murder. "And the jury found him guilty."

Rebecca forced herself to sit, then slid a stack of unsigned checks in front of her. The mindless act of signing her name allowed Clay Borger's words to gain her attention. Someone is lying. Jude Donovan's parents are convinced that their son is telling the truth. "Can you say the same about Nichole?" Myra had demanded. "Knowing what you know now, are you convinced that Nichole and Seth are telling the whole truth?" Rebecca's silence had answered her friend's question.

The intercom sounded, startling her. "Yes, Karen."

"Russell is here to see you."

Rebecca moaned. For a moment, she considered asking Karen to make an excuse for her. She should have let Russell know that a private investigator was looking for Nichole. Or did he already know? The truth was, she had not wanted to deal with his reaction. Now she had no choice, and she could not resist the obsessive sense that Russell was on the edge.

The sense heightened when he entered her office. His troubled face was drawn and flushed. His anxious expression, though not as desperate or pained, ignited a flash of memory of the night he showed up at her house and told her Callie was dead.

Rebecca motioned to the sofa, but Russell did not sit. He closed the door to her office, placed his palms on her desk, then leaned toward her. "Did you know there is a private investigator in town working for Jude Donovan?"

"He was at my house yesterday, looking for Nichole. I planned to tell you."

Russell popped the desktop with his palms, frustrated or angry, Rebecca could not tell which. "Well, you waited too long. The man showed up at Nichole's apartment this morning asking for her help."

"She spoke with him?"

Russell yanked back the armchair in front of the desk and sat. "The guy let her think he was working for the state, so she said she would be glad to do what she could to help. Why would you let Nichole get blindsided, Rebecca? Why didn't you warn us?"

"I planned to. I would have." She tried not to sound apologetic or defensive. She did not want a scene. "What did he ask her?"

"He had lots of questions about exactly where Calvin Canon was standing when Nichole first saw him, when she first drove up to the convenience store. And he seemed really interested and curious about Seth Palmer, what he said to Nichole after the shooting, but before the cops arrived."

"Maybe he wanted to be sure Nichole hadn't been pressured?"

"Pressured? By Seth? What do you mean by that?"

Rebecca's compliant attitude was eroding. "I didn't mean anything, Russell. And you need to back off. Your attitude is why I didn't contact you right away."

As if he had not heard her, Russell pressed on. "It's unbelievable. Borger was debating Emma Donovan at Saint Edward's, and now he's working for them. What does the man think he's going to find? Jude Donovan got a fair trial, and the jury found him guilty. Borger is blowing smoke. There is no new evidence to be found, and he knows it. He is just stealing their money."

"If you believe he won't find anything, Russ, then please let this go. You're ruining your health. Can't you see that?"

"What I see is this." He reached into his left shirt pocket and gently removed two pictures. Callie leaning against the Lone Oak. And a family photo of Derek Jaxson, his wife, and two young children. "I will not give up until there is justice for my daughter and this brave young man. Calvin Canon got what he deserved, but Jude Donovan is still alive. They can line up against us, but we are going to get justice for Callie and Derek."

"Who's lining up against you?" Rebecca asked, baffled.

"The do-gooders at Texas Innocence Initiative and that rag Texas Times Monthly. Catherine McKeon is going to make a run for governor. Did you know that?"

Rebecca shook her head, a silent omission of the truth.

"There was talk about it at the meeting I went to in Austin. You know why she's running, don't you?"

Rebecca shook her head again. Something akin to a conspiratorial quality had crept into Russell's tone.

"If McKeon is elected governor, she will stack the Board of Pardons and Paroles." He leaned toward Rebecca, lowering his voice, as if he might be overheard. "You see, the Board makes clemency recommendations to the governor. If she stacks the Board with people who think like she does, they'll recommend clemency for Jude Donovan and murderers like him."

"Russell, please," Rebecca implored. "Think what you're saying. Why would anyone want murderers to be set free?"

"Obviously, the woman thinks Jude Donovan is innocent." He spoke to Rebecca as if she were demented, underscoring each word. "She showed up at a Texas Innocence Initiative event to support Emma Donovan. You mark my words, Rebecca. Texas Times Monthly will start printing one article after another about Jude Donovan. They'll rally people to his defense, demanding to know how a defendant who didn't actually fire the murder weapon can get the death penalty."

Taking issue with Russell's speculation was futile. She would only antagonize him. Furthermore, he might be right about the magazine examining Jude Donovan's case. But concluding that Catherine McKeon would run for governor to exert influence over the Board of Pardons and Paroles was beyond far-fetched. It was delusional.

"People like Catherine McKeon would have a whole different opinion of the death penalty if it was her daughter who got shot to death."

The intercom sounded again. Rebecca picked up the receiver. "Yes, Karen."

"I'm sorry to interrupt, but I have a death call on line one. Jake is out of the building. Do you want me to take the call?"

"I'll take it." Sliding a death call notification form in front of her, she secured the name of the deceased and the caller, writing the names on the form. "Tell him I'll be right with him, Karen."

Russell sat hunched over in the chair, looking down at the photos cradled in his palms. His voice was little more than a whisper. "Catherine McKeon would have a whole different opinion if it was her child who got shot to death." His hand jerked when Rebecca said his name, and he slid the photos back into his pocket. Rising unsteadily from the chair, Russell spoke over his shoulder as he walked away. "You're Callie's mother, Becca. I thought I could always trust you."

CHAPTER 20

In his study, Mac listened in as Catherine spoke to Graham on the speakerphone. He was on his way to Austin from Plano for his weekend with Michaela. Catherine was making arrangements for him to pick her up. "She'll be at Brooke's for a swim later this morning. Would it be convenient for you to pick up Michaela there?"

"Sure, Catherine. No problem."

"Michaela wants to sleep in her own bed tonight, Graham, rather than the hotel. You don't mind, do you?"

"Whatever my daughter wants. You know that."

"I'll pick her up at your hotel after dinner tonight, then take her back to you on Sunday morning."

"That sounds perfect. And thanks for running interference, Catherine." Graham snickered. "I wouldn't want to run into Mac again. Your husband needs to get a grip."

"I'll tell Brooke to expect you around noon." Catherine ended the call and groaned. "What a pretentious, manipulative jerk that man is. And he can't resist the chance to get in a dig at you."

"You got what you wanted." Mac put his arms around his wife and held her close. "Michaela gets to sleep in her own bed tonight. That's what matters." He gave her a firm squeeze and said, "Let's go tell her the good news."

Michaela was in the family room, curled up on the sofa. Her cheek rested on the back of her hand, and she was still in her pajamas. She did not stir when they entered the room, acting as if she were asleep. Mac looked on as Catherine sat at the child's bare feet and stroked her leg. "Michaela."

Feigning drowsiness, she drew up her knees, curling into a ball. "I don't feel good."

"What's wrong, sweetheart?"

"My tummy hurts." She mumbled against her hand. "I don't think I better go with Dad today."

"I just spoke with him. He's looking forward to seeing you."

"But I'm sick."

"Are you?"

Michaela squirmed and sighed. "I guess he could see me here for a little while."

"That's an option, yes."

Mac caught Catherine's eye. "Could I speak to Michaela alone?" He took his wife's spot on the sofa. Michaela closed her eyes, ignoring him. "I know what you're worried about, but there's no need. I promise. Your dad is not going to take you away. You have my word. This is the plan. Graham will pick you up at Aunt Brooke's. You'll spend a few hours with him, have dinner, then Gran will pick you up at the hotel and bring you home. You'll sleep in your own bed tonight."

Michaela squirmed onto her back. Her cheek was red from being pressed against her hand. "Not at the hotel?"

"No. Your dad said that was fine with him. Then he'll see you again tomorrow morning before he heads back to Plano. You'll be home right after lunch." He patted her leg. "Now go put on your swimsuit and cover-up. Mom is packing your bag."

"No pajamas?"

"No pajamas. Remember to put on your watch."

As his granddaughter walked away, Mac sent a text to Travis Wheeler, giving him Brooke's address. Duty on at 11:30a. No overnight. M w/b at home. Ack rcpt. The man's reply was immediate. Copy that. I'm on it. Relax. M safe.

♦ ♦ ♦

MAC, SIERRA, AND MICHAELA followed Bryant through the house to the patio. Brooke had just finished trimming Sydney's nails. The dog had been set free to race around the pool when Bryant opened the sliding glass door. "Look who's here, Brooke. And they brought chocolate chip cookies."

Michaela came forth from behind her mother, bearing a plastic wrapped gift like a comical Magi. Her braids were pinned to her head in two poorly placed knots that looked like early season deer horns. Her cover-up was wrong side out and falling off one shoulder. The heel of one foot had slid off her flip flop. Mac could see disaster coming when Sydney spotted the child, then raced to greet her. Excited, Michaela began fast-walking across the flagstone terrace and stumbled. The cookies, fortunately on a plastic plate, clanked to the ground.

"Oh, no, you don't, Sydney." Giggling, Michaela snatched up the plate, then passed it off to Bryant like a football. He burst into laughter at the jumble of smashed cookies. "Nice presentation, Sierra."

Grinning, she shook her head and sat. "We know how to make an entrance, don't we?"

Michaela tore off her cover-up, tossed it on a chair, then raced Sydney to the pool. She jumped in, but the dog slid to a stop at the edge. "Good boy, Sydney." She stuck out her arm and showed him her palm. "Stay."

Mac pecked Brooke's cheek, then took a seat. "She'll notice you're here sooner or later."

Bryant poured iced tea while Brooke wrestled plastic wrap off the cookies. As they chatted, she picked up on her sister's somber mood. "Something bothering you, Sierra?"

"Just a little headache."

Brooke looked skeptical, but let it drop. "My head hurts from trying to get my brain around Mom running for governor." She grimaced at her father. "Why in the world would she want to be governor? She should be planning for retirement."

"Even when Catherine retires from the magazine, she'll stay busy. If she decides against running for governor, she'll accept even more speaking engagements than she does now. She won't slow down until she has to."

Bryant popped a cookie into his mouth. "Catherine would be a fantastic governor."

"No argument there," his wife agreed. "Mom would do a great job, but I repeat. Why would she want to? So where are you on all this, Dad?"

"On the fence."

"You?" Brooke exaggerated her disbelief. "You're never on the fence about anything. When does she have to commit?"

"By November, I think. But she'll need to make a decision fairly soon."

"You wouldn't have to live in the governor's mansion, would you?" Brooke laughed at the prospect. "That could be a problem. People under your feet every minute. No privacy at all. Of course, Sierra and Michaela could house-sit for four years. Right, Sierra?" Her sister did not react. She was watching Michaela fascinate Sydney by popping the surface of the water with a noodle. "Who decided that Graham would pick up Michaela here?" When her sister again did not respond, Brooke said, "I cannot tell you how eager I am to see him, Sierra."

"Who?"

"Graham."

"Really?"

"Of course not," Brooke screeched. "What is going on with you? And don't tell me you have a headache."

Sierra turned to her father. "Would you tell them, Dad? It involves them too."

Mac gazed out over the yard. It was such a peaceful setting. Huge oak trees mushroomed around the pool. Flower beds overflowed with a profusion of periwinkles and other annuals in intense, vibrant colors. Michaela was hanging onto the edge of the pool with one hand and petting Sydney with the other. Children should be worry free, but adults made it impossible.

"It has to do with Graham," Mac began. "Before he leaves town tomorrow, I'm going to tell him about a change in the visitation arrangements. Michaela doesn't want to be alone with him. She's afraid that he might run off with her again. I talked to an attorney friend of mine, and he recommended supervised visitation."

"Supervised?" Brooke repeated. "What does that mean exactly?"

"It means that a family member must be with Michaela when she's with Graham. Not Sierra or me, of course. But you or Bryant or Catherine."

"You can count me in." Bryant's earnest response was tinged with caution. "That is the perfect solution. But Graham— The man will go ballistic when you tell him that."

"I'm sure he will," Mac agreed. "But I will not allow Michaela to go through another weekend like this. She faked an upset stomach this morning so she wouldn't have to go with him by herself. Sierra's lawyer is drafting a new custody agreement, and Graham is going to sign it."

"He ought to do it willingly," Brooke insisted. "That inflexible jerk. What a pathetic excuse for a father."

Conversation ceased when Michaela climbed out of the pool to retrieve a ball from Sydney's toy box. It resumed when the child was out of earshot.

"Too bad you don't have some leverage over the guy," Bryant said, almost to himself.

Mac detected an exchange between his daughters, an intense nonverbal caution from Sierra to her sister. "What was that about?"

"What?" Sierra said.

"That look."

"There was no look."

"Brooke?" Mac pressed.

His daughter paused for a moment, as if hesitant about saying her next thought. "Just tell him, Sierra."

"Tell me what?" Mac went back in his mind, picking up the strings of the conversation. Bryant had said something about leverage over Graham, then Sierra had cut her sister a look. "What are you two keeping from me?"

Brooke hesitated, but then ignored her sister's expression of disapproval. "I'm sorry, Sierra, but Dad needs to know."

"Brooke, no."

"You're his daughter, Sierra. He needs to know." Brooke turned to Mac and leaned close, certain Michaela would not overhear. "Graham pushed Sierra down a flight of stairs."

"He did not," Sierra blurted. "I fell."

"Why did you fall?" Brooke demanded. "Because he exploded, and you were afraid."

Mac slammed the door shut on the exchange. "You fell down a flight of stairs? Where? When?"

"At home," Brooke answered, angrily. "The night before she moved out. She didn't want you and Mom to know."

"Why did you keep that from me?"

"I was embarrassed," Sierra admitted, her tone both defiant and resigned. "And I knew how you would react, Dad."

"Did you file a police report?"

"No." Her eyes widened and blazed. "Of course not. I got us out of there. The very next morning. And I've never looked back."

"You should have told me, Sierra Catherine." Mac reigned in his anger, tempering his tone. "That is not something you keep from your family."

"Now that you know," Brooke said, "maybe you can let up on her. My sister has been on the receiving end of Graham's rage, Dad. You haven't."

"I should have known the truth." But now I do, Mac thought. And now I have leverage over that abusive bastard.

CHAPTER 21

The phone jarred Rebecca awake. It was one in the morning. Her initial thought was that the answering service was reporting a death call or an inquiry of some kind. She rolled onto her side and fumbled for the telephone. "Rebecca Grant." Her voice was thick with sleep, but she was speaking to her landline dial tone. The ringing continued. Grumbling, she turned on a bedside lamp, then picked up her iPhone. "This is Rebecca."

"Hi, Rebecca. I'm sorry to disturb you. My name is Zeke Connor. I'm the manager at Four Oaks Apartments. You are listed as an emergency contact for Russell Shane."

Rebecca was instantly awake. "Is there a problem?"

"Russell wrecked his car tonight." The man's tone conveyed his distress. "He hit a tree here on the property."

Rebecca kept mental images at a safe remove. "Is he injured?"

"There's a cut above his eye. That's all I can see."

"Does he need medical attention?"

"I don't think so, but I'm not the person to make that decision."

"I understand." Rebecca forced herself to relax a little. "Where is he now?"

"In his vehicle. I haven't attempted to move him. You see, he's inebriated."

"Oh, no." Rebecca swung her legs off the bed, then stood. "I'll be there shortly."

Arriving at Four Oaks, she found Russell sitting on the curb next to his Tahoe. His upper body was slumped forward, his chin on his chest. The parking area was poorly lit. Two men stood in the shadows. Rebecca parked her car, then approached them. The larger man introduced himself as Zeke. "This is Abel. He lives here in the complex too."

The left front headlamp of the Tahoe was broken, the bumper askew, and the fender dented. Russell had hit an oak tree with sufficient force to damage his vehicle and to scar the tree trunk for life, but the airbag had not deployed. Rebecca knelt next to him and touched his shoulder. "Russ." With what appeared to be considerable effort, he raised his head and turned her way. Shadows fell across his face.

In every possible way, the man looked wounded. Rebecca was attempting to examine his injury when Russell toppled backwards. The men rushed to grab him but were too late. He landed on his back with a thud. Rebecca moaned. "Can you get him into his apartment?"

Zeke, the more muscular of the two, eased Russell back into a sitting position, then grasped him around the chest. Abel knelt next to him, then put Russell's limp arm around his neck. "Okay, buddy. We're going to help you to your feet. One. Two. Three. Lift." Russell groaned from the pressure on his chest but managed to remain upright as Zeke repositioned to his side. Together, the pair half-carried the staggering man across the parking lot while Rebecca backed the Tahoe away from the tree and parked it in Russell's assigned space.

By the time she entered the apartment, the men had deposited Russell on his rumpled bed and removed his sandals. Zeke pulled the bed linens up to his shoulders, then dabbed at the cut with a tissue. The injury was worse than Rebecca had thought. Blood was streaking down Russell's temple.

After the men left, Rebecca retrieved a first-aid kit from her car, treated the cut, then applied a butterfly bandage. Russell hardly stirred. This could not continue, Rebecca fretted, but what could she do? She had no legal authority to take action. None at all. She no longer had powers-of-attorney of any type. And even if she did, forcing an adult to seek or receive mental health treatment was impossible. She had no choice but to phone August. If anyone could get through to Russell, it was his father.

Sitting on the edge of the bed, Rebecca felt infinitely sorrowful looking down at this man she had loved so much for so long. She placed her hand on his chest, watching it rise and fall. The pain of losing Callie was devouring him, and there was nothing she could do. Tears of sorrow trickled over her lashes. It was like mourning another death as she leaned down and kissed his forehead.

Gathering herself, Rebecca adjusted the lighting in the room, then turned on the ceiling fan. He would probably sleep for hours, wake with a hideous headache, and have no recollection that she had even been here tonight. With that thought in mind, she opened the drawer of the bedside table. You don't think that's the only Glock I own, do you? The drawer was empty. Did he own a second pistol? Possibly. "But if he does, it would be here," she whispered, closing the drawer. "I'm sure of it."

In the living room, she walked past his cluttered desk. A stack of unopened mail had toppled over. Copied letters to the Board of Pardons and Paroles and to the governor lay where she had left them when she and Liam had come to check on Russell. Now, there was another, this one to Catherine McKeon. With a smothering sense of dread, Rebecca pulled back the desk chair and read the letter.

Ms. McKeon:

I have mailed this letter to your home to be certain that it reaches your hands. I have included photos of my daughter Callie Mae Shane and Derek Jaxson with his family. They were murdered in a convenience store near Katy. Callie was seventeen. Derek was twenty-six. Justice was served to one of their killers, Calvin Canon, but his accomplice, Jude Donovan, still sits on death row.

You attended a death penalty discussion at St. Edward's University. The Texas Innocence Initiative was represented by Jude Donovan's mother, a fact that she probably withheld because disclosing it would have tanked her credibility. I have sympathy for Emma Donovan. Not only is her son an accomplice in a double murder, but also she is being exploited by the Innocence Initiative.

Historically your magazine has been against the death penalty and sympathetic toward death row inmates. Your presence at the panel discussion suggests that readers can expect another slanted and biased look at the topic, including interviews from do-gooders at the Innocence Initiative. If so, I hope that you will at least be honest with your readers.

The mission of the Initiative is to spare the lives of the worst of the worst. Murderers currently on death row. Those offenders were sent there by jurors who actually heard the evidence presented at trial. If the Innocence Initiative genuinely cared about the innocent, they would not be trying to delay or stop executions of death row inmates.

The innocents, Ms. McKeon, are people like my daughter Callie and Derek Jaxson. If a member of your family had been murdered by the likes of Calvin Canon and Jude Donovan, I'm sure that your magazine would tackle the Innocence Initiative head on. You would advocate for the victims and their families, not the killers.

You have a chance to do the right thing, Ms. McKeon. I certainly hope that you do it.

Sincerely,

Russell Shane

Rebecca made a quick copy of the two-page letter. She would mail a copy to August. Reading it would help him appreciate the intensity of Russell's obsession with Jude Donovan and with anyone who might try to prove his innocence. Russell knew now that Catherine McKeon was considering a run for governor. He actually believed that her motivation was to position herself to influence the Board of Pardons and Paroles, to end the execution of death row offenders.

How had it come to this? Rebecca agonized, as she locked the apartment and returned the key to its hiding space on the lantern.

Walking to her car, she felt a familiar but unwelcome inner loneliness. She had an impossible decision to make about

Nichole and Seth Palmer. Nichole had lied about why they went to the convenience store the night of the incident. The credit card statement proved that she had bought gas before leaving Galveston. Beyond that, Nichole had initially allowed people to think she was fueling her car when the shooting erupted. "And she would have perpetuated that account if Dad hadn't caught her in a lie."

♦ ♦ ♦

REBECCA ARRIVED LATE to work. She had phoned August that morning. He would wait a day or two, then insist that Russell come for a visit. "Don't take no for an answer," Rebecca stressed. "He needs you."

She found Jake in the preparation room in full protective gear, but the mask dangled under his chin. Protective clothing, although necessary, could be constricting and smothering. The deceased man on the embalming table was, in funeral home parlance, a ship-out. He had died in a boating accident on Lake Travis, but would be buried in Knoxville, Tennessee. That afternoon, she and Jake would place his body in a shipping container, a sturdy corrugated box with a plywood base designed to safely and efficiently transport human remains in the cargo hold of commercial airliners.

Authorities had ordered a complete autopsy, including toxicological screening. Boating-while-impaired was not an uncommon occurrence. Jake had finished suturing the Y-shape incision on the man's torso. Now, he was sitting on a stool next to his head, suturing the ear-to-ear incision the M.E. had made in the man's scalp.

"How old is he?" Rebecca asked, standing next to the table.

"Twenty-seven. Thrown from a boat. Definitely has a broken neck."

Rebecca pulled on a pair of gloves, then removed the lid from a small container of liquid adhesive. Carefully, she painted the sticky substance over the incision to further seal it, admiring Jake's tight, precise, perfectly spaced sutures. "Nice work."

"Thanks." He sat upright and arched his back. "Would you do me a favor?"

"Of course."

"Make Kevin work seven days a week."

Rebecca chuckled, then finished brushing on the adhesive. The intercom sounded. "Rebecca, your father is on line one. Can you take his call?"

"Yes. Ask him to give me a minute." Rebecca peeled off her gloves, then patted Jake's shoulder. "Hang in there. You're almost done."

In her office, she settled at her desk, then picked up the phone. "Sorry, Dad. I was in the prep room. We got a ship-out. Boating accident." She skimmed the details, then said, "Well, what do you think? Is Myra right? Should I talk to Clay Borger again?"

"JoAnn and I agree with Myra. You have a moral obligation to disclose what you've discovered."

Rebecca's spirit sagged. That was not what she had hoped to hear. Or was it? She sat silently, waiting for her father to make his case.

"I am not advising you to contact Clay Borger, however. That is entirely up to you. I didn't meet him. You did. Borger has a stellar reputation, though. I had Sheriff Blankenship do some checking around."

"Thanks, Dad. I hadn't thought about doing that."

"JoAnn and I have talked about this at length. You are in an impossible situation, honey, and there is no easy way out. But we cannot ignore the possibility that Seth Palmer or Nichole, or maybe both of them, lied on the stand at Jude Donovan's trial. Think about it. If they were at the convenience store to buy drugs, then it is possible that Seth Palmer set up the transaction. If he did, then maybe Calvin Canon arrived with Palmer, not Jude Donovan. If that is the case, then Seth Palmer would have a powerful reason to lie. He could be on death row right now instead of Jude Donovan."

"But what about Nichole, Dad? Why would she commit perjury?"

"We're not convinced that she did. Maybe the girl actually did see Calvin Canon near Jude Donovan's car, but that does not mean he was ever inside it. That's something we cannot know." Rebecca heard her mother's voice in the background. "JoAnn wants to know if you've discussed any of this with Russell."

"No. He's in a terrible way. I can't bear to think how he would react if I so much as hint that Nichole was at the convenience store to buy drugs." She told her father about Russell's obsession with Jude Donovan and the Texas Innocence Initiative, about his anger because she had not warned Nichole that Clay Borger was looking for her, about the letters to the governor and the Board of Pardons and Paroles, even a letter to Catherine McKeon. "And he's drinking a lot, Dad. Last night he ran into a tree at his apartment complex."

"I'm really sorry to hear that, Rebecca. Believe me. Russell is a good man. But you cannot let your concern about how he might react prevent you from doing the right thing."

The right thing. It was the same phrase Russell had used in his letter to Catherine McKeon. You have a chance to do the right thing, Ms. McKeon. I certainly hope that you do it.

"You'll pay a steep price for coming forward, Rebecca."

"How steep?" she asked, wearily.

"That's something else we can't know. But this I do know. Nichole lied to me. I suspected it two years ago, and now I know for sure. If Nichole had not gone to that convenience store, Callie would be alive today."

CHAPTER 22

Sunday morning, Catherine and Michaela left to meet Graham at the Hyatt. Mac was at home, iPhone in hand, watching a flashing M move along a map of Tarrytown. Catherine's car headed east on Windsor Road, then stopped at Exposition. He pictured the two of them chatting away about who-knew-what, then they were on the move again. Travis Wheeler was in position in the hotel lobby. Catherine did not know that Mac had hired him or that Michaela's watch was a tracking device. Mac was not sure how she would react, and she had enough on her mind right now.

He had not told her about Sierra falling down the stairs either, the night before she left Graham. "I want to tell Mom myself," Sierra had insisted gently, "but not now. She's been asked to run for governor, Dad. What an honor. Let's not do anything to taint this time for her."

Sierra claimed that Graham had never hit or pushed her, but that his temper, his volatility were frightening, both for her and for Michaela. If Mac had known, he would have insisted that she move out months ago and get an order of protection. If he had his way now, Graham Hollister would be facing domestic violence charges.

Mac focused his attention on the map again. The vehicle was headed east on Lake Austin Boulevard toward downtown. Catherine and Michaela were minutes away from the Hyatt, minutes away from Graham Hollister. Mac loathed the idea of his grandchild being alone with the man, but two and a half hours from now, that would come to an end.

Mac's hand jerked when an email alert sounded. His nerves were on edge, even though he had all bases covered. The email was from Ben Morrow. He was ready to make an offer on the Donovan ranch. Mac felt a familiar surge of excitement, but it quickly dissipated. For the first time in his career, he dreaded telling a client he had an offer on their property. But for Emma and Lester's sake, he would push for an expedited closing. They needed the money and, in Emma's words, putting it off would not make things any easier.

Mac responded to the email but pressed Save. It needed proofing, but he could not focus. He closed the email, then turned his attention back to Catherine and Michaela. The vehicle was stationary. He zoomed in. They were at the hotel. Immediately a text tone sounded. It was Travis Wheeler. M with GH. I've got this. Relax.

Mac continued monitoring Michaela's movement. She and Graham were walking alongside Lady Bird Lake. Where was Travis? "You have to trust the man," Mac muttered.

Twenty minutes later, Catherine walked through the door of his study. Mac closed the app, then swiveled toward her in his chair. "How did it go?"

"Fine. She only asked me four times when I was picking her up. Thank God she has her new watch." She looked down at her own. "Has Sierra left for church?" Mac nodded. "If we hurry, we can make it too."

"Or we could not hurry at all and take a walk."

They opted for a walk. The late morning sun was burning through the cloud cover, but the tree-lined sidewalk remained in the shade. Tarrytown was a beautiful neighborhood, quiet and low key. Homes, whether modest or grand, were nicely maintained. They strolled in companionable silence, then Catherine brought up the letter she had received from Russell Shane. "I need to respond, but I can't seem to find the words. And those pictures, Mac. Both of those innocent young people are dead."

"And Jude Donovan was there when it happened."

"What do you think, Mac? About the verdict."

"I don't know, but Emma and Lester are convinced that one of the eyewitnesses is lying."

"They've lost their son, and now they're giving up their home in hopes of saving him. So much misery."

Mac's thoughts strayed, and he checked his watch. Two more hours and Catherine would return to the hotel. Where were Graham and Michaela now? He wished he could use the tracking app on his iPhone or that he could send a quick text to Travis. "He's on it," Mac mumbled. Relax.

◆ ◆ ◆

GRAHAM HOLLISTER WAS sitting on the patio outside Starbucks when Mac arrived. He did not look like a commercial property manager or a man suffering through a miserable divorce. He was tan, fit, and impeccably dressed in dark gray jeans, a light gray and blue shirt, and casual, lace-up shoes in black leather. He wore aviator style sunglasses, and his black hair was perfectly styled. "I've got to get back to Plano," he said curtly, "so let's cut to the chase. You wanted to talk to me about something."

"It's about Michaela." Mac paused, slowing the pace of what would be a contentious conversation. "She was upset the day you showed up at the club."

"Of course, she was. She saw you shove me."

The words hung in the air between them, but Mac ignored them. He would not be baited. "Michaela told me she's afraid."

"Afraid? Of what?"

"Michaela is afraid you'll take her away again."

"She didn't say anything about that to me." Graham leaned back and crossed his arms over his abdomen, the picture of defiance. "I want to hear that from her."

"I'm telling you this in confidence, Graham. Michaela is afraid, and we cannot let it continue." Mac had to force himself to use the word we. He loathed any association with this man. "We have to be sure she feels safe."

"What are you getting at?" Graham snapped.

"For the time being, I think it's best for a family member to be with Michaela during your visits."

Graham angled his head, then screwed up his face. "You cannot be serious."

"It wouldn't be Sierra or me. Maybe Brooke or Bryant. Or Catherine."

"You're telling me that I shouldn't be alone with my own daughter?"

"This is not about you, Graham. It's about Michaela. You kept her from her family for ten days. To a child that is an eternity."

Leaning forward, the man tapped the metal table with a rigid finger. "I am her family, Mac, and don't you forget it."

Mac chose his words carefully. He detested this colossal bully. "Having another person around when you're with Michaela is not ideal, but we have to make it work."

"The hell I do." Graham pounded out his next point with his fist, rattling the metal table. "Short of a judge's order, it's never going to happen. And no judge is going to order me to submit to that crap, like I was a danger to my child, or some kind of pervert."

The man was fuming. Mac disciplined his voice, maintaining control. "No one wants to involve the court. I hope it won't come to that, but that depends on you."

"That woman put my life through a meat grinder, and now she thinks—"

Mac chopped off the sentence. "That woman?" The words were a declaration of war. "Is that what you just called my daughter?" This time Mac jabbed the tabletop. "You listen to me, you arrogant, abusive bully. Sierra's lawyer is drawing up a revised custody agreement, and you are going to sign it."

"The hell I will."

Mac had held back as long as he could. It was time to drop the hammer. "I know what happened the night before Sierra and Michaela moved out."

There was a slight pause, then Graham said, "I don't know what you're talking about."

"Sierra fell down a flight of stairs." Anger hung between them like an invisible dagger. "She was trying to get away from you."

"She's lying." Even through Graham's sunglasses, Mac could see the fury in his eyes. "Do you really want to go head-to-head with me, Mac?"

"Do you want another run through that meat grinder?"

Graham's chest was heaving as the threat went unanswered. Long seconds later, he smirked. "Fine. Send your little custody agreement to my lawyer. We'll take a look at it. I want what is best for my daughter." He stood, smoothed his shirttail in the waist of his jeans, then adjusted his sunglasses. "Oh, and one other thing. Give Sierra a message for me. Tell her I'm aware that she contacted my insurance agent. Then remind her that I own her life insurance policy. I pay the premium. And I'm the beneficiary."

CHAPTER 23

Rebecca looked on as Myra, with her bare hand, swept broken twigs and brittle leaves from a concrete bench, then sat on the hard, unwelcoming slab. Before leaving Sparrows Cove and driving to the secluded park, they had stopped by Sacred Grounds and bought three iced coffees. Despite the rising temperature that morning, Clay Borger's drink would still be chilled by the time he arrived.

"I cannot believe we're doing this." Rebecca placed a document on the picnic table, then anchored it with her purse. "Sneaking out of town to meet a private investigator in an isolated county park."

"You don't want anyone to know you're talking to him." Myra's tone was compassionate. "That's understandable."

After speaking with her father, Rebecca had fretted for days. Nichole had lied about why she had been at the convenience store. Rebecca had to speak up, to do the right thing. Should she hire an attorney and let her handle it? Should she disclose the information to the District Attorney's office in Harris County or to Jude Donovan's attorney? She had raised other options, but one by one, she had shot them down. Hiring an attorney would be expensive, and she did not want to spend the money. Contacting the DA's office would mean battling a bureaucracy. The case was closed. The office had racked up another victory. What reason would they have to poke a sleeping bear? She had considered contacting Jude Donovan's trial attorney, but he had been an unimpressive man. Rebecca had no interest in speaking with him. But what about Clay Borger? she had pondered. The man had seemed well-intentioned, genuine, and humble.

Any moment now, he would be sitting across the table, and Rebecca would be committing an act that seemed in one moment honorable and in the next profoundly disloyal.

A black Chevy Silverado slowed on the two-lane county road, pulled onto the parking lot, then rolled to a stop. The driver's heavy door swung open slowly, and Clay Borger stepped out. He was dressed in neatly pressed jeans, a white shirt with the sleeves rolled back, and polished black boots.

The three shook hands when Clay Borger reached the table, and Myra slid the cup of iced coffee his way. "I have this for you too." She handed the man a dollar bill. "That is what you and Rebecca agreed on, right?"

"Precisely." He folded the bill and put it in his pocket. "I'm officially retained."

"Just so you know," Myra teased. "My son is an attorney. If you violate confidentiality, he'll file a complaint, then sue you."

Clay Borger snickered, then removed the lid from the coffee cup. "I am officially warned, and I'm officially on the clock."

Rebecca welcomed the man's good humor, then thanked him for driving all the way from Waco. "I hardly know where to start."

"How about the end?"

"The end? Most people say start at the beginning."

"But that can take a long time. Something is troubling you. I'm betting it has something to do with Nichole, and the night your Callie was killed. Am I right?"

"Yes. Nichole lied about why they were at the convenience store."

Clay Borger cocked his head. "Well, I didn't see that coming." He took a gulp of coffee, then swiveled on the concrete bench to gain some leg room. "Now, let's start at the beginning."

Rebecca began by detailing the only account Nichole had given her about the night Callie died. She ended by saying, "That conversation occurred the day after the incident. There is no doubt in my mind that Nichole said she had been putting gas in her car when she heard gunfire. No doubt at all. But then two weeks later, she changed her story."

"How did that happen?" the man asked.

"My dad and I went to Houston, to the convenience store. I had to see where my daughter died." Rebecca told Clay Borger about the sketch her father and Nichole had generated the night before the trip. "The drawing showed where all three vehicles were parked. The Honda. The Mercedes. And Nichole's Mazda. But on our way home, my father realized that what Nichole said could not have been true." She lined up two sugar packets on a napkin, then took a pen from her purse, marking on the napkin where the pumps were located as P-1 and P-2. "This is Seth Palmer's Mercedes." She marked the sugar packet by pump one with the letters SP. "Nichole said she parked behind his car. The problem is, the fuel door on a Mercedes is on the passenger side, but the fuel door on Nichole's Mazda is here." She tapped the second sugar packet. "On the driver's side."

"Interesting. So Nichole parked on the wrong side of the pumps."

"Yet the day after the incident, she told me she had been putting gas in her car when Callie was shot."

"She was lying," Myra interjected. "And she admitted as much to Nelson, Rebecca's father, when he quizzed her about it. Nichole got very flustered and claimed that she had forgotten that detail."

Rebecca continued. "She told my father that she was nervous and in a rush. That's why she parked on the wrong side. But before she could reposition the Mazda, the gunfire erupted."

"What did she testify at trial?" Clay Borger asked. "Do you remember?"

"Not specifically. As I recall, she said she stopped there to buy gas. More than that, I don't remember."

"But there's more, Clay. Go ahead, Rebecca," Myra urged. "Show him the credit card statement."

Rebecca slid the document from under her purse. "This is a copy of my ex-husband's credit card statement from two years ago. Nichole was using it at the time. I highlighted a specific charge." She handed him the paper.

"July thirty-first. Thirty-two dollars and twenty-five cents. Texaco. Galveston." Clay Borger frowned and nodded knowingly. "July thirty-first. That was the day of the shooting."

"Nichole filled her SUV in Galveston," Myra underscored. "Then she drove seventy-five miles or so and pulled into a convenience store. She told numerous people that she was there to buy gas, but that girl is a total liar."

"Myra's right, not that Nichole is a liar—"

"Which she is," Myra insisted.

"But it makes no sense that she would stop for gas that soon."

"None at all," Clay agreed. He continued considering the document. "If you had to guess, why do you think she was there?"

"We think they were meeting Seth Palmer." Rebecca picked up the coffee cup, but then set it down again. She was suddenly incredibly nervous. "Possibly to buy drugs."

"Seth Palmer and Jessica Hart are involved," Myra explained. "We don't know for how long. And there is every indication that Jessica does drugs. Most likely meth."

Clay Borger stared at the document. Rebecca and Myra sat quietly, allowing the man mental space. Leaves rustled in the oak trees. Noisy blue jays screeched, as if warning smaller birds of a predator. Clay looked up, studied the birds, then turned to Myra. "If the girls were there to buy drugs, then that means Seth Palmer could have set up the buy."

"Of course, he could have," Myra maintained. "He's a sleazy, conniving kind of guy. I wouldn't trust him any farther than I can spit."

Rebecca and Clay exchanged looks. Amusement sparked in his eyes, but then he grew serious again. "If what you suspect is true, Palmer had a compelling reason to lie about what happened, even if it meant implicating Jude Donovan."

The sound of the man's name still had a jarring effect on Rebecca. Jude Donovan was an accomplice in Callie's murder. Or was he? Rebecca became suddenly nauseous. She could feel the color drain from her face.

"Are you okay, Becca?"

She nodded, the untouched coffee quivering in the cup. "Where do we go from here, Clay?" Her voice was as thin as the breeze tousling her hair.

For a long moment, Clay Borger considered the question. "There are three people still alive who know the truth about what happened that night. Seth, Nichole, and Jessica. So far, they have stayed united. The weak link, as I see it, is Jessica."

"No question," Myra agreed. "But how do we get her to break from the other two?"

"We have to get her to turn on them."

"I think I know how," Rebecca said, flashing back to the intimate moments she had witnessed between Nichole and Seth.

"What do you have in mind?" Clay Borger asked.

"Tell her that Seth is cheating on her with Nichole."

"Is he?"

"I think so." She told them about the secretive gesture she had witnessed at Zoe Hewlett's memorial when Nichole and Seth had held hands with Jessica literally in their presence, and later witnessing the pair embracing outside Russell's apartment. "Nichole has always gone after what she wants, no matter who she tramples."

Myra flicked a fallen leaf off the table. "The girl is as disloyal as Judas himself."

Rebecca and Clay again exchanged looks. She liked this man, maybe even trusted him.

"What you need," Myra continued, "are some pictures of Seth and Nichole together. Better yet, a video. You could get that. Right, Clay? Then you could show it to Jessica, get her completely rattled. Then tell her that you know they were buying drugs that night, that they framed Jude Donovan, and that all hell is getting ready to break loose."

With jittery fingers, Rebecca retrieved the credit card statement. Russell Shane. She returned the paper to her handbag and was suddenly assaulted with guilt. What was she doing? Nichole was Russell's daughter. He had been furious that Clay had spoken to Nichole. What would he do when he finds out that his daughter was being accused of buying drugs and lying about it? A decision that got Callie killed. Rebecca's body went suddenly limp. She released a long, slow audible breath. You have a moral obligation to do the right thing, her father had said. You can't let worrying about how Russell might react prevent you from doing the right thing.

"I think Myra's plan might work," Clay Borger said. "And the truth is, Jessica Hart never implicated Jude Donovan. It was Seth and Nichole's statements to police that put Jude in the line of fire."

"Of course, it was," Myra insisted. "You must convince Jessica that she is home free if she tells the truth. They were at the convenience store to meet Seth Palmer and buy meth. Nichole sent Callie inside that damn store to get her out of the way."

Fighting back tears, Rebecca nodded agreement. Myra stroked her back. "You deserve to know the truth. Callie was your daughter. You deserve to know the truth."

Clay Borger reached across the table to squeeze Rebecca's hand. "She's right, you know. You deserve the truth, and so do Emma and Lester Donovan."

CHAPTER 24

Mac could have secured Emma's and Lester's signatures on the contract electronically, but he opted to hand deliver it. Ben Morrow had had a family emergency, so several days had passed since his email indicating that he was prepared to make an offer. But now, Mac had the forms in hand. He had intended to take the helicopter to Kerrville, but changed his plan when Catherine said she would like to go along with him. On a previous flight to Corpus Christi, they had hit several minutes of turbulence that even Mac had to admit had been severe. Catherine had not boarded the helicopter since.

On the way out of Austin, they commiserated about decades of poor planning that had resulted in the city's ever increasing traffic snarls. Miles later, as so often happened, the conversation shifted to the children. Catherine asked about the custody agreement.

"Graham's lawyer received it. He said it's all in order, but he will advise Graham not to sign it. He called it unnecessary, onerous, and offensive."

"That doesn't sound promising."

Respecting Sierra's desire, Mac had not told Catherine about their daughter's fall down the stairs the night before she and Michaela left Graham. Had the fall actually been an accident? Would Sierra admit it if Graham had pushed her? No matter how it happened, Sierra could have been badly injured, and Mac had no qualms about using the incident as leverage. Even a man like Graham Hollister did not want to be labeled a domestic abuser. "We'll give him a few more days. I think he'll sign it."

"I admire your confidence, but why would he?"

"Self-preservation." If Graham were not Michaela's father, Mac would not think twice about ruining the man's life with a few well-placed phone calls to associates in the Dallas metroplex. But as it was, Mac would protect Michaela while, at the same time, taking Graham Hollister down a few notches.

Mac had passed along to his daughter Graham's message about the life insurance policy, omitting the man's confrontational tone. Sierra admitted to having contacted the agent about the possibility of accessing some cash via the policy. "I want to pay back the thirty-thousand dollars we owe you, Dad." Mac regretted that Sierra had been troubled over the loan and reminded her that he had a second lien on the Plano house. "The title company will cut me a check at the closing. But I'm not signing a release until I'm sure you get your community property share."

Mac understood the wisdom of carrying life insurance on a spouse when children were involved. But, God forbid, if something were to happen to Sierra, Graham Hollister would not need money to take care of Michaela. Mac would never allow the man to take his grandchild away from her family.

"Enough about Graham Hollister," he said to his wife. "I don't want to think about that guy."

"Agreed." Catherine gazed out the window as they made their way west through the hill country. "The offer you're taking to Emma and Lester, is it a good one?"

"Full price. Ben Morrow wants the place, and he's not a haggler. It's a cash sale, so the deal should close in short order."

"How sad for Emma and Lester, though. What are their plans?"

"They'll put most of their furniture in storage, then rent a place closer to Livingston."

"What about their jobs?"

"Lester said that being an architect allows him to work from anywhere. It will require some travel on his part, but he will deal with it. Emma will get a job wherever they end up living. She said she's never waited tables, but she's willing to learn."

"No matter where they move, word will get out that their son is on death row. What could be worse?"

"Believing your son is innocent."

According to Lester, Jude's depression was worsening. The chaplain had told them not to despair, that what their son was experiencing was not uncommon, and that they should continue to pray. As if they needed to be told, Mac thought. Don't despair. Easy for him to say.

"So much pain," Catherine whispered, "from one horrific crime."

Mac sat silently, his right wrist resting on the steering wheel. He let his mind wander back to a week ago, when he had listened to Clay Borger condense the prosecution's case against Jude. And then there are the victims and their families, he had said in closing while wiping a water ring from the tabletop. Derek Jaxson was a fine young man. And Callie Shane was as innocent as the day is long. Mac had gotten the impression that Clay would go to Sparrows Cove right away to try and talk with Callie's half-sister and the other witness.

Sparrows Cove. Mac recalled how stunned he had been to see the return address on the letter Catherine had left on his desk. "Honey, did you respond to the letter from Russell Shane?"

"I did," she answered, reaching for her purse. "But I haven't mailed it. I wanted your opinion." She retrieved a single, typewritten page from her bag and unfolded it. "Dear Mr. Shane: Words cannot express how moved I was to receive the photograph of Derek Jaxson with his family and the picture of your precious daughter Callie. The loss you have suffered is unimaginable. You have my deepest sympathy. You also have my respect for seeking justice for your daughter and for Derek Jaxson. My familiarity with the Texas Innocence Initiative is limited. My presence at St. Edward's the day of the panel discussion you referenced was not meant as a sign of support of their mission."

"Wait," Mac interrupted. "I'm not sure about that part. Russell Shane has it in for the Innocence Initiative. Are you sure you should mention it?"

"I wondered about that. I don't want to sound defensive." She marked through the lines and continued to read. "Your point is well taken with respect to any future articles that might appear in Texas Times Monthly concerning the criminal justice system. You are correct to underscore that we have an obligation to our readers to cover all issues in a balanced and intellectually honest manner. In closing, you have my heartfelt sympathy for your loss, and my earnest respect for your courage and determination. Sincerely, Catherine McKeon."

"Perfect."

Catherine thanked him, then re-read the edited letter silently. "There is one other thing I could acknowledge. Callie Shane was murdered July thirty-first. The date stayed in my mind because that was Mother's birthday. The thirty-first is just a few days from now. Perhaps I should acknowledge it."

Mac agreed, then glanced at his wife as she inserted a sentence in the second paragraph. That done, she still seemed to be troubling over the letter. "Something bothering you?"

Before Catherine could answer, her cell phone rang. It was not synced with the Tahoe's Bluetooth, so Mac heard one side of his wife's conversation with her assistant. "Tell Phil to look at his calendar. First of next week would be better for me." She ended the call, then dropped her phone back in her purse. "The word is getting around that I was asked to run for governor. Apparently, the rumor is causing a stir."

"It's only been two weeks since Phil approached you," Mac reminded, his tone impatient. "Are you feeling pressured?"

"A little, yes, but it's actually been helpful."

Mac tensed. For two weeks, he had watched his wife's interest in running for office gain traction. Catherine had always been restless for fresh horizons, but she was a methodical thinker and a savvy woman. She arrived at conclusions, decisions, and positions; she never leaped there and then retreated. Now, if Mac was reading her accurately, the process was complete. She had reached a decision, and he had made a colossal miscalculation. He had meant to give Catherine time to think and to silently celebrate the honor of being asked to run for governor. But now, he worried that he had come across as ambivalent. He had been too passive. Now, he had no choice but to change course. He would not allow his family to be thrust into the spotlight, to have their privacy invaded, and their fragile routine derailed.

"Mac, I've decided not to run."

Her words, sudden and unexpected, were like debris on the highway. Mac actually tapped the brake and tightened his grip on the steering wheel. I've decided not to run. His relief was so profound that he released a deep, protracted but silent sigh. "You're not running? When did you decide?"

"Last night."

Mac remained silent, but his mind was racing. How had he misread Catherine so badly? Or had he? Had something happened to change her mind? It didn't matter. She had decided not to run. That was the end of it. There was no need to worry that she would backtrack. No one could persuade her to change her mind, not even Phil Kuykendall. "Tell me about it. How did you decide?"

Catherine extended her hand and Mac took it. "We both know that I've put my career before my family twice. First, when the girls were young, and I took the political beat at the Statesman. I knew the job would require travel and insanely long hours, but I took it anyway. Why? Because I also knew that you would pick up the slack. The second time was when I left the paper and took a job at a start-up magazine with an uncertain future." She squeezed his hand. "I also took a hefty pay cut, although the job meant more travel, more pressure, and even longer hours. Again, I knew the girls would be fine because of you."

"Do you regret your decisions?" Mac asked, hoping that she did not.

"Regret them? No. But am I proud to admit that I put my career before my children? No, again. Were they harmed by it though? Of course not. They had you."

"We made it work." Max felt himself relax as relief circulated like blood through his veins. "Is that why you decided not to run? Because you would be putting yourself before us again?"

"Again?" Catherine chuckled. "You didn't have to put it that way exactly. But yes. I don't want to do that again. My family needs me more than the governor's office does."

Mac lifted his wife's hand and kissed her folded fingers. "I cannot tell you what a relief this is."

"I figured as much." Catherine smiled tenderly, then turned to look out the passenger window. "Sierra is in so much pain. She needs us both. And so does Michaela." She squeezed his hand again, then released it to wipe sudden tears from her eyes.

Catherine was rarely emotional, and Mac knew not to attempt to comfort her. The conversation had taken her to an uncomfortable place. He waited, knowing she would not stay there long.

"My next step is to properly thank Phil and Lillian." Her voice had reclaimed its disciplined quality. She was ordering her steps. "Then I need to thank some other people who privately encouraged me to run. I will need to make some sort of public statement too. That's the only way to put an end to any further speculation."

"And it gives you a chance," Mac interjected, "to let people know how honored you are to have been asked." His wife's smile, warm and beautiful, reached deep into Mac's heart. "You would have been a great governor. I'm so proud of you."

CHAPTER 25

Rebecca's day began at four in the morning when she abandoned any hope of sleeping. She had re-sent a text message to Russell at midnight, but he still had not responded, nor had he returned her phone call. She had to tell him that Nichole had fueled her car before leaving Galveston and that his daughter had lied about why the girls had stopped at the convenience store the night Callie was killed. For now, though, Rebecca would not tell him that she was teaming up with Clay Borger.

Wearily, Rebecca threw on her workout clothes, then drove to her parents' house. Sparrows Cove was sound asleep, its streets deserted. Last night, she had confided in her parents about Clay's and her plan to talk to Jessica alone, away from Seth or Nichole. "We must get to the truth, and Jessica is the weak link. We'll confront her with the credit card statement, then keep the pressure on." It was then that her father had brought up the convenience store sketch that he and Nichole had generated. "I'm confident I still have it, honey. It would be in the file cabinet in my study. The tab reads Callie."

The exterior lights at her parents' home were on a timer, giving the house a lived-in appearance. Rebecca parked in the driveway, then used her key to enter. The air conditioner had been off for nearly a month. The house was stuffy and warm, but it still had the lingering scent of "sea breeze," her mother's favorite home fragrance.

Rebecca had grown up in the house. It was a typical, hill country lake house with walls of windows framing the coveted view, ceramic tile floors, worn rugs scattered here and there, and casual wicker and upholstered furniture that her parents had collected over the years. She and her brother Adam had had a happy childhood. "Come to Geneva sometime, Becca. You would love it here." And maybe someday she would.

Her father's study was in the front of the house. The desk lamp was on a timer, too, so the room was dimly lit. A metal file cabinet stood in the corner of the room, the drawers neatly labeled. She pulled open the top one, then thumbed through the tabs. Callie. Removing the entire Pendaflex, she opened it on her father's desk. Cards of all kinds spilled out. Birthday. Grandfathers Day. Valentines. Christmas. Even a handwritten card for Veterans Day.

Rebecca whispered Callie's words. "Dear Granddad, Veterans Day is an opportunity to fly the flag. Mom and I are doing that. It is also an opportunity to thank men and women who have served our country in the military. So thank you for your service, Granddad. I'm proud to be your granddaughter. Love, Callie." Rebecca placed her palm over her daughter's words, hungering to hear her child's voice. What a precious girl Callie had been.

She attempted to read the printed lines of a birthday card but had to stop. Her heart was sinking, but she could not look away from the handwritten words. "Granddad, I hope your birthday is as happy as you made mine! Callie." Rebecca closed the card when her eyes began to burn. Tears pooled in them, then began to stream down her face. The ache in her heart was suddenly unbearable.

With her vision blurred, she rifled through the cards, trying not to take in more greetings or images. So touching, she thought, that her father had kept these cards from Callie for years. Amid the cards was a folded piece of white paper. It was the sketch, exactly where her father had said it would be.

♦ ♦ ♦

JESSICA HART ARRIVED AT eight o'clock. Clay Borger had arrived at Rebecca's house an hour earlier and was now out of sight in the kitchen. That morning, he and Rebecca had decided that a tag team approach to prying Jessica loose from Seth and Nichole had a higher likelihood of success than Clay talking to her alone.

Jessica was clearly anxious, fearful even, when she took a seat on the sofa. She had large, timid eyes, and her thinness made the feature even more pronounced. Her sundress was crinkled cotton in a pale pink. She wore a lacy jacket over it, but the skimpy garment did nothing to camouflage her skinniness, nor did her foundation conceal a raging acne outbreak. "Why did you ask me to come here, Rebecca?"

"I have someone I want you to meet." Rebecca paused, then Clay stepped out of the kitchen. "This is Clay Borger. He's a private detective."

Jessica cut the man a look. "I know who he is. That man is working for Jude Donovan. What is he doing here?"

"We need to talk to you," Rebecca said curtly, still standing.

"I don't have anything to say to him." Jessica sprang from the sofa, but Rebecca blocked her way. "Move, Rebecca. You can't make me stay here."

"You can leave if you want," Clay said, lowering himself into a club chair perpendicular to the sofa. "But you are making a huge mistake if you don't hear me out."

"Jessica, he's right. You don't have to stay. You don't even have to talk. But you need to listen." Rebecca continued to block the girl's exit. "Sit down."

Jessica plopped onto the sofa again, folded her arms, and locked them. "That man is a liar. He told Nichole he was working for the cops or somebody."

"You're right," Clay conceded nonchalantly. "I let Nichole think that at first, but I'm going to be truthful with you."

"I don't believe a word you say." Her icy insolence persisted.

"Then believe what I say," Rebecca demanded, sitting next to Jessica, now clearly feigning defiance. "You are facing a massive mountain of trouble." She picked up one of two papers lying face down on the cocktail table. "You lied about what happened the night Callie was killed. So did Seth and Nichole. Do not bother denying it because I have proof right here in my hand."

Jessica gave the papers a quick, dismissive glance. "I don't care what you have. Clay Borger is the one who's lying." Her combative attitude was escalating, and she pressed on. "He's trying to get Callie's killer out of prison."

"That is exactly what I'm doing." Clay moved to the edge of the seat, leaning toward Jessica, his expression a warning. "And believe me, young lady, I will mow down anybody who gets in my way."

Rebecca held a document before the girl's face. "Look at this, Jessica. That is Russell's credit card statement from two years ago. There is a charge for thirty-two dollars and twenty-five cents. The charge is for gasoline bought at a Texaco station in Galveston."

"Look at the date," Clay demanded. "Recognize it?"

With the document still in Jessica's face, Rebecca said, "You and Nichole lied. She fueled her car before you left the island. You were not at the convenience store to buy gas."

"Or bottled water," Clay said, contemptuously. "You were there to buy drugs, Jessica."

"Drugs?" Her voice shrilled.

"And Seth Palmer was your dealer."

"That is crazy." Jessica slapped the document away, wrinkling it. "Seth does not sell drugs."

"And two years ago—" Clay jabbed at the girl with his forefinger. "Calvin Canon was his supplier."

"You are insane."

Jessica's combative attitude was beginning to erode. Rebecca tossed the statement face up on the table, then picked up the second document. "And then there is this. Nichole and my dad drew this sketch two years ago. It shows exactly where Nichole parked her Mazda at the convenience store gas pumps. Right behind Seth Palmer's Mercedes."

"So?"

"Nichole parked on the wrong side of the pump, Jessica, but she didn't care. She was not there to buy gasoline. She was there so that you could buy drugs from Seth Palmer."

"That never happened."

Clay pointed from one document to the other. "Those papers are called evidence. And Monday morning, I am taking them to the district attorney in Harris County. And then all hell is going to break loose."

"Jessica, you need to listen to him," Rebecca pressed, knowing Clay would not do that. He understood that she had to speak to Russell first.

"All three of you lied. Seth. Nichole. And you, Jessica." Clay continued to pound away at the girl who was visibly crumbling. "You lied to the police. That is a felony. You lied to the district attorney. That is obstruction of justice. Another felony."

"I did not lie to anybody."

"And you lied on the witness stand. That, Jessica, is perjury in a capital murder case."

"I did not lie." Jessica was on the edge of panic. Her pupils were enormous black holes. "Never. Not one time."

"You told the police you were at the convenience store to buy gasoline."

"Nichole told them that. I didn't."

"And you told them that Calvin Canon got out of Jude Donovan's car."

"You are wrong. I never said that."

"Fine," Clay conceded, giving Rebecca a we-got-her look. "That was Seth Palmer's lie, but you kept your mouth shut, Jessica. You are as guilty as he is."

"No. None of what happened is my fault."

"Of course, it is. And that is how the District Attorney will see it. I guarantee it."

Jessica grabbed Rebecca's wrist, clenching it with trembling fingers. "This is not my fault, Rebecca."

"Yes, it is, Jessica. Stop lying." The girl's hand was like a heating pad. Did she have a fever? Rebecca wanted to throw off her hand but resisted. "You all lied. But it is not too late for you to tell the truth."

"I am telling the truth. I had nothing to do with—" She released Rebecca's wrist and tried to stand, but her trembling legs would not allow it. "I want out of here. You cannot keep me here."

"Suit yourself, but you are making a huge mistake." Clay settled back in the chair, his body language suddenly passive. "Look, Jessica. You are in love with Seth Palmer. I get that. You are protecting him, being loyal to him. But he is not loyal to you."

"Of course, he is. Seth is a great guy. He loves me."

"He is a liar. And he's cheating on you." Casually, Clay pulled a photograph from his shirt pocket, then tossed it atop his briefcase lying on the cocktail table. "Does that look like a great guy? Does that look like a guy who loves you?"

Jessica stared at the photograph and recoiled. It was Seth and Nichole embracing, the lake in the background. For a moment, Rebecca almost felt sorry for the girl. But no. Callie was dead because Jessica and Nichole put her life in jeopardy. Derek Jaxson was dead because Seth Palmer and Calvin Canon decided to commit a crime at the young man's workplace. And Jude Donovan. Oh, God. Jude Donovan.

"Listen to me, Jessica." Clay's voice was startlingly loud. He was clearly intent on keeping the girl off balance. "When all this comes out, the three of you are facing serious charges. And who do you think Seth will protect then? You? Of course not. Nichole? Maybe at first. But when the D.A. comes after him,

Seth Palmer will drop both of you like a hot rock. The guy will do whatever it takes to save his own sorry hide. You can be damn sure of that. You are a fool if you do not protect yourself. Two innocent people are dead, and you are at fault."

"No," she shrieked. "Derek Jaxson and Callie are dead because of Calvin Canon. That maniac killed them."

"Because you three unleashed him on them."

"We could not have known." The panicked girl pivoted awkwardly on the couch, the last vestige of defiance falling away. "Rebecca, please. How could we have known that that lunatic would go inside the store and start shooting people? We hardly knew him."

"But Seth knew him, didn't he?"

"Maybe he had seen him around, but Calvin Canon came up to the three of us on the beach that weekend." She gasped for breath as words spilled from her mouth. The camera hidden in Clay's briefcase captured them all. "None of this was supposed to happen. We didn't mean for any of this to happen. But it did. And what were we supposed to do? Callie was dead. Derek Jaxson was dead. And we could not change anything. None of it. Calvin Canon killed them. Not us. It was not our fault. We did nothing wrong."

Clay snatched up the papers and the photo, then hurled them into her lap. "Tell that to Jude Donovan."

CHAPTER 26

Mac had not seen the Cessna Citation since Bryant and his partners had had the aircraft refurbished. Wanting to take a look, he had offered to deliver Michaela and her friend to Austin Executive Airport to meet Brooke and Bryant for their trip to Chicago. They were scheduled to be wheels up at ten, although Sydney's competition was not until the next morning.

Mac and the girls arrived fifteen minutes early, then pulled to a stop at the security gate. Michaela and Anna Rose strained at their seatbelts, taking it all in. He pressed a call button on a pole-mounted speaker, then provided the tail number to the pleasant woman whose voice routinely greeted him. The gate rolled aside, and Mac drove through. The jet was parked under a canopy attached to the building, a rare convenience at an FBO. Aircraft of various brands and sizes were parked nearby, others in enclosed hangars, among them his company's helicopter.

The jet had never looked better. Its silver paint glistened in the morning sunlight. Two broad stripes, deep red and dark navy, swept from under the nose and upward, broadening as they reached the tail. It was a striking and sophisticated look.

Mac pulled his vehicle alongside the plane in time for the girls to see Sydney race up the stairs and disappear inside the cabin. Michaela and Anna Rose erupted in laughter. Brooke waved to the girls, then boarded, leaving the ground crew and Bryant to deal with the mass of gear and luggage in the SUV. No question, Mac thought, that most of the storage space would be consumed by Sydney's necessities.

Mac greeted his son-in-law, then the two pilots. He knew them both from previous flights. They were topnotch. The ground crew stowed the girls' luggage, and the pilots welcomed them aboard. Mac and Bryant followed behind. Immediately, Mac was struck by the handsome interior which smelled of leather and fresh carpet. "Looks like new, Bryant. They did a great job."

Sydney was sharing Brooke's seat, the Boston terrier's ears twitching as the girls settled opposite him in rear-facing club seats. Bryant sat across the aisle from his wife, then reminded Mac that it was not too late to change his mind. "Anna Rose's parents had to bow out, so there's plenty of room. We'll be back tomorrow night."

Brooke raised her eyebrows at the girls and whispered loudly. "Granddad can buy jammies and underwear in Chicago, right?"

Michaela and Anna Rose exploded in giggles, covering their mouths, squirming in their seats. Mac captured their joyfulness with a rapid series of pictures on his cell. He stole a priceless shot of Sydney looking up at Brooke as if to say, "What's so darn funny?"

Suddenly, Mac regretted not making the quick trip to Chicago with his family. Sierra had bowed out too. Her best friend Jenny was having a tea at the club that afternoon, a birthday gathering for her mother. Sierra and Catherine would both attend. Tonight, Mac and Sierra would accompany Catherine to a retirement party for a longtime colleague at the magazine.

Mac leaned over his granddaughter and kissed her forehead. "Have a good time, sweetie." He noted that she was wearing her watch, then exchanged a look with Bryant. Yesterday, Mac had told his son-in-law about the tracking device. After installing the app on his iPhone, Bryant had been mesmerized by the technology and mastered it in record time. "Don't worry about a thing, Mac. I'm all over this."

Wishing them a pleasant flight, Mac told the crew to take good care of his family and deplaned. From inside the terminal, he watched the aircraft taxi gracefully to the runway and stop for clearance to take off. Seconds later, the jet was on the move, speeding down the runway like a bullet. Mac glanced down at his watch. 10:05. The aircraft was wheels up and soaring into the sky.

♦ ♦ ♦

AUSTIN COUNTRY CLUB was one of the oldest existing clubs in Texas. Mac had played the Pete Dye course for nearly thirty years, but today its forced carries, uneven lies, and menacing bunkers gave him a beating. The design of the 18th hole offered players a chance to lose a ball, but Mac's approach shot into the green was well struck, and he ended the round on a positive note. The foursome settled up their meager bets in the locker room, then Mac headed for Tarrytown.

Sierra and Catherine had just returned home from the tea they had attended at Westwood. The two chatted about how lovely everything had been, then Sierra checked her text messages. "Brooke says all is well in Chicago. The girls are having a ball." She chuckled and held up her phone. "Is this adorable?" It was a picture of Michaela, Anna Rose, and Sydney sitting on a park bench amidst a crazy-quilt burst of zinnias. Mac examined it and smiled. The child looked so happy, and she was wearing her watch.

The retirement gathering that evening was for Braden Case, a writer-at-large since Texas Times Monthly was established. At the hotel, Mac let Catherine and Sierra out of the car near the front door and was stunned when a nearby parking space became immediately available.

In the hotel lobby, he found Catherine and Sierra chatting with Phil Kuykendall and his wife. Mac had seen Phil earlier at ACC. "It's our loss," the man had said when Mac brought up his and Lillian's meeting with Catherine. "She would have been a great candidate and a phenomenal governor. But I understand. Life is all about timing."

Early next week, Catherine would hold a press conference and put to rest speculation that she might run. Mac and the rest of the family would be at her side. He still felt a massive sense of relief that she had decided against entering the race, and that the decision had been hers alone.

A receiving line of sorts had formed inside the door of the banquet room where Braden Case greeted guests. Case was a large man, blustery, and white haired. A lifelong bachelor, he was a notorious womanizer, but he greeted Catherine with affectionate respect. The room was soon full. Mac was not surprised that his wife knew almost everyone there. She was a warm, gracious, people person, and masterful at remembering names.

Leaving Catherine and Sierra to chat with other guests, Mac ordered a vodka soda from a waiter, then asked him to take champagne to his wife and daughter. Two of the buffet tables were set with arrays of fresh fruit and cheeses. Mac walked past them both and headed toward the hot hors d-oeuvres. He picked up a plate, then scanned the tented cards, ignoring anything he did not recognize or could barely pronounce. He chose a charred beef skewer with bleu cheese, two pieces of bacon-wrapped Texas quail, and a chipotle chicken empanada. At a table of cold hors d-oeuvres, he maneuvered a bundle of prosciutto-wrapped asparagus onto his plate, but then frowned at the cream cheese and white truffle oil.

The chief of police waved Mac over. He joined the group at a large, round table. Daren Grissom was a controversial fellow, equal parts law enforcement officer and politician who attracted the press like a magnet. The chief greeted Mac as if they were old friends, then introduced him to the few at the table Mac did not already know.

During the evening, which turned out to be an enjoyable time, Mac exchanged text messages with Brooke. The final one from her read: Wish you were here. M luvs you this much." The picture captured Michaela in her pajamas with her arms held wide apart. Mac smiled at his phone, keenly aware that it had been months since he had felt worry free about his grandchild's security. Soon, Graham would sign the revised custody agreement, the Plano house would close, and Sierra would be legally free of the guy.

When something akin to a roast began, Catherine nodded toward the door. Mac, his wife, and daughter slipped out of the gathering unnoticed, then took the elevator to the lobby. When Sierra said that she had enjoyed herself, Mac believed her. Several times during the evening, he had seen her laugh. It was a beautiful sight. She was wearing a slim, yellow dress with a lacy white jacket that did not quite reach her waist. He knew she had layered it over the dress to conceal her thin shoulders and arms. He slapped away the image of his daughter tumbling down a flight of stairs, as they made their way across the hotel lobby.

They left the building through a side entrance. Mac was mildly surprised to find a handful of reporters on the sidewalk, accompanied by a couple of TV cameras. The press had no doubt assembled to question the police chief about a public spat between him and the city manager. A skinny blonde with short, red fingernails noticed Catherine, impulsively poked a microphone in her face, then shouted over sudden street noise.

"Ms. McKeon, have you made a decision about running for governor?"

Momentarily startled, Catherine quickly gathered herself and said that she had no comment. The woman jostled another reporter aside, pointing the microphone at Mac. "Mr. McKeon, could I get a comment?"

Instantly annoyed, Mac nudged his wife and daughter forward, resisting the urge to slap the mike away from his face. Instead, he ignored the woman and placed his hand on the small of Catherine's back. "Just keep walking." He glanced over his shoulder. Sierra was keeping pace, but then the strap of her bag slipped from her shoulder. When she bent down to retrieve her purse from the sidewalk, a cameraman bumped into her, nearly knocking Sierra over.

"Back off," Mac ordered. His temper was peaking, but then he remembered the cameras. This could be on the news tonight. "Step back, please," he insisted, feigning calm and undeserved courtesy. The group complied, stepping back in unison like a flock of mindless sheep.

With Catherine slightly in front of him and Sierra at his side, Mac said, "Let's get out of here."

Seconds later, they reached the sedan parallel parked on the street. Mac opened the passenger door for his wife. She had one foot inside the car when Mac heard in the distance a muffled pop, pop, pop. The sound registered, jarring, and unmistakable.

"Gun!" he shouted, flinching at the instantaneous ping, ping, ping of metal on metal. Rounds were hitting the car. "Get down!" With one hand, he shoved Catherine into the front seat of the sedan. "Get in! Get down!" Screams erupted. Mac shouted above the roar. "Sierra, get down!" Wrestling with the car door, he banged it against his wife's ankle.

Reporters. Crew. Pedestrians. All scattered like litter in a gust of wind. Shouting. Screaming. Running for cover. Gunfire erupted again. Pop. Pop. Pop. Mac ducked, scanning the area. Where the hell was it coming from? Was it getting closer?

Sierra dropped to her knees by the rear car door. She covered her head with one arm and reached for the door handle with her free hand. Pop. Pop. Ping. Ping. Mac lunged for his daughter, smashing her to the sidewalk face down. He threw himself over her, blanketing her with his body.

One of the cameramen, staggering backwards, wrestling with his camera, filmed the chaos. The blonde reporter was making a run for the hotel. She tripped, stumbled, and fell to her knees. Dazed and panicked, the woman scrambled to her feet, then raced toward the door, ducking and dodging. A businessman in a summer suit dropped to the ground, then crawled away on all-fours, dragging his briefcase. Shouts and curses mingled.

Mac's heart hammered in his chest. He cupped his mouth close to Sierra's ear. "Stay put, honey. Just stay put." He raised his head slightly and scanned the area again. The sidewalk was deserted now. Everyone had scattered, taking cover. Mac's heartbeat battered against his ears, muffling the ceaseless hum of downtown traffic. Then the squeal of car tires broke through the din. "Sonofabitch!" Was it the shooter? Was he coming after them?

"Mac!" Catherine yelled from inside the car. "Sierra!"

"Stay down!" Mac looked frantically about. The gunfire. The pings. The echoes. The screaming. He had no idea where the shots had come from. "Call 911," he shouted, still covering Sierra's head and upper body with his.

"Dad." Sierra's cheek was flattened against the concrete, muffling her words. "What is happening?"

"I don't know." Mac eased his weight off his daughter, but still shielded her motionless body. "Are you hurt?"

"I don't think so," she mumbled, groaning. "Mom?"

"In the car. She's safe."

A woman yelled from the hotel entrance. "Cops are on the way. They're on the way."

The gunfire had stopped, but the pounding in Mac's head was relentless. Was it over? He had to get Sierra into the car. "Don't move." Unsteadily, Mac rose to his knees, hunched over, staying low. Was he gone? Or was the shooter slamming another magazine into his gun and heading their way?

A young man in shorts and a black tee shirt rushed to them, hunched forward. He tossed off his backpack, then knelt beside Sierra. "Can I help?"

"Let's get her into the car." Mac opened the door, then clambered into the space between it and Sierra. The stranger knelt opposite him. They carefully eased Sierra onto her back. She moaned with each movement. Her cheek was badly scraped and bloody. One eye was swelling, the lid torn. "We're putting you in the car, honey." Sierra's hair fell away from her face. Her earring had torn through her lobe. Blood trickled into her hair. "Crazy bastard," Mac muttered, frowning over his daughter's battered face and the fear in her eyes.

Mac and the stranger grasped Sierra by the shoulders and lifted her upper body. She paled and whimpered as her lacy jacket front opened. A moment passed. Mac moaned. He and the stranger exchanged silent glances. Blood. A bright, burgundy flow oozed from his daughter's chest. Without a word, the stranger yanked open his backpack and grabbed a neatly folded tee shirt. Silently, he pressed it against the gunshot wound, securing it with both hands.

"Sierra." Catherine stumbled out of the car, then rushed hunched over to her daughter. "Oh, God. Mac."

"Mom." Sierra's voice was weak and raspy. "Can't breathe."

"Help is on the way, honey."

Mac watched helplessly as Catherine lifted their daughter's hand. Sierra's grasp was urgent, her knuckles white. Her lips quivered, and her eyes jittered with panic. But for the blood smears, her face was colorless.

"We're here, Sierra," Catherine said calmly. "You're safe. We're right here." She leaned down and kissed her daughter's forehead, smoothing her tangled hair. "Honey, breathe. Just keep breathing."

Sirens screamed in the distance. The sounds grew louder with each pounding beat of Mac's heart. The wail was ear-piercing as he scrambled to his feet, then stood by the rear of the sedan, hands in the air. Patrol units rounded the corner and squealed to angular stops, blocking the one-way street. Mac shouted, "Over here. We need help. Over here."

Uniformed officers spilled from their patrol cars, guns drawn. Some spanned out, barking orders to onlookers from nearby buildings. "Get inside. Now!" Other officers raced toward what was left of the chaotic scene. Mac stepped over Sierra's legs and knelt next to his wife. Catherine still held Sierra's hand, but now her fingers were limp.

CHAPTER 27

I t was Friday afternoon. Rebecca stood at the window of her room at the Broadmoor in Colorado Springs. Her parents were in a suite on the other side of Cheyenne Lake. Tomorrow marked the date of Callie's death two years ago. On Rebecca's phone were already a dozen text messages, none of them from Russell. Praying for you, my friend. Thinking of you. From Myra, You know I'm here for you. And I know your heart is heavy. And from her brother Adam, Sending strength and much love.

Her parents, headed home after their trip to Wyoming, had insisted that Rebecca meet them in Colorado Springs at their favorite luxury resort. "You need to get away, honey, and we need to know you are all right." Yearning to be with them, Rebecca had agreed. "But just for one night. I'll feel closer to Callie if I am at home Saturday night."

From the window, Rebecca watched her parents make their way across the footbridge spanning Cheyenne Lake. As they often did, they walked hand in hand. The sight of them was infinitely comforting. Her father was only a couple of inches taller than her mother. Neither looked their age. Seventy. They enjoyed the outdoors, particularly boating and hiking. As a result, they were both admirably fit. This fall they would celebrate forty-eight years of marriage.

She met them on the mezzanine level of Broadmoor Main at a beautiful lakeside bar. They hugged, and Rebecca felt herself relax. It was late afternoon, and the sun was low in the sky. The Broadmoor was an exquisite property in a magnificent setting in the Rocky Mountains. Even in the summer, its highest peaks glistened with patches of snow. Deciding to dine outside, they requested a table in the warm glow of a stone fireplace.

"Did you take a nap this afternoon?" her mother asked as they settled around the table.

"I did," Rebecca fibbed. Actually, she had been too exhausted to sleep. She had caught a painfully early flight out of Austin that morning.

The confrontation last night with Jessica had left her physically and emotionally depleted. Nearly twenty-four hours had passed, but she still could not fully comprehend the scope or the magnitude of what had happened. Much of what she had believed for two years about the night Callie died had been shattered. Piecing it together meant reliving it all, and it was a brutal process. "But now you know the truth," Myra had said tenderly. "You are the bravest woman I know."

Clay had an appointment with Jude Donovan's attorney that afternoon in Houston. After the meeting was over, he would drive to Kerrville and share the news with Jude's parents. "Lester and Emma will have a million questions," Clay had told her. "I want to have most of the answers before I tell them what you and Myra uncovered. And what that sorry threesome did to their son."

Rebecca thought back to the evening at the Highline Grill when Nichole had asked if she thought Jude Donovan would be put to death. It was impossible that Nichole or Jessica would have kept silent and let an innocent man be executed. Surely they would not have done such a monstrous thing. But she could not ignore that they had allowed Jude to be convicted, to be sent to death row. Had Seth Palmer somehow convinced them that the jury would find Jude not guilty? After all, Jude had not fired a gun. He had not even been inside the store. Or was it possible that both Nichole and Jessica were totally without conscience?

So much could have happened since last night or could be happening now. Had Jessica confronted Seth and Nichole? How much legal trouble were the girls in? Seth Palmer belonged in prison, but did they? "It's out of your hands," her mother had reminded Rebecca. "You did what you had to do." But questions and worries battered Rebecca, and she still had not been able to speak with Russell. He would reach out to her tomorrow, though. She was sure of it. The timing was dreadful, but he had to hear the truth from her, no one else, about the night Callie died. And she had to be the one to explain why she had joined forces with Clay Borger.

Determined to fend off the onslaught of anxiety and uncertainty, Rebecca opened the menu. She scanned the offerings, but focusing was impossible. Closing it, she gazed out over the lake, praying silently. Please phone me, Russ. Please.

Last year, on the date of the shooting, Rebecca had phoned Derek Jaxson's wife. DeAnna had been touched by the call, but would she be this year? There was no way to be certain.

A realization ruffled through her mind like wind on water. God only knew when, but Jude Donovan would be released from prison. DeAnna needed to know, to prepare herself for the media storm that would surround the announcement.

"Rebecca." Her father touched her hand. "This young man is waiting to take your order."

"Oh, I'm sorry." How could she not have noticed that the waiter was standing there? "I will start with Grey Goose and soda with lime."

"She means tonic," her father corrected. "And bring her a small order of crab cakes with a green salad. Soy ginger dressing. Does that sound good, honey?"

"Perfect," Rebecca answered. The waiter thanked them, then walked away. "You two aren't eating?"

"We already ordered," JoAnn answered patiently.

"I'm sorry," Rebecca apologized again. "My mind is all over the place."

"Of course, it is. How could it not be? Any word from Russell?"

"None. The apartment manager hasn't seen him. August spoke with him briefly a couple of days ago. Of course, I don't know about Nichole."

◆ ◆ ◆

IT WAS AFTER NINE O'CLOCK Saturday night when Rebecca reached Sparrows Cove. The quick trip to Colorado Springs had been time well spent. As much as she loved her cove, she was drawn to mountain destinations as well. Being with her parents had calmed her internal turmoil. Tomorrow morning, they would head home too.

Despite the late hour, lights were on at the funeral home. Jake had not advised her about a death call, which he normally did, but his car was in the back parking lot. Still in casual clothes,

Rebecca parked at the rear of the building and entered through the back door, going directly to the preparation room. Only one bank of lights was on, so the space was dimly lit.

As she had anticipated, a body lay on the embalming table, draped with a crisp, white sheet, signaling that the procedure was complete. The deceased was female. Her hair was still damp from having been shampooed and hung off the end of the table. It was board straight and dark blonde. The woman was tall, Rebecca observed as she approached, but terribly thin. Her coloring, even after embalming, had an odd gray cast. A horizontal cut angled across a large lump on her forehead. What were the marks on her face?

Rebecca froze in midstride and gasped. A paralyzing sense of disbelief held her still. It was Jessica. "No," she moaned, inching toward the table. "No, Jessica. What happened to you?" The door to the preparation room opened, startling her. "Jake, what happened to Jessica? Tell me it wasn't suicide."

"Meth abuse is always suicide." Jake crossed the room and stood at Rebecca's side, pity claiming his expression. "But no. Ruled a natural death."

"And the cause?"

"Cardiac arrest."

"Oh, my God. Did you wait on the family?"

He nodded. "Patsy and her son."

Patsy was Jessica's mother. Her son was in his early teens. "How did it happen?"

"Jessica showed up at her mother's house at three in the morning, pounding on the door. Patsy made the mistake of letting her in. Jessica was demanding money and making all sorts of threats. Her brother recognized the signs and called 911. He had seen it before. Aggression. Sweating. Nonstop talking. Poor kid told dispatch that his sister was strung out on meth again, and that he needed help fast. When the deputy arrived, he tried to put cuffs on her, but Jessica fought like a maniac. He and Brady took her to the floor and managed to restrain her."

"That's how she got this?" Rebecca pointed to the injury on her forehead.

"Actually, no. Brady did that. He hit his sister with a tennis racket trying to protect his mother."

"Jake, no."

"The deputy knew Jessica was in bad shape, so he called for an ambulance. She was feverish, incoherent, and confused. When they finally got her into the ambulance, she had multiple seizures on the way to the hospital and went into cardiac arrest. The EMT's restored a heartbeat, but she died in the emergency room."

Rebecca touched Jessica's sheet-covered hands crossed on her abdomen. "When did this happen?"

"Early this morning. Rebecca, I know what you're thinking." Jake's tone was at the same time tender and firm. "You and Clay Borger had no role in this."

"Didn't we? I knew Jessica was in a fragile state when she left my house that night. I should have let Patsy know."

"How much were you prepared to tell her? Anyway, what could Patsy have done? Law enforcement would have been no help. They couldn't arrest Jessica for something she might do to herself. Jessica chose to start doing meth years ago. Sadly, this is the consequence."

"Why didn't you phone me when you got the death call?"

"I talked to Nelson instead. He said I should tell you in person." Jake gave her a gentle hug. "I'm sorry you found out this way. Today of all days."

On the way home, Rebecca drove to Russell's apartment. His parking space was empty, and so was the apartment when she used the hidden key and went inside. It was excruciatingly hot. The air conditioner had clearly been off for hours, if not days. She checked his closet, but it was in such disarray she could not tell if he had packed a bag or not. There was no luggage in the closet, but she was not even sure that he owned any.

The second bedroom offered no clues either as to where he might be. In the kitchen, she found the refrigerator empty but for three cans of beer, a block of sharp cheddar in a Ziploc bag, and a plastic container of molding carrots. Clearly, Russell had not been home in days. But where could he be? He had so isolated himself that there was no one Rebecca knew to call. "Other than Nichole," she muttered, allowing the refrigerator door to close on its own.

Had Jessica confronted Seth and Nichole before she spun out of control? Had she told them that their lies had caught up with them? And where was Seth living? With Jessica? Or in Houston? But what did it matter? He would be brought in for questioning soon enough. And so would Nichole.

After leaving Russell's apartment, she drove by Nichole's. Her Mazda was parked in front of her apartment. The fuel door. Such a minor thing, but why hadn't the police noticed when they investigated the shootings? She had asked Clay about it. "That was a brutal crime scene, Rebecca. Three victims. Traumatized witnesses. A BOLO for a black Honda. The last thing on their mind was how cars were parked at the gasoline pumps."

At home, she sent Clay a text, asking that he phone her ASAP. He did exactly that. She told him about Jessica's sudden death. His reaction was the same as hers. "Was it suicide?"

"Natural causes. Cardiac arrest." As Rebecca explained the circumstances, Clay peppered her with questions as any investigator would do. "I don't know if she confronted Nichole and Seth or not. I have no idea what they know."

"Have you spoken with Russell?"

"Not yet. But I will. I'm positive. How did Jude's parents react when you told them the news?"

"I haven't seen them yet. Lester and Emma are both in Livingston, trying to see Jude. The poor boy is going through a really rough patch. The chaplain described it as a psychotic break. I'm waiting to hear from Lester and Emma. I'm in Kerrville now."

They talked a while longer, then agreed to speak soon. "Stay strong, Rebecca." Clay paused to clear emotion from his throat. "You have been through so much."

At ten-thirty, Rebecca went outside onto the deck. With the lights off, she leaned against the wooden rail, gazing out over the inky water. The moon hurried from one dark cloud to another, finally hiding her face entirely. Water rippled gently against the shoreline. The Lone Oak towered, its branches rigid in the stillness.

Her cell phone rang and broke the silence. Rebecca flinched. Night owl. It was Russell. With jittery fingers, she slipped the phone from her pocket. "I am so glad you called, Russ. I knew you would."

"Of course." The connection was poor, but the despair in his voice was unmistakable. "She was the best of us both, Becca."

"Yes, she was." Darkness pressed down on her, suddenly oppressive. "Where are you?"

"Nowhere. Where are you?"

"On the deck. In the dark." Rebecca's eyes ached with unshed tears. "Looking at Callie's oak."

"She loved you with all her heart." Russell's voice was tender and tranquil. "And so do I. I'm sorry for what I said, Becca, that I couldn't trust you."

"It's all right, Russ." Rebecca's voice cracked, but she could not piece it back together. "Where are you? I need to see you, to talk to you."

"I'm all right, Becca. Please don't worry."

"But it's important, Russ. Please."

"Get some sleep. Sweet dreams of Callie."

"Russ?" Rebecca pressed the phone hard to her ear. "Russ?" He was gone. Mournful tears streamed down her face. "And so is Callie."

Memories closed around her, filling her fragile soul with longing. Callie. She raised her cell phone and swiped up the screen with her thumb. Text messages sailed past. With a trembling finger, she tapped the final one. Stopping for gas. Almost to Katy. Sorry.

CHAPTER 28

The surgeon's scrubs were moist with perspiration when he entered a private waiting room at Seton Medical Center, then closed the door behind him. It was one o'clock in the morning. The man's narrow face was darkened with stubble, and his expression, Mac feared, looked grave. Taking a chair opposite the sofa where Mac and Catherine sat, he leaned toward them, bracing his elbows on his knees, his hands dangling between them.

After four hours, Sierra was out of surgery and was being moved to intensive care. She had been shot twice. One bullet entered her shoulder, nicking her collar bone. "We removed the bullet, all the bone fragments, and repaired a damaged vessel." The other round had passed through her chest wall, lodging in her left lung. "There was considerable damage, so we had to remove a section of the lower lobe."

Almost against his will, Mac pictured Sierra on the sidewalk before the paramedics arrived, gasping for air, wheezing out blood in a fine mist or in droplets. He had nearly gone mad before the police had allowed the EMT's to approach the scene. By then, Sierra had been coughing up clots of blood, and her breathing had become so shallow that Mac thought she was dying. She had been unconscious when the team loaded her into the ambulance and screamed away.

"… a chest tube in place," the surgeon was saying. "And she's on a ventilator. I can't say for how long, but we always try to remove tubes as quickly as we safely can because of potential complications."

"What kind of complications?" Catherine asked, clenching Mac's hand.

"Most commonly, pneumonia. But gunshot wounds are also laden with possible complications. Sierra is being treated with antibiotics to prevent lung and wound infections. And, of course, she's on pain medication to keep her comfortable."

"Do you know if she ever regained consciousness?"

"She did not, Catherine," he answered. "Your daughter was in shock when she arrived at the ER and had lost a lot of blood by the time we got her into surgery. Her blood pressure fell very low, and she just wasn't getting enough oxygen."

For a fearsome moment, Mac felt a surge of panic. "To her brain?"

The doctor nodded. "That sounds very frightening. I understand. But know this. Your daughter is receiving the best possible care. A team of specialists will be treating her. You should know, though, that Sierra is not out of danger. She has undergone major surgery and, as I said, gunshot wounds are fraught with potential complications."

"When can we see her?" Catherine asked.

The man moved to the edge of his chair, reached across, and patted Catherine's forearm. "Give the nurses some time to get her settled in, then keep your visit very, very brief. It's best not to stimulate her. Sierra needs to rest."

After the doctor left the room, Mac's gaze lingered on his wife. Her ankle was swollen and badly bruised. He had slammed the car door on it during the gunfire. With each shallow breath, her weariness seemed to grow. Her expression was vacant. He had no idea what she was thinking until she finally spoke. "What time does their plane land?"

It was the same question she had asked just before the surgeon entered the room. Mac glanced at his watch. "Two fifteen."

Knowing Brooke had had some sort of event that evening, Mac had phoned Bryant from the hospital. The exchange had been brief and surreal. Sierra's been shot. She's in surgery. Get home as fast as you can.

"I can't go home, Mac." Catherine choked out the words. "I cannot leave her."

"You don't have to, honey. When Brooke gets home, she can gather a few things for you and bring them here."

"You'll have to talk to Michaela alone." The message in her eyes was full of regret. "What will you say to her?"

"I have no idea." For now, Mac refused to think about it. He had to get through the next few hours. "How could this have happened, Catherine? Who could have done this?"

There was a tap at the door, then it opened slowly. It was Daren Grissom. Mac nodded the chief in without speaking. Grissom took the chair the doctor had vacated, assuming the same sympathetic posture. "How is your daughter?"

Mac told him Sierra was out of surgery. "She was shot twice. In her shoulder and in her chest. They had to remove part of her lung." It occurred to Mac that the bullets were probably on their way for ballistics examination. "Tell us what's going on, Daren? Do you have any idea who did this?"

"No, but we will. My investigators are working nonstop. We'll catch him. I'm sure of it. There are lots of cameras downtown, and we're in the process of reviewing everything that they captured."

"It must have been a random shooting," Mac insisted. "No one would want to harm Sierra."

"We're making no assumptions. The investigation will take us wherever it takes us." Grissom leaned a little closer. "I wish I had more to tell you. The reason I'm here, though, other than to inquire about Sierra, is to thank you for talking to my detectives earlier. The timing was tough. I can only imagine how frantic with worry you both were, but we needed information that only you could provide." The chief's cell phone sounded. He apologized, excused himself, then stepped into the hall.

Mac put his arm around Catherine, pressing her head on his shoulder. They embraced in stunned silence. How could this be? No one would harm Sierra. It was insane. Impossible. It had to be a random shooting. Sierra had no enemies. No one in the family had enemies. Oh, God, Mac mourned. What would he say to Michaela?

"Mac, we have to tell Graham." Catherine lifted her head from his shoulder. "We can't let him hear it on the news. That would be cruel."

"I know. I thought I would let Bryant call him."

"Why Bryant? He detests Graham."

"Who doesn't?" Mac gave her a weary, half-smile. "But I'm not talking to him. You're sure not. You can't expect Brooke to do it."

"I guess Bryant drew the short straw." Catherine's voice was as flat as a tabletop. "I hope Graham doesn't come here. There is nothing he can do but make things worse."

"That won't stop him. Anyway, the detectives will want to talk to him. You know how it goes. Process of elimination." The conversation was surreal, bizarre. The heaviness in Mac's chest felt like a stone. A harrowing headache pounded his forehead. "Do you have any aspirin? My head's killing me." He flinched at his own words. Had someone tried to kill Sierra? The question was locked in his mind, but it did not belong there. No one would want Sierra dead. The shooter could have been aiming at your wife, the detective had said. Or at you, Mr. McKeon. Or it could have been completely random.

"Here, honey." Catherine pressed two aspirins in Mac's hand. "If you find bottled water, would you bring me one?"

The chief was still in the hallway when Mac left the waiting room. He was talking to the two detectives Mac had spoken with earlier. He had already forgotten their names. "Any news?"

"We have an image of the shooter," Grissom answered. "Several actually. They're not good quality, so we're in the process of enhancing them."

Mac's throat tightened, his head pounding. "Are you sure it's him?"

The chief looked at the older of the two detectives, drawing him into the conversation. Bostic, Mac recalled. Lieutenant Bostic. "We are positive. He is our shooter. No question. We'll need you to look at the video, Mr. McKeon. Will you be here?"

"I'm going home shortly. My granddaughter …"

"I'm sorry. How old is she?"

"Almost five."

"Is Graham Hollister her father?" When Mac nodded, Bostic continued. "Earlier, you said the divorce was acrimonious. Are they on good terms now?"

"Good enough, I guess. They have very little direct contact."

The red-haired detective spoke for the first time. "Do you know if Sierra has life insurance?"

"She does."

"Who's the beneficiary?"

"Hollister."

"I hope you don't take this the wrong way, but is it a large policy?"

"I don't know. I never asked. But recently Hollister told me to remind Sierra that he paid the premiums, and that he is beneficiary."

The chief, with practiced humility, said, "I don't want to offend you, Mac, but has Graham Hollister ever been violent toward Sierra or anyone else, for that matter?"

"Physically violent? Not that I know of. But he does have a temper. The night before Sierra moved out of their home in Plano, Graham was raging about something, and she fell down a flight of stairs." The three men exchanged looks. Mac had the eerie feeling that they knew something he did not. "Is there something you're not telling me?"

"No," the chief answered quickly. "You have my word. When was the last time you spoke with Hollister?"

"Sunday a week ago."

"How did that go?"

"Not well. We butted heads about the visitation agreement, then he headed back to Plano."

"Angry?"

Mac nodded. "Look, men, Graham Hollister is an arrogant, overbearing SOB. I don't think he is capable of harming Sierra, but he damn sure deserves to be treated like a suspect."

◆ ◆ ◆

BROOKE'S FACE BORE NO telltale signs that she had been crying. She was tough like her mother, and Mac knew that she would not have broken down in front of Michaela and her friend. Anna Rose's parents had picked up their daughter at the FBO. They had been horrified about the shooting and told Brooke that it was all over the news.

Brooke had put Michaela to bed. "She was exhausted, Dad. I told her what you said, that her mom was not feeling well and was spending the night in the hospital."

"I don't know how you did it." Mac opened his arms, and his daughter stepped into them. He closed his arms around her, and an image exploded in his mind. Sierra face down on the sidewalk. He had blanketed her body with his, but he was too late.

Are you hurt?

I don't think so. Mom?

Mac held Brooke tightly when sobs erupted and her shoulders began to shake violently. He whispered in her ear. "Let it out, sweetheart."

"Who did it?" She choked out the words through sobs. "It was Graham, wasn't it? He did it. He tried to kill my sister."

The accusation was stark, chilling, and completely unexpected. Mac looked at Bryant who had clearly heard the words before. "We don't know who did it, sweetheart. It's too soon." Gently, he kissed the top of Brooke's head. "We have to let the police do their job, while we take care of Sierra and each other." Holding his daughter tightly, Mac allowed her sobs to subside. By the time she inched away, tears had soaked through his shirt front. "I know you have a million questions, Brooke, but I need you to get to the hospital. Your mom is there alone. There is a tote bag on the shelf in her closet. Pack her a change of clothes, toiletries, whatever else you think she will need." Mac stroked his daughter's cheek. "And take a couple of throws. The waiting room gets a little chilly."

Brooke inched farther away, her spine literally stiffening. "I'll take care of Mom. But what about you? You shouldn't be alone, Dad."

"I'll be all right." He wiped smudges from under his daughter's eyes with his thumb. "Go take care of your mom."

After Brooke left the room, Mac collapsed into his favorite chair, but Bryant sat on the edge of the sofa. "How can I help, Mac?"

"I'm afraid you drew the short straw. I need you to call Graham."

"I can do that. How much do I tell him?"

"Everything you know. The three of us were leaving a hotel downtown and a man opened fire on us. Sierra was hit twice. Once in her left shoulder. Once in her chest. They had to remove part of her lung. She went into shock from blood loss. She made it through surgery, and now she is in ICU. If Graham asks about Michaela, say she doesn't know yet, that I'm telling her later this morning."

"I'll take care of it."

Mac rubbed his throbbing forehead. "The police have the shooter on video, Bryant."

"Have you seen it?"

"Not yet. They're enhancing it. But the shooter is definitely a man." Mac felt as if he were being devoured by despair. "One of the detectives asked if Graham was ever violent with Sierra."

Bryant's expression was unchanged. "I know how Brooke would have answered them. But, Mac, Graham would have to be deranged to do something that vicious. And in front of you and Catherine. And why now?"

Mac sagged in the chair, weighed down with a heavy, sodden dullness. "Life insurance. Retaliation. He was furious about supervised visitation." He pictured Hollister pounding the metal table outside Starbucks, enraged at being treated like an abusive parent or a pervert. "I pushed him hard, Bryant. Sign the papers or I'll put your life through a meat grinder."

CHAPTER 29

Myra Perriman stood at the lectern and adjusted the microphone. She had been a lector at All Saints Episcopal in Sparrows Cove for years. She read the scripture in a conversational way, with ease and genuine interest. The timbre of her voice made her far easier to listen to, Rebecca thought, than the rector who sounded as if he were perpetually at battle with strep throat.

Myra's husband Bob Perriman was out of town, so she and Rebecca would spend Sunday afternoon together aboard the Silver Star, a cabin cruiser belonging to Myra's father. A picnic lunch was packed and ready at Rebecca's house. All she had left to do was to assemble her famous chicken salad sandwiches and place them in the basket.

Myra came directly to Rebecca's home after church, changed into her swimwear, and emerged from the powder room tying the sash of a sassy black cover-up. She was five years older than Rebecca and looked multiple years younger. Rebecca smirked at her— "Tan and toned." —and then did an awkward pirouette. "Pale and puny."

Myra laughed, tossing her beach bag by the front door. "You could put on a few pounds. And thank God for sunscreen. You are as pale as a perch belly."

Rebecca threw a wad of foil at her friend, then they loaded their gear into Myra's car. The fifteen-minute drive to the marina would take them past Nichole's apartment. If her car was there, they would attempt to speak with her. Last night, before finally hearing from Russ, Rebecca had phoned Nichole. The call had gone to voicemail and was ignored. Rebecca still did not know if Jessica had confronted Nichole and Seth.

Tomorrow, Jude Donovan's attorney was scheduled to meet with the prosecutor in Harris County. Did Seth and Nichole know they would soon be in the DA's crosshairs? More importantly, did Russell know? Rebecca had not had the chance to tell him last night or to explain the role she had played.

"Becca, have you had any contact with Jessica's mother?"

"I spoke with her this morning."

"At the funeral home?"

"I was arranging flowers in Jessica's stateroom when Patsy walked in. I was a nervous wreck when she asked if I had a minute to talk."

"How much did she already know?"

"Everything, as best I could tell. She definitely knew that Clay and I had confronted Jessica about the night Callie died." Rebecca had been prepared for the grieving woman to light into her, but she had not. "She blamed everything, including Jessica's death, on Seth and Nichole."

"Works for me."

"I didn't tell her that Clay and I had to drag the truth out of Jessica."

"Why cause the woman more pain?" Myra slowed the car suddenly and pointed to the right as they neared Nichole's apartment building. "There they are."

It was Nichole and Seth. They were loading boxes and clothing into his Mercedes. "Looks like she's leaving town. Let's go talk to her."

Pulling onto the parking lot, they watched as Seth closed the trunk. Hand in hand, the pair walked away, then disappeared into the apartment, leaving the door fully open. Myra parked next to the Mercedes. Together, she and Rebecca entered Nichole's apartment without knocking. Hastily labeled boxes were stacked in the corner. Walls and floors were bare. An empty bookcase stood just inside the door.

Nichole stood across the room near the kitchen, bundling a vacuum cleaner cord. She dropped it when Rebecca said her name, startled as a burglar. "What are you doing here?"

"I see you're moving." Rebecca stood next to the bookcase, Myra a few steps behind her. "Does your dad know?"

Seth appeared at the mouth of the hallway carrying a black garbage bag filled with bed linens. "What's it to you, Rebecca?" He tossed the bag on the sofa.

Rebecca ignored him. "When was the last time you talked to Russell?"

Nichole snatched the cord from the floor and began wrapping it. "None of your business."

"How much does he know, Nichole?"

"About what?" She yanked angrily at the cord, whipping it toward her.

"Stop being a smartass," Myra barked, still standing just inside the open door, her lemon-yellow tote bag hanging from her shoulder. "You know exactly what Rebecca's talking about. Answer the question. Does Russell know that you two degenerates sent an innocent man to death row?"

"Shut up, Myra." Nichole turned her back and began placing cleaning supplies in a plastic laundry basket. "And get out of my house. Both of you."

"Answer my question," Rebecca demanded. "How much does Russell know?"

Seth strode toward her, stopping an arm's length away. "What's the problem, Rebecca?" His hand shot out. He grabbed her by the throat and shoved her against the empty bookcase. "Are you worried that your ex knows what a backstabbing bitch you are?"

"Get your hands off her." Myra's shout echoed in the near-empty room.

Pinned to the bookcase, Rebecca was too stunned to speak. Seth's grip was like a vice. She grabbed his wrist with both hands and tugged with all her strength, trying to break free, but he tightened his hold.

"Let her go." Myra lunged at him, but he stiff-armed her, knocking her off balance.

"That's why you're here, right?" His voice was a growl, his face inches away from Rebecca's. "You're worried that Russell knows what you did. That you colluded with Clay Borger. That the two of you manipulated Jessica into telling a bunch of lies about me and Nichole before she killed herself."

Thoughts rocketed through Rebecca's mind. A wave of dizziness surged through her. Seth knew everything, and he was furious. This was a nightmare. How had this gone bad so quickly? Unable to turn her head, she cut Myra a panicked look. Get help!

Myra jammed her hand in the tote. The bag slid from her shoulder. Its contents spilled onto the floor. Robot-like, she raised both arms shoulder high, hands together, feet planted. What was she doing? Rebecca questioned, still tugging at Seth's hands.

"Let her go." A small, shiny handgun wobbled in Myra's hands, but her voice was steady, her demands clear. "Let. Her. Go."

Nichole shrieked, then cupped both hands over her mouth. Seth's face froze. He looked as shocked as if Myra had shot at him. Nichole mumbled through her hands. "Do what she said, Seth. Let go of her."

The man's chest heaved with anger. He glared at Myra, then slammed Rebecca's head hard against the bookcase, throwing off her feeble grip and stepping back.

"Get over there," Myra demanded, jerking her head toward the stack of boxes, keeping the gun trained on Seth. "Get on the floor." When he complied, she ordered Nichole to sit next to him. The girl stumbled across the room and collapsed to the floor, her face pathetically pale. "Becca, call 911." Myra nudged her phone toward Rebecca with her shoe. "Are you okay?"

"Wait." Seth raised both hands in a don't-shoot position. "Just wait a minute. Don't call the sheriff. I'm sorry. There is no need to call them. I apologize."

"You apologize?" Disbelief sent the words soaring. Rebecca rubbed the knot swelling on the back of her head, then massaged her neck. "You choked me, you maniac." She picked up Myra's cell phone and pressed 911.

"Rebecca, please," Nichole whined. "Don't do that. Please. They'll arrest us both. We're already in trouble. Think about Dad."

Myra kept the gun trained in their direction. "Shut up, Nichole. You make me sick. Who were you thinking about when you sent Callie into the convenience store? Who were you thinking about when your lies sent Jude Donovan to death row?"

CHAPTER 30

Mac had been nine years old when his father died of a brain aneurysm. His mother had been too distraught to tell her children about his sudden death, so her brother had taken on the task. Mac's uncle had seated him and his younger sister at the kitchen table. Before that day, the table had been nothing more than a round piece of wood furniture, a place to eat bacon and scrambled eggs, Frosted Flakes, or oatmeal with maple syrup. But in a matter of moments, everything had changed. "Kids, something terrible happened to your dad while you were at school. He got a really bad headache, so your mom rushed him to the hospital."

Mac had no specific memory of what his uncle said after that, what words the man had chosen to tell two unsuspecting, innocent children that their dad was dead. With each passing week, though, Mac had grown more and more bitter, slowly swelling with rage, not at his uncle, not consciously anyway, or at his mother, and certainly not at his dad for dying, for leaving them and never coming back. For some inexplicable reason, he had directed his fury at the kitchen table. He hated the thing. Every time he looked at it, the piece screamed out. Sit down. Your dad is dead. He won't be coming back.

Now, Mac had to take on the same task his uncle had tackled nearly fifty years ago. Thank God, Sierra was alive, but somehow Mac had to find the words and the place to tell Michaela that something terrible had happened to her mom. The shooting was public knowledge now, so he could not keep it from her for long, nor could he risk Michaela hearing it from another child or from a parent who let something slip.

Throughout the night, Mac had weighed his options. How much should he tell the child? How much would she understand? How much could she bear? Unable to sleep, he had gone online and researched how to tell a child about tragedy. The approach that made the most sense to him was to provide facts in tiny bits, then to take cues from the child as to what to offer next.

Somehow, Mac would tell his innocent grandchild the brutal truth, but he would not tell her in her bedroom, or in the family room, or at the kitchen table, not on the terrace, or in the master bedroom where she delivered his orange juice. He would tell her in the living room, a lifeless space the family rarely used. If on the off-chance Michaela focused her emotions on a room or a piece of furniture, as he had done, she would not have to stare it down for months on end.

Michaela was still in her pajamas when Mac lifted her onto his lap. Her hair was a mass of messy curls, and she had drowsy, crusty eyes. "How did you sleep?"

"Good." She answered through a yawn. "I dreamed I could fly."

"Like birds? Or butterflies?"

"No, silly. Like pilots."

Mac chuckled. "I see. Maybe someday you will." He noticed a dark smudge of some sort on her ankle and pointed to it. "What is that?"

"Oh, yeah." Michaela pulled up the leg of her pajamas. "It's a tattoo."

"What? You got a tattoo in Chicago?"

"Aunt Brooke let me. It's called ink."

Mac feigned his angry adult expression. "Aunt Brooke is in a heap of trouble."

"I'm kidding." The child giggled and smoothed down her pajamas. "She told me to say that. It'll wash right off. I promise." Drawing up her knees, she locked her arms around them and yawned. "Is Mommy coming home today?"

"I'm afraid not, sweetie." Mac stroked her back. "The doctor needs to keep her in the hospital for a while longer."

"Why? What's wrong with Mommy?"

"Her chest is hurting, so she needs a special machine to help her breathe."

"Why is her chest hurting? Does she have a bad cold?"

Honest answers, he reminded himself. Information in small bits. "No. She doesn't have a cold. The doctor had to operate on her chest last night."

"Operate? Why?"

For Mac, the back-and-forth between them was like flinchingly, cautiously removing a bandage from a wound. At some point it was going to hurt like hell. "The doctor had to repair one of Mommy's lungs, to help her breathe."

"What happened to her lung?"

Mac disciplined his voice, steadied himself, then ripped off the bandage. "It got hit by a bullet."

The child winced, as if her flesh had been pinched. "A gun bullet?"

"Yes."

Michaela's dark eyes looked wounded. "Somebody shot my Mommy?"

Mac could do nothing more than nod. His throat ached, and his eyes burned.

"Why, Granddad?"

"I don't know. The police are trying to figure that out."

The child's body went limp, but her fists were clenched. "I want to see my Mommy." Her tone was insistent, without a hint of whine. "I want my Mommy."

"I'll make that happen. But I can't say when."

Michaela's cheeks reddened, and her lower lip began to quiver. "Promise?"

"I promise." Mac wrapped his arms around her little body, a precious bundle, but said nothing more. He had to get her out of this room.

♦ ♦ ♦

MAC TOOK MICHAELA to Brooke's house mid-morning. Catherine would not leave the hospital, no matter who coaxed her or how insistently. He had spoken to her several times. "There is no change. Sierra is heavily medicated, so she won't fight the ventilator. One eye is swollen shut, and her cheek is scraped. No infection."

"Michaela needs to see her."

"I don't think the staff will allow it."

"Yes, they will," Mac snapped. "She needs to see her mom."

He was on the way to the hospital alone when his cell phone rang. It was Lieutenant Bostic, asking if Mac could stop by the station. "We need you to look at some video."

Mac agreed and was taking a seat in an electronics room fifteen minutes later. It was a dim, cramped space with marred gray walls and mottled charcoal floor tiles. A rectangular, metal table occupied most of the room. Four chairs on casters had been haphazardly pushed against it. Mac picked up the scent of tomato sauce, then noticed a pizza box jammed in a trash bin in the corner. Cords, keyboards, monitors, and other equipment completed the chaotic look.

Mac and Bostic settled in at the table. The detective slid a keyboard in front of him and began clicking. A grainy black and white video appeared on the nearest monitor. Mac recognized the historic building immediately. The spires, the pointed arches on doors and windows, the massive wooden doors. It was Saint Mary Cathedral. Pedestrians walked casually along Tenth Street. Bostic explained that the images had been captured by cameras on a nearby state office building. "Do any of those people look familiar?"

Mac examined them closely. Two women walking together. Three men, each walking alone. "No. Maybe if I could get a closer look."

"You will." The detective cued up the next video and played it. "This was shot from a federal building."

"That's one of the men who was walking past the church, right?" Mac confirmed.

"Yes. He's headed south now on San Jacinto. Does he look at all familiar?" When Mac shook his head, Bostic paused the video and zoomed in. "There is a better look."

The man was average in every respect. Medium height. Average weight. He wore a gimme cap of some kind and sunglasses, making it impossible to get a good look at his face.

He was dressed in jeans, sneakers, and had left the tail of his plaid shirt outside his jeans. Mac studied every detail, then shook his head.

The detective released pause, and the video rolled. "He's two blocks from the hotel now. Look at his body language, Mac. The way he walks. Anything look familiar?"

Again, Mac shook his head. "Definitely not Graham Hollister."

"Agreed. Far shorter and not nearly as fit." The video ended. Bostic explained that cameras briefly lost sight of the man, but that another camera picked him up again less than a minute later. He cued up another video. "The guy is a block from the hotel now. Watch closely. He starts looking around. Getting nervous. And there. See that?"

Mac watched intently as the man reached back, then ran his hand under his shirttail. "He's feeling for the gun."

"Exactly," Bostic agreed. "When we see him again, he's across the street from the hotel."

Mac shifted uneasily in the chair, trying to ease the tension that was building in his body. This was the man who shot Sierra. *Who is he?* Mac agonized. *And why did he do it?*

Now, the man was lingering next to a parking meter, standing behind a dark SUV, maybe a Jeep. The camera captured him from the waist up. He was looking toward the hotel and in the general direction of Catherine's car.

"There he takes out his cell phone," Bostic explained, "and looks down at it. Maybe checking his texts or to see what time it is. Then he is on the move again. Headed south on San Jacinto. But notice how he repeatedly looks over his shoulder."

"Toward the hotel and our car."

"Exactly. Now, he's at the end of the block. He pauses, turns, then heads back north again. This pacing goes on for twenty-three minutes, so I'll fast forward."

A creeping uneasiness settled in the pit of Mac's stomach. "He waited twenty-three minutes for us to return to the car."

"Lying in wait. There is no other explanation." Bostic tapped a key, resuming normal speed. "Now, he's headed back toward the Jeep, which is not his car, by the way. Notice how he starts picking up his pace. He spotted you. You and your family have just walked out of the hotel, past some members of the press, and are headed to your car. In fourteen seconds, he will open fire."

Mac waited for Bostic to click the keys, his insides writhing. "Let's see it."

"But that's when he opens fire, Mac."

"I understand that."

Bostic let the video roll. The man, hiding behind the Jeep now, pulled down on the bill of his cap, then adjusted his sunglasses. His right arm bent at the elbow. "He's reaching back for the pistol. Now, you can't see it, but the weapon is in his hand. He's holding it low, straight down, in front of his thigh. Next, brace yourself, he takes aim."

Mac's whole body stiffened, his nerves at full stretch, his fists clenched on the desktop. The shooter slowly raised both arms to shoulder height and extended them. He steadied the pistol, left hand under right, and fired. The video was silent, but blood roared like gunfire in Mac's ears.

CHAPTER 31

For the first time in her career, Rebecca felt as if she did not belong at a service under the direction of Baker and Grant Funeral Home. It was the residual guilt she felt over Jessica's death. The funeral mass was being celebrated at Queen of Angels in nearby Spicewood. Before leaving for the church, Jake had reminded her, "You are not to blame, Rebecca. Jessica made choices and lots of people paid the price, including her."

But now, sitting at her desk, unable to focus on anything productive, she could not ignore or deny how hard she and Clay had shaken Jessica, determined to jar the truth from her. We tag-teamed her, Rebecca thought remorsefully. And when Jessica shrieked that she had done nothing wrong, Clay had hurled papers onto her lap. The sketch and credit card statement. The photo of Seth and Nichole. "Tell that to Jude Donovan."

Rebecca had not spoken with Clay since Saturday night. He had been in Kerrville, waiting for the Donovans to return from their long, round trip to Livingston, waiting to tell them about Jessica's confession. Today was Monday. Did Jude know now? Had Clay and the Donovans driven back to Livingston to tell him in person? Jude Donovan and his parents had been living in hell for two years. What would happen to him now? Jude's attorney was meeting with the Harris County prosecutor today, but the judicial process moved at a glacial pace. How long would it be before Jude was released? Rebecca recalled something Clay had said, that Jude was going through a rough patch. The chaplain had even described his condition as a psychotic break.

Her thoughts diverted to Russell, and her heart ached. She had not heard from him since Saturday night either. He had struggled so intensely in the past month, as the date of Callie's death neared, and Rebecca had closed her heart to him. At August's birthday party, she had been harsh and judgmental, throwing off his hand when he grasped her arm. At his apartment, the day she and Liam had startled Russ from sleep, Rebecca had read his letters to the Board of Pardons and Paroles and the governor's office. But the only interest she had shown was to inquire about the enclosures. "A picture of Callie, and one of Derek Jaxson with his family. Without a picture, they're just names." Russ had agonized over the Texas Innocence Initiative, fearing that their efforts would undermine the jury's decision to put Jude Donovan to death.

As she had done repeatedly, Rebecca pictured Russell slumping forward and raking his fingers through his messy hair. "I have this picture in my head, Becca. Callie lying on that filthy floor. Scared. Bleeding. Dying." Instead of opening her heart and comforting him, she had shielded it, as she had so often, and left the room in search of his handgun. On her way out the door, she had, in his words, lectured him. "Callie loved you, Russ. You loved her with all your heart, but this is not the way to show it."

The urge to apologize to Russell was intense, but she also had to tell him the truth about what happened the night Callie died, the atrocious truth about Nichole, Seth, and Jessica. She was running out of time. Surely Jude's attorney would go to the press, possibly even tomorrow. A wrongful conviction of a death row inmate was a huge story. The media would be like vultures, feeding on every sensational detail.

"Nichole should be telling her dad what she did," Rebecca fumed. "Not me. Miserable coward."

The tension in Rebecca's body was rising like an outdoor thermometer. She had to get out of there or she would go insane. Her parents were driving in this evening from their road trip, and there was not a morsel of food in the house. She grabbed her purse and headed for the grocery store.

An hour later, she was juggling overflowing grocery bags through their kitchen door. More were in her car. She plopped the bags onto the island and started putting things away, aware of a gathering headache. The lump on the back of her head had stopped throbbing, but it was sore to the touch. The confrontation with Seth Palmer, so sudden and unexpected, had left her shaken. Never had a man put his hands on her in anger, but Seth had actually smashed her head against the bookcase and squeezed her neck hard enough to leave bruises. The rage in his eyes had been frightening, but it had dissolved quickly enough when Myra pointed her gun at him. Not until the deputy arrived had Rebecca seen the word MACE on the grip. "Pepper spray?"

"If I'd had a firearm," Myra had snarled, "I'd have shot him."

Seth had been arrested and taken away in handcuffs. He had probably bonded out by now and headed back to Houston with Nichole. But Rebecca couldn't think about that now. All that mattered was Russell. How much did he know? How much had Nichole told him? Not the complete truth, that was certain.

With the groceries put away and the air conditioner on high, Rebecca ran the Swiffer over the floors and dusted the furniture, burning nervous energy. Just after seven, her cell phone rang.

She retrieved it from her pocket. Night owl. Finally. "Russ, hi. I'm so glad you called."

"Are you busy?"

"Not at all."

"I need to see you, Becca."

"Of course. Where are you?"

"On 71. Headed your way." He spoke in a neutral manner, without inflection. "Could you meet me?"

"Yes, of course. Anywhere."

"Lakeview Park? We could watch the storm roll in."

"I'd like that." She did a quick mental calculation. The park was half an hour away. "Can you be there by eight-thirty?"

"See you then. Drive safely."

"You too. See you soon."

Hurriedly, Rebecca finished getting the house ready for her parents' return. Then she put away the cleaning products, turned on lamps, sprayed home fragrance about, then wrote her parents a quick note. "Welcome home. I've missed you like crazy. Meeting Russ at Lakeview Park. Must tell him the truth. Text me when you're home safe and sound. See you tomorrow. Much love, R."

Clouds were moving in when Rebecca left for the park. It was a quarter of eight, and the sun was sinking rapidly toward the horizon. She sent up silent prayers for God's grace and help. Minutes into the drive, a gentle rain began to fall. The thump of windshield wipers set her nerves on edge and worsened her headache. A text tone sounded. Instinctively, Rebecca reached for her phone. She reconsidered and pulled off the road seconds later. It was from Clay. FYI. Jude's atty to make public statement tomorrow. Prepare yourself.

"Tomorrow," Rebecca whispered, tossing her phone aside. "It's all coming out tomorrow."

With each passing mile, the rainfall grew heavier, drumming on the roof of her car. Twenty minutes into her drive, Rebecca turned off Highway 71 onto a county road leading to the park about a mile toward the lake. It was a two-lane blacktop, narrow and winding. The wet surface hissed under the tires of her RX350. She turned her headlights on high beam and slowed her speed. She hoped Russell had not been drinking. The road could be dicey, particularly when the blacktop was slick with rain.

Oak trees towered on both sides of the narrow road, their branches reaching toward each other like twisted arms. She had driven the road countless times, the most recent when she and Myra had met Clay at the park. That was less than a week ago. Each day had bled into the other.

The park was minutes away now. A hard wind blew debris across the blacktop. Lightning cracked the charcoal sky. Cautiously, Rebecca slowed her speed, negotiating a treacherous curve. With terrifying suddenness, taillights glared up ahead like warning flares. She floored the brake pedal and clenched the steering wheel, locking her elbows. Fishtailing on the rain-slick blacktop, the Lexus fought for traction. Water sprayed against the tire well. Interminable moments later, the car slid off the shoulder and ground to a jarring stop. The headlights shone directly at a mud splattered vehicle, pitched into the ditch at an impossible angle. It had smashed into a tree. A jagged limb creased the hood and roof.

"Russell, no!"

Frantic, Rebecca steered her SUV back onto the blacktop. She had to get to a safe spot off the road. Waves of dread passed over her as she maneuvered around the rear of the Tahoe, then drove a short distance to an unmarked lane. The Lexus slid to a stop on the loose gravel. Rebecca slammed the gear into park, killed the engine, and flung open the door. Blowing rain pelted her face. Gusts of wind shoved her toward the Tahoe.

A single headlamp shone into the woods. The beam coned around a shape, something thrashing and struggling. Rebecca choked back a cry. Russell? Had he been thrown from the car? Please, God, no. Lightning ripped and dazzled, then the flailing slowed. Rebecca cringed at the sight. A deer. Bloodied. Struggling. Twitching.

Looking away from the dying animal, she was instantly assaulted by the sight of the wrecked Tahoe. Crumpled front end. Jagged, broken tree limbs. Blood-smeared hood. Russell. Bracing herself, she skidded clumsily into the ditch, grappling with brush to slow her stumbling descent. Wrestling for balance, she grabbed the outside mirror. Then, without thinking, she fumbled for the door handle and pulled. The door swung open under its own weight, knocking her to the ground. Stunned, Rebecca scrambled to her knees, to her feet, then froze. The air bag had deployed, littering the vehicle with debris. Russell. His body was held upright by the shoulder harness. Eyes closed. Head dangling. Chin on his chest. Blood oozing from his forehead and streaming from his nose.

"Russ." Rebecca's voice was a frantic croak. "Russ, it's me. Becca. Are you okay?" She picked up his left hand, warm and limp. "Russ, can you hear me?" She felt a faint squeeze. "Good. That's good. Talk to me." Rain came in noisy sheets, smearing blood across his face, fading it from red to watery pink. "Are you okay? Talk to me." A moan rose from deep in his chest. His eyelids fluttered open, but then closed again. Rebecca grasped his bloody face, supporting his head, saying his name again and again. Slowly, he raised his head, squinting and groaning. "Careful, Russ. Easy."

"What …?" Blood and saliva drooled from his mouth. "What happened?"

"You hit a deer." Blood poured from his nose, a river of red flowing onto his pale blue shirt. "I need to call an ambulance."

"No." He gripped Rebecca's hand with surprising strength. "No ambulance."

"But you're bleeding."

"I … said … no." He struggled clumsily against the seat belt. "Let me out."

"Wait, Russ. Please." Supporting his head with one hand, Rebecca pressed against his shoulder with the other. He grasped her forearm and tugged. "Okay. I won't call an ambulance, but we must stop the bleeding."

Rebecca freed her hand from his grip, then gently pinched the soft tissue of his nose, holding his head slightly forward with her free hand. The cut at his hairline was seeping like a soaked sponge. She had to keep blood from his eyes. "I need my first aid kit, but you must keep pressure on your nose. Can you do that?" He mumbled and raised his hand, clumsily feeling for his nose. Rebecca positioned his fingers and held them in place. "Do not let go. I'll be right back."

Cautiously, she closed the car door to the rain, scrambled out of the ditch and onto the blacktop. Averting her gaze from the dying deer, Rebecca raced to her car, her clothes rain-soaked and clingy. She popped the rear door and snatched a first aid kit that was Velcroed to the carpeted wall. Should she call an ambulance? Not yet, she decided, closing the door, then trotting back to the Tahoe.

Russ was still sitting upright, his nose pinched between his bloody thumb and forefinger. His shirt was soaked now. He looked as if he had been in a fist fight in a thunderstorm.

Rebecca opened the door to the back seat, shoved aside an unzipped duffle bag, and climbed in out of the rain. Opening the first aid kit, she glanced at the duffle bag, hastily stuffed with clothes. Atop them lay a crumpled white cap. Stitched on the front was a spinning rod with a bowed tip and a line pulled taut by a colorful fish. TIGHT LINES BAIT AND TACKLE.

"You did it, Russ," she said, twisting the lid from a bottle of hydrogen peroxide. "You went fishing with your dad."

CHAPTER 32

Mac lifted Michaela onto his lap. They were in the living room again. This time, they were preparing to leave for the hospital. Catherine had been home only once since Sierra had been admitted almost forty-eight hours ago. Brooke was staying at her mother's side so that Mac could focus on Michaela. The head nurse had put up no resistance when he had asked what time would be convenient for Michaela to have a brief visit with her mother. The woman had suggested early afternoon, and Mac had offered to give half an hour notice.

That morning, he had held a conference call with his partner and the staff at LSL&R. His assistant would bring Don up to speed on all the deals Mac had working, handle all his calls, and brief Mac at the end of the day with a single email. "I know you'll stay on top of everything, Amelia. Pay special attention to the Donovan deal. They need the sale to close ASAP." He had received a text from Lester last night, brief and no doubt heartfelt. *No matter how hard we try. Can't always keep them safe. Deeply sorry.*

Mac cuddled Michaela closer. She had not said a word since he lifted her onto his lap. She was resting her head on his shoulder and holding onto his middle three fingers, something she had done for as long as he could remember.

Can't always keep them safe.

Graham had arrived in Austin at noon. Mac would leave it entirely up to Michaela whether or not she saw her dad while he was in town. He would not let the child be pressured, and under no circumstances would they visit in a public place, not while the maniac who shot Sierra was still out there somewhere.

Lieutenant Bostic had scheduled an interview with Graham. Interview. It would be an interrogation. Mac was certain. "The shooter was clearly not Hollister," Bostic had said. "But we can't rule out the possibility that he hired the man. We're following the evidence and the facts. And the fact is that Hollister is a controlling, volatile guy who took out half a million dollars in life insurance on his young, healthy wife."

Dread and anxiety gnawed at Mac's stomach as he stroked Michaela's hair. Can't always keep them safe. Her father was everything Bostic said and more, but only a psychopath would hire someone to shoot the mother of his child. "Sierra," Mac whispered.

"Is Mommy going to be okay?"

Mac flinched, aware of an unmanageable sense of disorientation that he had to overcome. He gathered his thoughts, reminding himself to give short, honest answers. "We'll know more about how your mom is doing when we get to the hospital."

"Promise I can see her?"

"Yes. For a few minutes."

"Eleven?"

Mac gave the child a squeeze. Eleven. It was Sierra's and her favorite number. They were both born on October 11. He spent the next few minutes doing his best to prepare Michaela for the sights, smells, and sounds of the ICU. "Mom's taking medicine through a needle in her arm."

"What for?"

"One is to keep her comfortable, and another is to help her sleep."

"Will Mommy be sleeping when we get there?"

"Probably, but you can talk softly to her. Of course, she can't talk to you because of the breathing tube, but the doctor is pretty sure Mom can hear you." Mac was prepared for Michaela to ask what she should say, but she did not. The child had been heartbreakingly quiet, withdrawn even, since the shooting. "What time do you have?"

Holding her watch so they both could see it, Michaela studied the digits with fierce concentration. "Hmmm. Twelve and a half?"

"That's it. Half past twelve. Let's eat a bite, then head to the hospital."

They arrived at Seton Medical Center an hour later. Mac parked the Tahoe as close to the garage elevator as he could, then rushed Michaela toward it. "Slow down, Granddad."

"Sorry, sweetie."

"Why are we running? Is Mommy okay?"

Catherine and Brooke met them in the lobby. Some women would have dropped to her knees, Mac thought, urgently sweeping a child into her arms, but not Catherine. Instead, she bent down and hugged Michaela, warmly, calmly, reassuringly, then whispered in her ear. "I'm so glad you're here. I've missed you."

Brooke was doing battle with her emotions when she embraced her niece. "Are you and Granddad taking good care of each other?" Michaela nodded but didn't speak. "What did you have for lunch today?"

"Grilled cheese."

"Yum. Gran and I are hungry for tacos and tea, so we'll meet you in the cafeteria after you visit your mom."

Mac stepped in when Michaela only nodded. "We won't be long." He took the child's hand, tiny and cold, and headed for the Intensive Care Unit. Michaela's pace seemed to slow with each step. Was she having second thoughts? Had he made a terrible mistake by bringing her here? Her mother was lying in a hospital bed with a tube down her throat. Machines beeped and hummed. Nurses studied charts, speaking in a language of their own. No child should have to go through this.

Anger swelled inside Mac, escalating with each step to heart-pounding fury. Some sonofabitch had opened fire on his family. Shot his daughter. If the cops didn't solve this case, he swore, he would track down the bastard if it took him the rest of his life and every dime he had.

"Granddad." Michaela squeezed his hand. Her voice seemed to come from somewhere far away. "I'm being brave."

Mac felt as if he were under emotional assault. Fury and frustration. Heartache and helplessness. And the sickening fear that Sierra would not recover. Gently, he drew the child to a stop, pausing to gather himself. Kneeling on one knee in front of his granddaughter, he took both her hands in his. Tears burned his eyes. He swallowed over the painful knot in his throat. "You are being brave. But I want you to know something, Michaela. People can be brave and scared at the same time."

"Are you a little scared?"

Mac nodded. "But we'll get through this together, sweetie." He stroked her cheek. "Are you ready?" He kissed her forehead when she nodded, stood, then pressed a button on the wall.

The doors to the ICU quietly swung open. Mac led Michaela past the nurses' station, praying that she was blocking out the eerie unfamiliarity of the place. "Your mom is in a bed behind that curtain." Michaela crept forward, her fingers like icicles. "She might be asleep, or she might just be resting with her eyes shut."

Mac eased the curtain aside, and they entered the crowded space hand in hand. Sierra's beautiful face was scabbed on one side. Her right eye was swollen and black. He had smashed her to the sidewalk trying to protect her. *No matter how hard we try. Can't always keep them safe.* Catherine or Brooke had obviously brushed Sierra's hair, letting it fan out a little on the pillow. Her chest rose and fell in rhythm with the whoosh and click of the ventilator. A stool Mac did not remember seeing before had been rolled into the space, and he lifted Michaela onto it.

Carefully, the child grasped her mother's fingers, steering clear of the IV tubing. "Hi, Mommy. It's me. Michaela." Her voice was paper thin but steady. "You don't have to open your eyes. You need to rest. I know you're scared, and that's okay." She eyed the monitor above her mother's bed, the bagged IV pole, and finally the ventilator as it ticked and hissed. "This place is really noisy, and it stinks like Clorox, but the nurses and doctors are taking good care of you."

Not wanting to hover, Mac stepped back, blocking the narrow opening into the space.

"I'm sorry your chest is hurting, Mommy, but the machine is helping you breathe, like my vaporizer when I have a bad cold." Michaela leaned in closer. "Granddad let me sleep in your bed last night. Your ceiling fan wobbles, but he'll get it fixed by the time you come home. I wish you could come home today, Mommy. I miss you." Her voice broke like a snapped twig. Mac forced himself to stand back. She had to do this. But the sound of her tiny, fragile voice was heartbreaking. He could hardly bear it. "Gran said we all have a job to do, Mommy. My job is to take care of Granddad and to be honest about what's on my mind. Your job is to rest. That's all you have to do." Michaela looked over her shoulder at Mac, her lower lip trembling. "Can you pick me up?"

"Sure." Mac lifted the child from the stool, holding her tight as she leaned down and kissed her mother's cheek.

"Sleep tight, Mommy. I love you. Sweet dreams."

Mac carried Michaela out of the unit and into the hallway, her face buried in his shoulder, her arms locked around his neck. "You're a brave little girl," he whispered, then lowered her feet to the floor. He wiped tears from her cheeks and smoothed back her hair. "Don't let me forget to get that fan fixed, okay?"

Catherine and Brooke appeared from around the corner. What were they doing there? Mac wondered. They couldn't possibly have eaten already. "What's going on?"

"Change of plans." Brooke gave him a look, a warning of some sort. "We'll get something later."

Catherine drew Michaela to her side. "Why don't you and Granddad head home? He looks as if he needs a nap." Then she hugged Mac and whispered in his ear. "Graham is on his way here. Hurry and you can avoid him."

♦ ♦ ♦

MAC CLOSED THE SHUTTERS in Michaela's bedroom, blocking the afternoon sun. He turned on the ceiling fan, then told her to have a good nap. She would sleep for at least an hour. She always did. That would give him plenty of time to go to Starbucks and deal with Graham. Bryant had left the office early and was waiting in the family room. "Appreciate your coming over."

"Anything I can do to help." Bryant sank back into the sofa cushions and shook his head slowly. "Michaela sure was quiet. It's just brutal seeing her like that."

"The worst." Mac's cell phone vibrated. It was a text message from Catherine. Phone me ASAP. She answered his call right away. "Are you all right? What's happening?"

"I just met with Dr. Chesney. He had bad news, honey. Sierra's white blood count is very high. That and a sudden fever says she has an infection. He has ordered more blood work, but this is not good."

Awash with sudden dread, Mac thought back to what the surgeon had said. Gunshot wounds are laden with potential complications. But Sierra had been on antibiotics since she was moved to ICU. Why weren't the drugs working? "Do you think Chesney knows what he's doing? Or do we need to bring in another specialist?"

"I mentioned a specialist. He had already planned to bring someone else on board."

"Who?" Mac did not wait for an answer. "Tell him we want Jack Beckett."

"I agree. Yes. I'll tell him."

"Better yet, call Jack yourself. Sierra's not Chesney's only patient. We can't risk the guy dragging his feet."

"I'll call Jack myself. Yes."

"Right away," Mac pressed. "Or maybe I should call him."

A moment of silence was followed by a terse, "Mac, I said I would take care of it."

Mac released a noisy, frustrated sigh. "I'm sorry, honey."

"Don't be. You're right. We must stay on top of things." Catherine's voice faltered but could not regain its footing. "I have to be vigilant. Sierra is completely helpless, and I'm her mother."

The sound of Catherine crying jabbed at Mac's heart. Why had he pushed so hard? His wife had seen their daughter shot right before her eyes. She was scared, worried, and exhausted. "I'm so sorry, honey. Maybe you should take a break. I can be there in ten minutes. Graham can cool his heels for a while." He waited for his wife to respond, but heard a muffled, shuffling sound. "Catherine?"

"Dad, it's me. She'll be okay. Mom just needs to eat something."

"Do I need to come, Brooke?"

"No. Go to Starbucks. Tell Graham Hollister I hope he burns in hell. He's behind this, Dad. I know it."

Twenty minutes later, Mac pulled into Casis Village and parked in front of Starbucks. Graham was waiting for him outside, sitting at the same table they had before. Just over a week had passed. How was that possible? It seemed like an eternity.

Mac pulled back a chair. The scrape of metal on concrete set his nerves on edge. "Make this quick, Graham. Why did you want to see me?"

"Where's my daughter? I told you to bring her."

"Michaela was too tired. It's not a good time for a visit."

"Her mother is in intensive care, and it's not a good time to see her father?" The man stirred in the chair, perspiring and agitated. "So the McKeons are circling the wagons. Is that it? First the hospital won't let me see Sierra, and now you're keeping my daughter from me."

Circling the wagons. It was a telling choice of words. That was what people did when they were under assault. "You have no right to see Sierra, legal or otherwise."

"But I have a right to see my child."

"Not today you don't." Mac shoved his warning across the table. "You listen to me, Graham. Michaela has rights too. And she did not want to see you."

"You think you have the upper hand now, don't you?" His glare was like a declaration of war. "Did you really think that if you sicced Barney Fife on me that I would go slinking out of town with my tail between my legs? I had nothing to do with what happened to Sierra. Nothing."

"I don't believe you."

"I don't care what you believe, but don't you dare let Michaela think—"

"Think what? That the man who pushed her mother down a flight of stairs tried to have her killed?"

"Is that what you told the police? That I pushed Sierra? That I hired a hit man to shoot her?"

"What's got you so worried, Graham?"

"Have you lost your mind, Mac? I had nothing to do with the shooting. Nothing. I know you want me out of your family's life, but accusing me of hiring somebody to shoot my wife is—"

"She's not your wife." Mac pushed back his chair. "I'm not listening to another word out of your mouth."

"You're going to hear this." Graham stepped into the narrow aisle between the tables, blocking Mac's way. "I am Michaela's father. Nobody can change that. Not even the powerful Mac McKeon."

"Get out of my way."

Graham held his ground. "Hopefully Sierra will pull through this, but if she doesn't, you are not raising my daughter. You will not keep Michaela from me."

"We'll see about that. Now get out of my way."

Graham stepped to the side. "Tell Michaela I'll see her in a few days. By the way, she is crazy about the watch you gave her. It's a Smart Watch, isn't it?"

A wave of fury passed over Mac. His body went rigid, and he clenched his fists.

"Face it, man." Graham smoothed his shirt front, his expression a smirk. "You've met your match."

CHAPTER 33

Blood-stained clothes soaked in the utility sink in Rebecca's laundry room. Russell was resting in the guest room. He had refused medical treatment tonight, but he had agreed to see a doctor tomorrow morning. Persistent, anxious thoughts battled for Rebecca's attention. Russ could have been killed tonight or grievously injured. Nothing suggested he had been drinking when he hit the deer, but he might have been. Why had he asked to meet her at Lakeview Park? What had he wanted to talk to her about? Did he know that she had teamed up with Clay? Did he know the truth about the night Callie was killed, and that Jude Donovan was an innocent man?

"Stop it," she ordered herself, dropping into a chair in the family room. "Who but Nichole could have told him? No one. Russ knows nothing."

The silent house was suddenly oppressive and stifling. Rebecca picked up the remote from the chairside table, then turned on the television. The ten o'clock news would air shortly. Tomorrow, Jude's attorney would make a public statement, but could the story have been leaked to the press already? Was there anything about Jude's exoneration on the Internet? She worried about August. That dear man could not hear such horrific news about his granddaughter from the media, not even on a telephone call from Russ.

"It is Nichole's responsibility to face her family," Rebecca muttered angrily. "No one else's. She is the reason Callie is dead. She is the reason Jude Donovan is on death row."

Rebecca turned up the television volume. Her thumb jittered on the button. The stress of the past two weeks and the shock of seeing the wrecked Tahoe was catching up with her. "When will this end?"

The lead news story was the shooting of Sierra Hollister. A grainy, inferior picture of the suspect appeared on the screen. The man's body was half hidden behind a vehicle. His cap was drawn low, and he was wearing sunglasses. How could anyone possibly recognize him? In a brief recorded statement, the police chief asked for the public's help, ending with an assurance that the shooter likely worked alone and that investigators were working nonstop. "This man carried out a brazen, brutal attack on the McKeon family, and he will get what he has coming to him."

The remainder of the newscast mentioned nothing about Jude Donovan. Rebecca turned down the volume and set the remote aside. A maddening mixture of anger and resolve spread through her like a virus. Nichole should get what she had coming too. Attempting to contact her by phone was a waste of time, Rebecca decided. Nichole would not accept her call. "I could leave a message. Tell Russ your side, or I'll tell him Jessica's." But even that threat might not be enough to force her to face her dad. There had to be another way.

A thought erupted, exploding in Rebecca's mind with such force that she gasped. Russell's phone was on the dresser in the guest room. Surely Nichole would take a call from her dad. Rebecca popped from her chair and paced the room. Somehow, she would lure Nichole to Sparrows Cove. She would force her to face her dad.

A plan took shape in Rebecca's mind, but first she had to protect August. She called her parents' home, apologizing when her mother answered. "I know it's late, Mom, but I need your help." Quickly, she told her about Russell's accident. "He's at my house. He'll be fine." She told her that Jude's attorney was going public tomorrow. "I'm worried about August. Will you call him? He doesn't have to know about the accident, but he must be told the truth about Nichole."

"Of course. August is family. We'll phone him first thing in the morning. Better yet. We should tell him in person."

"But, Mom," Rebecca protested. "It's a long drive to Hillsboro. A hundred fifty miles. You just got home tonight."

"We'll be fine after a good night's sleep."

"But there is more rain on the way."

"Then I guess we'll have to use the windshield wipers."

Rebecca chuckled, despite the tears gathering in her eyes. "Thank you so much."

"Are you okay, honey?"

"Don't worry about me. Just take care of each other and August."

Rebecca set her phone aside. She felt shaky when she stood. Had she eaten anything today? She couldn't honestly remember. Steadying herself momentarily, she slipped down the hall and into the dimly lit guest room. Russell was dozing, his head lolled to the side, his lips slack and parted. The bandage on his forehead covered the cut, but not the bruise spreading toward his brow. His cell phone lay on the dresser next to his wallet, keys, and the fishing cap. She had set the cap aside in her search for Russ's pajamas wadded in the duffle bag. Again, she felt a rush of gratitude that he had taken time to visit his dad, and that August would not be alone when the disastrous news broke about Nichole.

Quietly, Rebecca picked up the cell phone and stole out of the room. The screen was black, the battery dead. But the device was an iPhone like hers, and at her desk in the family room, she plugged it into her charger. The phone soon came to life.

As Rebecca had anticipated, the passcode was the year of Russell's birth. He never bothered to change it. She tapped Contacts and then swept up, locating Nichole's name, and an unfamiliar number. "Changed your number, huh?"

Staring at the screen, Rebecca rehearsed what she would say if Nichole answered. Then she took a deep, steadying breath as she tapped the number and brought the phone to her ear. She tensed when the ringing began and jerked when Nichole answered.

"Hi, Dad."

"Nichole, it's Rebecca." She spoke rapidly, determined to make her point before Nichole could hang up. "Russ was in a car accident. He needs your help."

"Is he okay?" Her tone was curt, icy even.

"When can you be here?"

"I asked if Dad's okay."

"And I said he needs you. When can you be here?"

"Where are you?" Nichole's frosty tone was melting. "Is Dad in the hospital?"

Rebecca's thoughts stalled. Nichole might not come to Sparrows Cove if she knew Russ was at her house. "I didn't hear you," she lied, buying precious moments to untangle her thoughts. "You're breaking up. Just listen. You are in charge of health care decisions. You need to come."

"Where is he?"

"I'm having trouble hearing you. The medical power-of-attorney is at my house. When can you be here?"

"I'm an hour away," Nichole answered, almost breathless. "I'll leave now. Will Dad be okay?"

"You're breaking up again." Lowering the phone, she tapped the screen and ended the call. "It worked. She bought it."

Rebecca was suddenly crawling with nerves. She had assumed that Nichole was in Houston, three hours away, that she wouldn't come until tomorrow. But she was only an hour away. But where? Her heart hurt for Russell, but he had to know the truth, and Rebecca was running out of time.

♦ ♦ ♦

REBECCA CLOSED HER LAPTOP and pushed back from her desk. There was nothing on the Internet about Jude Donovan's wrongful conviction, not even on the Innocence Initiative's website. It was ten forty-five. Nichole was probably fifteen minutes away. Should she wake Russell now or wait until Nichole arrived?

"I thought you would be in bed by now."

Rebecca gasped. "Russ, you startled me." Gathering herself, she tucked his phone out of sight, then turned off the desk lamp. "How are you feeling?"

"I'm okay."

"Can I get you anything?"

"No thanks." Hunched over, Russell walked slowly across the room, flinching when he sat. "I feel like I spent seven seconds on a bronc."

"I'm sure you do." Rebecca sat next to him on the sofa, noting how very thin Russ had become. Painful memories reminded her that grief and worry could melt the pounds right off a person.

"Becca, I wasn't drinking tonight. I want you to know that."

"That's good to know." Rebecca felt a familiar tenderness stir inside her. "I was horrified when I saw your Tahoe. When I heard the deer thrashing in the ditch, I thought the worst."

"I'm sorry." Russell picked up a throw pillow and clutched it to his abdomen, locking his forearms across it. "I'm sorry about the way I treated you at Dad's birthday party too. It was nice of you to be there, but I acted like a jerk. You deserved better. You were like a daughter to my parents."

"Your mother used to say that I wasn't her daughter-in-law. I was her daughter-in-love."

Russell smiled, a barely detectable tip of his lips. "Dad and I had a good time fishing together. Been too long. I told him what a good man I think he is."

"I'm so glad you took the time. It runs out sooner than we want to think." Rebecca checked the clock again. She had waited as long as she could. "I need to talk to you about something, Russ. I wish I didn't have to, but I don't have any choice. It's about Nichole. She's on her way here."

"You called her? There wasn't any reason to do that. I'm fine."

"I know you are," Rebecca said tenderly, turning her body toward him on the sofa and placing her hand on his shoulder.

"That's not why I called her. Nichole has been keeping something from you, and it cannot continue."

"What are you talking about?"

"It's about the night Callie was killed," Rebecca continued. "You don't know the truth, Russ, and neither did I until recently."

"What are you getting at?"

Before Rebecca could answer, headlights shone through the front shutters. "That's Nichole now. Make her tell you the truth, Russ. She lied to us. So did Seth and Jessica. They all lied." The car engine went silent, the headlights dark. A single door slammed shut. "I'm genuinely sorry, Russ, that you have to go through this."

Rebecca crossed the room, turning on a lamp near the door before opening it. Nichole was dressed in faded jeans and a tee shirt. Her face was free of makeup, her hair in a haphazard ponytail. The porch light cast shadows on her face, darkening the circles under her eyes. Rebecca stepped aside, allowing Nichole to enter.

Instantly, the girl's face paled. "Dad. What are you doing here? She said you were in the hospital."

"It was the only way I could get you here," Rebecca confessed with a diminishing measure of satisfaction. "You have to tell him the truth, Nichole."

Russell's forehead wrinkled, creating furrows in the bandage. "What's this about, Nichole? Rebecca said you've been keeping something from me, something about the night Callie was killed."

Nichole turned on Rebecca, her lips tremoring. "How could you do this? Do you hate me that much?"

"Tell him the truth," Rebecca demanded, unfazed. "Sit down and tell your dad why you were at the convenience store that night."

"I can't," Nichole whined. "He'll hate me. Like you do."

"Tomorrow what happened that night will be all over the news, Nichole." Rebecca closed the front door. "This is your chance to tell Russ your side of the story."

Russell sat with the pillow still across his abdomen, but now his fists were clenching. "What is she talking about, Nichole? You were at the convenience store to buy gas. What is she talking about?"

Nichole's eyes zigzagged in their sockets. She inched her way across the room, standing now with a cocktail table between her and her father. "It was Jessica, Dad. I had to get her some meth."

"Meth? You went there to buy meth?"

"I didn't want to. I had no choice." Nichole crept forward, as if she were picking her way through land mines. "Jessica was in a bad way. I couldn't let Callie see —"

"You took your sister to a drug buy?"

"Please, Dad," Nichole pleaded. "I didn't know what else to do."

"So you called Seth," Rebecca interjected, her pulse racing. The look in Nichole's eyes was like terror. "That's what you did, isn't it?"

"I had to. I needed his help. Seth knows what Jessica can be like." Nichole lowered her body onto the sofa, her hands gripping the edge of the cushion. "I'm so sorry, Dad."

"Sorry?" Russell's voice grew suddenly strong with angry disbelief. "You put your sister's life in danger. You got your sister killed."

"We didn't know that lunatic had a gun. We didn't know he would go into the store and start shooting people."

"But you did know Calvin Canon, didn't you?" Rebecca pressed, standing behind an armchair, gripping the upholstered wings. "You met him on the beach. You and Seth and Jessica."

"He was there. Yes. But we didn't know him. Not really." Nichole was speaking more and more rapidly, her knuckles whiter than her face. "We didn't know he would come to the convenience store high on meth. We couldn't have known."

Rebecca struggled to control her raging impatience. "But you knew Jude Donovan didn't bring him there, didn't you?"

"What are you talking about?" Russell's face contorted in confusion. "Of course, Donovan brought him there."

"No, he didn't, Russ," Rebecca insisted. "Calvin Canon was with Seth Palmer that night. Not Jude Donovan. Wasn't he, Nichole?"

"Yes! But Seth was just trying to help." Her voice broke, and tears burst from her eyes. "Jessica was about to spin out of control. All I wanted to do was get her fixed up and get home. I was just trying to get home."

"You lied about Jude Donovan?" Russell demanded, his breathing almost a pant. "That cannot be true. Nichole, tell me that's not true."

"I'm sorry, Dad. Everything spun out of control. Callie was dead, and we panicked. When we described the car, when we gave the cops a partial license number, we never expected they would find it. Never. We didn't mean for any of this to happen. I'm sorry. I'm so sorry."

"You got Callie killed. You got my innocent Callie killed." Russell hurled the pillow across the room, knocking a lamp to the floor like a wounded animal. "An innocent man went to prison. What have you done? What have I done?"

"Dad, please, forgive me." Nichole's plea was frantic and desperate. "I need you."

"Get out!"

"Dad, don't do this." She grasped at her father's forearm, but he yanked it back. "I never meant for any of this to happen."

Russell's hand shot out with the quick brutality of a switchblade. He slapped Nichole across the face. Her shriek shrilled over his words. "Go! Get out!"

CHAPTER 34

Mac left the attorney's office and headed for the parking lot, scanning his surroundings. Early August was too hot for even a light jacket, but the layer kept his holster out of view. He had been licensed to carry for years. Rarely had he felt a need to do so, but he did now. Would it have changed anything the day Sierra was shot? No, but he was not taking any chances. Bostic had reminded him that there was no way to know for certain that Sierra had been the target. "You and your family need to take precautions." Short of hiring bodyguards, Mac did not know what else he could do. Brooke had promised that she and Michaela would not leave the house today. Catherine, Mac had to believe, was safe within the walls of the hospital.

Victoria Casey, recommended to Mac by his friend who practiced family law, had a reputation as an aggressive child custody lawyer. She was well connected and a fierce litigator. Right away, she had gained Mac's confidence. Now, she had to deliver. "Breathe easy," Victoria Casey had said, as she wrapped up the hour-long conference. "Hollister has a volatile temper. He's a suspect in the attempted murder of his wife. And the man's an outsider. You and your wife are pillars of the community. No judge will ever rule in Hollister's favor." She waved off the absurdity with a flip of the hand. "Michaela is not going anywhere."

Mac had contacted Victoria Casey yesterday after the confrontation with Graham. The insufferable jerk was staking his claim to Michaela, making plans for being half a million dollars richer if Sierra died. The man thought that Mac would capitulate if he was combative enough, if he showed that he was up for the fight and would not be intimidated. Mac felt like a fool for thinking that a tracking device was the answer to keeping Michaela safe. The thing had done nothing more than tip his hand. But now, Mac was done playing by the rules. I'm afraid my dad will take me on vacation again. He would do whatever it took to keep Michaela safe.

Before meeting with Victoria Casey, he had placed a call to Bostic. The detective had described Graham Hollister as slicker than a snake in wet grass. "When I asked him if he would be willing to take a polygraph, he agreed. But then he hedged, saying that his attorney might advise otherwise." Mac doubted that Graham had consulted with an attorney, but he took a lot of satisfaction in knowing that the man was beginning to sweat.

Ironic, Mac thought, that Victoria Casey had told Mac to breathe easy. After almost seventy-two hours, Sierra was being weaned off the ventilator. The respiratory specialist was monitoring her closely. It was possible that the breathing tube could be removed today. He hoped to be at the hospital when Jack Beckett arrived. Sierra was receiving a broad-spectrum antibiotic, but her white blood count was not improving. Gunshot wounds are laden with possible complications.

Mac and Brooke were swapping duties today. Michaela was spending the afternoon with her and Sydney. He would pick up Michaela before bedtime, but Brooke would spend the night in her own bed. Catherine's close friends were functioning like a crisis intervention team. Years of close friendship made the question "What can we do to help?" a waste of words. Each one of the women, it seemed, had faced a crisis of some sort. They knew what to do for each other and how to do it. Tonight, one of them would spend the night at the hospital with Catherine. Brooke wasn't the only person who needed a night in her own bed, but trying to convince Catherine to leave Sierra was a waste of breath, and everyone knew it.

At the hospital, Mac found his wife alone in the waiting room, studying something on her iPad. Relief swept over her face when she looked up and saw him. "I'm so glad you're here."

They embraced when he sat beside her and kissed. "How is she?"

"She's off the ventilator, honey. The tube is gone."

"When?"

"About an hour ago. I started to phone you."

"It's okay. Have you seen her?"

"Briefly. She's still heavily medicated, so she probably didn't know I was there. But it was such a relief to see her without the tube. Of course, she's on oxygen, but Sierra is breathing on her own, Mac."

"Thank God. Now, she has to keep fighting off the infection. Has Jack made rounds yet?"

"He's with her now. He'll stop by before he leaves." Catherine's eyes left Mac's face for a moment, as if she were trying to recapture an elusive thought. "How did your meeting go? What did you think of — I forgot her name."

"Victoria Casey. She's smart and tough. Just what we need. She assured me we have nothing to worry about, and neither will

Sierra when she gets out of here. Michaela is not going anywhere."

Catherine frowned. "Mac, you don't really think Graham is behind this, do you?"

"I hope not. For my family's sake. But until the police find out who is, then I want Graham Hollister to sweat." There was a price to pay for all that he had done. Hollister had intimidated and bullied Sierra. He had taken Michaela to Vancouver to visit his girlfriend without Sierra's permission. He had led Michaela to believe that her mother needed time away from her. And worst of all, the man had caused Michaela to be afraid. *I'm afraid he'll take me on vacation again.* "It's time for that man to know what fear feels like."

Catherine picked up her iPad and tapped in her passcode, quickly locating a video of the shooter. "Who is this man?" She sounded stunned, baffled. "Why did he shoot her? Or was he aiming at me or at you?"

The door to the waiting room opened. Jack Beckett, tall and rugged, crossed the space in long, slow steps. He told Mac to keep his seat, then eased into a chair opposite them. "I just examined Sierra. I was pleased to see she is off the ventilator. That is a big plus for so many reasons."

"And the white count?" Catherine asked.

"Still climbing," he answered. "And she has a persistent fever."

"It was a hundred two earlier. What is it now?"

"Hundred four. We're attacking the fever in multiple ways. Trust me. But getting the infection under control is critical. I've ordered more tests. The nursing staff knows to call me if there is even the slightest change."

"How did her lungs sound?" Mac asked.

"Better than I would have expected," Beckett answered, with a cautionary lift of his hand. "But I'm not going to mislead you. Sierra is in critical condition. Gunshot wounds. Major surgery. On a ventilator for nearly three days. And now infection and persistent fever." The doctor shook his head, almost indiscernibly, and sighed loudly. "But Sierra is putting up a good fight, and she is getting the best possible care."

"Is there anything more we can do?" Mac pressed.

"No. Not at this point." Grimacing, Beckett kneaded the muscles in the back of his neck. "Do the police have any idea who did this to her?"

"Not yet."

"Chief Grissom himself is asking for the public's help. The video is everywhere. Somebody will recognize the guy."

"That's what we're counting on."

"Grissom was tight lipped about the investigation," Beckett continued. "He's not even acceding that Sierra was the target."

"We don't know that she was," Mac agreed. "We're all being cautious until they make an arrest."

"Unbelievable. I am so sorry about all this." Beckett shook his head, glanced at his watch, then stood. "I have another patient to see. Catherine, you have my cell phone number. Do not hesitate to reach out if you have questions or concerns. I'll examine Sierra again first thing in the morning."

Mac and Catherine followed the doctor into the hallway, said goodbye, then made their way to the ICU. The unit was quiet, but for the steady beep of monitors and the muted conversations among staff. Sierra's bed was straight ahead. Seeing her without the breathing tube was an enormous relief. Her face looked less puffy, but her right eye looked worse than before. The right side of her face was covered with a bandage now, protecting it, Mac assumed, from the straps holding the oxygen mask in place. He leaned over her and kissed her forehead. It was unbelievably hot. "You did it, sweetheart. The tube is gone."

Catherine placed her hand on Sierra's chest. "You're breathing on your own." She put her lips close to her daughter's ear and whispered. "I knew you could do it, but now it's time to rest. Michaela is with Brooke. They send their love." She kissed Sierra's forehead, then smoothed her hair. "I love you, my precious daughter. Rest well."

The suffering on Catherine's face was unbearable. How could this have happened to their beautiful, innocent daughter? A rush of bittersweet remembrance about the day of the shooting intruded. Mac recalled taking Michaela and Anna Rose to the airport to meet Brooke and Bryant. The girls had been so excited, straining at their seatbelts to get a first glimpse of the plane. On board, he had taken pictures of the girls, giggling after Bryant had asked Mac to go with them, then Brooke had said, "Granddad can buy jammies and underwear in Chicago, right?" Had he ever looked at the pictures? He couldn't remember. That afternoon he had played golf at the club, just as he had done most Saturdays for thirty years. He had seen Phil Kuykendall in the locker room. "It's our loss. Catherine would have been a phenomenal governor." The retirement dinner had been an enjoyable affair. Several times during the evening, he had seen Sierra laugh. She had looked so beautiful in her yellow dress with the lacy, white jacket.

It was inconceivable that a deranged stranger had been pacing up and down San Jacinto Street. Waiting. Watching. Knowing.

Mac flinched as an image flashed in his mind like a lightning bolt. Blood. A bright, burgundy flow oozing from Sierra's chest. He squinted his eyes shut and groaned. A wave of nausea came over him, and the room felt suddenly hot as a furnace. He had to get out of there.

Mac leaned over and kissed his daughter's forehead again. "I love you so much, sweetheart. You're going to get through this."

Suddenly, Sierra's entire body jerked. Her head pitched back at an impossible angle, smashing the pillow. Both arms went suddenly rigid, but her torso writhed and thrashed. Terror stabbed Mac's chest. "What's happening?"

"She is having a seizure." Catherine's voice shrilled with alarm. "Get her nurse. She's having another seizure."

Mac staggered back and slapped the curtain aside, almost hitting a nurse who was rushing into the space. "She's having a seizure."

"Step outside, please." The woman brushed past Mac. "Sierra. Sierra, you're okay." A second nurse hurried into the room. After a rapid, urgent exchange, he darted out, insisting that Catherine and Mac wait in the hall. "We'll take care of her. Wait outside, please."

Blindly, Mac raced out of the unit and into the hall, leaving Catherine behind. Beads of sweat popped on his forehead. His breathing was harsh, his pulse rapid, as he paced the hall. A seizure. Sierra was having a seizure. But why? Why was she having a seizure? Had Catherine said another seizure? Yes. He was sure of it.

The doors swung open and Catherine emerged, eyes filled with concern. Mac glared at her and gestured toward the ICU. "Why didn't you tell me? When did she have a seizure?"

"Earlier today. I was going to tell you."

"When?" he demanded. "When were you going to tell me? You have no right to keep me in the dark. None."

"Mac, honey." She approached and gently grasped his forearm. "You need to sit down."

"I need to know what is going on in there."

"Please, Mac. Your face is flushed, and you're perspiring." She nodded toward chairs at the end of the hall. "Please, let's sit down."

Mac brushed off his wife's hand. "What else are you keeping from me? You know how I feel about that, Catherine."

"Of course, I do." Her voice was soft and eminently reasonable. "I was going to tell you earlier, but then I wanted you to take courage in the fact that Sierra is off the ventilator, that she is breathing on her own. I would have told you about the seizure. You know that."

Mac wiped the back of his hand across his forehead, smearing drops of sweat. Can't always keep them safe. The thought whipped in quickly. An image flashed. Sierra. Her body thrashing on the bed. Her neck cords stretched and rigid. And her arms. Stiff and thin as metal rods. A harrowing headache pounded Mac's forehead. Sierra. Tears of fear trailed down his face. He reached for his wife, and she stepped into his arms.

CHAPTER 35

Rebecca knotted the sash of her robe, stepped into her slippers, and made her way down the hall. It was five in the morning, dark as pitch outside. She had slept a miserable two hours, thrashing about in bed like a fevered child, reliving the gut-wrenching confrontation between Russ and Nichole. The girl had fled the house in tortured sobs. For a moment, Rebecca had felt sorry for her, but the emotion had passed like a summer storm. Nichole's decisions had wreaked havoc on an unimaginable number of lives, and the end was nowhere in sight.

The door to the guest room stood ajar. Rebecca inched it aside, then peeked into the dark and silent space. Russell was asleep with his back to the door. If the bed linens were any indication, he had endured a miserable night too. The duvet had slid off the bed, and one of the pillows lay on the floor. The top sheet was twisted around Russell's arm like a wrinkled sling. Rebecca had not anticipated that Nichole would come last night, so soon after Russell's car accident. "But at least it's behind you now," she whispered, knowing that it never really would be.

Passing by her desk on the way to the kitchen, Rebecca turned on her computer. Her parents would be leaving for Hillsboro in a few hours to break the news to August. She was concerned about the weather. Interstate 35 was a nightmare under the best of circumstances, but heavy rain and truck traffic made it a dangerous highway. Later, she would text Clay. Hopefully, he would have more information about the timing of Jude's attorney's public statement.

But for the light above the sink, the kitchen was dark. Rebecca wanted it that way. Moving about the space with a heavy dullness, she poured a glass of cranberry juice and put eggs on to boil. An English muffin would not suffice this morning. She felt weak and nauseous, but she had to get Russ to a doctor this morning. She was deeply worried about him, not only his physical condition after the blow to his head, but also his psychological state after the emotional assault he had endured last night.

They had said little to each other after Nichole left. The few words Russ did utter were slow and tortured, his face devoid of affect. But some things could get better for him now. Obsessing about Jude Donovan could stop. Writing letters to public officials, even to Catherine McKeon, could come to an end.

Leaving the eggs to cook, Rebecca slipped back down the darkened hall to retrieve Russell's duffle bag. He would need fresh clothes for the day. She suspected that those in the bag needed washing. She picked up the fishing cap too. In all the confusion last night, the bill had been smeared with a swipe of blood, and she was hoping to clean it.

In the laundry room, she set the cap aside, emptied the contents of the bag onto the counter, then separated darks from lights. Blood stains on the shirt soaking in the sink since last night had almost disappeared. She treated the remaining tinges with a pre-wash spray, then tossed the shirt in the washer, along with tee shirts, underwear, and a blue and gray plaid shirt, the one Russ had worn to August's birthday party.

"Oh, August," Rebecca whispered, pouring in detergent and adjusting the settings. "I wish you never had to know."

Rebecca pushed aside the thought and looked at the cap. It was just a small blood stain. Deciding to try a white cloth and a squirt of Dawn, she picked up the cap and made her way back toward the kitchen, stopping at her desk. She tapped her computer to life and clicked on her favorite news site pinned to the start menu. The weather forecast warned of heavy rains moving east from West Texas. Interstate 35 North was squarely in its path. But her parents were both excellent drivers. If things got too dicey, they would find a place to safely pull off the highway and let the worst of it move through.

Clicking on the news tab, she scrolled through the headlines. There was nothing about Jude Donovan, no mention of an innocent Harris County man who had been sentenced to death row. Russell's anguished words echoed in Rebecca's mind. An innocent man went to prison, Nichole. What have you done? What have I done? Rebecca had wanted, after Nichole left, to assure Russ that nothing that happened was his fault. He had been seeking what he thought was justice for Callie and Derek Jaxson. But what good were words when he was faced with the unimaginable? He had spent the last six months of his life determined to see an innocent man put to death. What have I done?

Rebecca recalled the day Russ had shown up at the funeral home, angry at her for allowing Nichole to be blindsided by Clay Borger. He had sounded delusional when he began fretting and speculating about what Catherine McKeon might do to stop executions if she were elected governor. He had called Catherine McKeon and her ilk bleeding-heart do-gooders, fuming about what she would think about the death penalty if her child had been shot and killed.

Tragic, Rebecca thought, that the McKeon family had become targets. But sadly, that was the plight of many high-profile families. Fortunately, unlike Callie, Sierra Hollister had survived. "At least I hope she did."

Rebecca tapped on the story. The headline read AUSTIN SHOOTER AT LARGE. POLICE CHIEF RENEWS PLEA FOR HELP. The first paragraph recapped the assault on the McKeon family and Sierra Hollister's injuries. Quoting Chief Grissom, the article indicated that FBI experts had enhanced the photo released to the public. Rebecca scrolled past the story to the photo. She detected little change from the blurry, black and white image she had seen on television last night. Perhaps, she conceded, the contrast was a bit sharper.

Looking at the photo, she remembered the first time she had seen a picture of Calvin Canon taken by the convenience store camera. With tattoos crawling up his neck and a sneer on his lips, Canon had looked like a thug. She had instantly despised him. The mug shot of Jude Donovan had evoked a different reaction, though. He had looked shell-shocked and helpless. But for the starkness of the photograph and the placard positioned across his chest, Jude had looked like the decent, young man next door.

Considering the photo of the man on her computer screen, Rebecca felt much the same. There was nothing about him that would have attracted the attention of passersby. Nothing about him seemed out of place, nothing about him to alarm. The photo simply depicted a man standing next to a dark SUV wearing sunglasses, a light-colored plaid shirt, and a ball cap of some sort. But was that a ball cap?

Rebecca leaned in, squinting, scrunching her forehead, trying to make out the decal on the crown. "What is that?" she muttered. And what were the words stitched just above the bill?

A creeping unease gathered inside her. Rebecca's gaze crawled from the picture to the cap lying on her desk, then back to the picture again. Then her eyes began to race between the objects. Her chest constricted so tightly she could hardly breathe. The plaid shirt. The sunglasses. The cap with the leaping fish. It was glaringly obvious.

"Russ, no." She jerked her hands away from the keyboard, jamming her clenched fists to her mouth. Her heart hammered so hard in her chest it sent vibrations through her body.

A hand touched her shoulder. A thunderbolt of shock jagged through her. Russ. Rebecca whirled toward him on the chair, her eyes jittering in horrified disbelief. He was staring at the image of the shooter. His eyes were hooded, his face collapsed. Even the dim light in the shadowy room could not hide the fierce pain in his eyes, the wounded look of a dying animal.

"Oh, my God, Russ."

After moments of dead silence, the image on the screen released its lock on Russell's stare. His lids fluttered. His eyes gravitated to Rebecca's. They met and caught. Tenderly, he placed an icy palm to her cheek and nodded mutely. An avalanche of thoughts cartwheeled in Rebecca's head. She tried to shield herself, but they crashed down on her. Russ shot Sierra Hollister. It was brutally, shockingly true. Callie's father attempted to kill an innocent young woman because she was Catherine McKeon's daughter.

Russell's left hand dropped to his side. He looked away, then turned toward the French doors leading onto the deck. Slowly, he crossed the room, his bare feet silent on the wood floor. What was he doing? Rebecca agonized.

When Russell disappeared through the opening, a motion-activated light swept the deck in misty silver. A light rain had begun to fall. Rebecca pushed up from the chair and steadied herself, lightheaded with shock and confusion. Why was he going outside? It was raining. He was barefoot and in his pajamas.

A single, lucid thought pierced Rebecca's mind. You don't think that's the only Glock I own, do you? Fear and panic penetrated like shrapnel. She rushed clumsily across the room and onto the deck. Russ was standing in the yard now, facing Callie's oak tree. Without pause, he raised his arm, crooked at the elbow, and positioned a dull black object near his temple. "Russ, no!" The crack of gunfire was soul shattering.

CHAPTER 36

Mac took four slices of soft French bread from a bag, then laid them on the cutting board in front of Michaela. In a haphazard manner, she slathered two slices with mayonnaise and the others with Dijon mustard. Mac sliced a ripe, red tomato, wiped the knife clean, then returned it to the knife block.

"Good job, Granddad."

Mac grinned and picked up a meat fork. He scooped up thin slices of warm, juicy meatloaf he had thawed and heated, then arranged them on the bread. Michaela layered on the tomatoes, then seasoned them generously with salt and pepper. When she was finished assembling the sandwiches, she pressed them firmly with her palm. "There we go. All done."

Mac retrieved a serrated knife and cut one of the sandwiches in half. "What shape do you call those?"

"Triangles."

He cut the second one. "And these?"

"Hmmm." She puzzled over the pieces, then said, "I'm guessing rectangles."

"Good guess. Four sides. Two long. Two short."

"If the sides were all the same long, it would be a square, right?"

"You got it." Mac put the triangles on his plate next to a pickle and a pile of kettle chips.

"Granddad, if the sides were all the same short, would it still be a square?"

Mac stifled a laugh. "It would, yes. It doesn't matter how long the sides of a square are. They just all have to be equal in length."

Satisfied, Michaela put the rectangles on her plate, righting one of them when it toppled over. She had gone to bed early last night and awoke in a cheerful mood. Each time Mac had checked on her, she had been sound asleep. She hadn't seen her mother in three days. Every day, she had asked to visit, but Mac had manufactured a reason to postpone. He could not risk the child being in the room if Sierra had another seizure. She had had only one since the day Mac was there, but Catherine had assured him that it was mild. "The anti-seizure medication is doing its job. She's responding well." The seizures, according to the neurologist, could be fever related or triggered by the infection.

"Granddad, I said the blessing. Were you listening?"

"Oh. Yes, sure."

"Then say, Amen."

Over lunch, they chatted about Michaela's play date yesterday with Anna Rose. He had assured the girl's mother that the children would not leave the house, and that Mac would be close by. I'll understand, he had added, if you decline. He had been relieved and grateful for her reaction. "Of course, Anna Rose can come. Michaela is her best friend. She's missed seeing her at the club. Hopefully this will all be over soon."

"Granddad, can we go to the hospital today?"

He had expected the question. "I'll check with Catherine and see what she thinks." To redirect the conversation, he took a bite of his sandwich, then bragged about it. "Your mom makes great meatloaf, doesn't she?"

Michaela popped chips into her mouth and chewed noisily. "It's a lot better than Gran's."

Mac chuckled. "Who do you think is the best cook in our family?"

Without hesitation, she answered, "Uncle Bryant."

"What? You're kidding me." Mac swigged his tea. "What does he cook?"

"Italian." Michaela took another big bite of her sandwich. Mustard smeared her upper lip and fingertips. "Spaghetti and meatballs. Ravioli in naranara sauce."

"You're just messing with me, right?"

"Seriously, Granddad. When Aunt Brooke bringed the spaghetti last time, Uncle Bryant said he made it. Even the meatballs." She raised her hands, palms up, her eyes large and round. "Aunt Brooke did not do a thing but boil the water and buy some garlic bread."

For the first time in days, Mac laughed out loud. Michaela joined in, her giggles contagious and genuine. Mac reached over and tousled her curls. "You're a hoot. You know that?"

Mac's cell phone rang. He picked it up from the table and swiped the screen. APD. BOSTIC. "This is Mac. I'll be right with you." He whispered to Michaela to finish her lunch, then took the call in his office. "Do you have some news for me?"

"We do. Where are you?"

"At home."

"Can we talk there?"

"Sure."

"We're leaving the station now."

Mac ended the call but stood staring at his phone. The police had a lead. That had to be it. The detectives would not come to the house otherwise. Or maybe it was more than that. Could they have identified the guy? Maybe even made an arrest?

On edge now, Mac returned to the kitchen to finish his sandwich. Michaela was done with hers and was eating chips out of the bag. He had to keep her occupied while the detectives were there. It was early for her nap, but she could read a book or play in her room.

She chose to read a book and curled up on her bed. Mac turned on her bedside lamp. Her watch was in her bluebonnet bowl where she faithfully kept it. It was no use, now that Graham suspected that it was a tracking device. Can't always keep them safe. No matter how hard you try. Had the detectives tied Graham to Sierra's shooting? For Michaela's sake, he hoped not.

Mac pulled a light throw over the child's feet and legs, leaned down, then kissed her on the forehead. Her eyes glistened in the lamplight when she looked up at him. "Granddad, why did the bad man shoot my mommy?"

Mac's heart fell. It was the first time she had mentioned the shooter since he told her five days ago. He sat on the edge of the bed, looking at her over the top of the open book. "I don't know yet, but the police are working hard to find him."

"Does he know where we live?"

"I don't know that either." He was poised to tell the child not to worry, but that was what adults had told him after his father died, and he had hated it. "It's reasonable to ask questions like that, sweetie. And I'll always do my best to be honest with you. Is there anything else you need to ask me?" Michaela shook her head. "Then I need to ask you something. What can I do to help you?"

Her eyes flooded with sudden tears. "Take me to see Mommy."

♦ ♦ ♦

MAC MET CATHERINE at the front door. Bryant had picked her up at the hospital and brought her home. Michaela was asleep. Grissom and Bostic had left the house an hour ago. Mac had been so stunned, so shocked by what the chief had told him that his brain had slowed to a crawl by the time he asked his last question.

Catherine's face looked tired and drawn. She set her purse on the entry table, then stepped into Mac's arms. He hugged her tight and asked about Sierra. She hadn't had a seizure in twenty-four hours. "Her white count is dropping, and so is her fever. Oh, Mac. She may be making the turn." She rested her head on his chest. "Where's Michaela?"

"In her room. Napping." Mac stroked her hair. "Let's go in the living room. I have some news."

"Why the living room?"

Mac ignored the question and took his wife by the hand, leading her through the foyer and into the lifeless room. The chair under the window was where he and Michaela had sat when he told her that her mom's chest had a bullet in it. A gun bullet? Someone shot my mommy? He motioned to Catherine to take the sofa, then sat next to her. Michaela could wake any minute, and he had a lot of ground to cover. God, help me.

"Grissom and Bostic were here earlier. That's why I asked you to come home. They've identified the shooter." Catherine's delicate fingertips flew to her lips, but she said nothing. "It's over." He allowed the words to penetrate. "Everyone is safe."

Slowly, she lowered her hands, then clenched them in her lap. "Are they sure?"

"Positive."

"Who is he?"

"The man is no one we've met, but he is someone we've heard of." Mac looked directly into her eyes. Short, honest answers. "It was Russell Shane. Callie Shane's father."

Catherine squinted, her brow furrowing. "Russell Shane shot Sierra? I don't understand. Why?"

Mac could not bring himself to answer her question, so he answered a different one instead. "Rebecca Grant, Shane's ex-wife, came forward. She saw the picture the police released and recognized the cap the man was wearing. There is no doubt. The shooter is Russell Shane."

"Have they arrested him? Is he in jail?"

"Actually, honey, Shane is dead. He killed himself." Mac sat silently, allowing his wife to process what she was hearing. She looked tired, pale, and overwhelmed.

"He wrote me a letter, remember?"

Mac nodded, hoping she still had it. Shane hadn't left a suicide note, but according to Rebecca Grant, he left town on Thursday morning for Hillsboro to go fishing with his father. He had returned to Austin on Saturday afternoon and shot Sierra that night. Questions cramped Mac's mind. How had the man known they would be at the hotel? Had he followed them from the house? Had he actually intended to kill Sierra?

"Why, Mac? Why did he shoot our daughter? I don't understand."

Mac hated that he had to explain, to defend the man who shot Sierra, but what choice did he have? He had to temper the agony in the conclusions his wife would inevitably draw. "Russell Shane was a troubled man, honey. He was devastated when Callie was murdered and deeply depressed. Rebecca told the police that he was taking an anti-depressant, but that he had started drinking a lot lately. After the trial, Shane became obsessed with Jude Donovan. He wanted the man to die. He was tormented over the possibility that Jude's sentence would be commuted to life, or that someday he might be released."

"But what does that have to do with Sierra? I don't understand."

"There is no way to understand it." The heaviness in Mac's heart felt like a stone. "Why he did it. His motive. It makes no sense."

"But to him it did," she insisted. "Russell Shane's daughter was murdered. Why would he try to kill our daughter?"

The intensity of Catherine's struggle was gut wrenching. Mac had to give her more information. "He was trying to send a message to people who are against the death penalty. He wanted to force them to answer the question: Would you still be against the death penalty if it was your own child who was murdered?"

"But why us? What do we have to do with the death penalty?"

"We don't, Catherine, but Shane was a troubled man. Rebecca even used the term delusional. Over time, I guess you could say, he fixated on us. Shane became aware that I attended the event at Saint Edward's to hear Emma speak. He drew conclusions because she is associated with the Innocence

Initiative. Then he learned that you were considering a run for governor. All those facts got tangled up in his tormented mind."

"So he saw me as a threat?"

"Shane saw enemies and adversaries everywhere, Catherine. He was afraid, if you became governor, you would stack the Board of Pardons and Paroles, and that they would place a moratorium on the death penalty."

"And Jude Donovan would never be put to death." Catherine let her head fall back onto the sofa cushion and closed her eyes. The weight of her lids pressed tears from them. The drops trickled down her cheeks. Mac feared that he knew what she was thinking. The letter. Was there something they had missed in Russell Shane's letter? If they had shown it to the police, could this tragedy have been prevented?

CHAPTER 37

Jake Spencer stood at the foot of Russell's casket. Under other circumstances, Rebecca would have taken the position. She guessed that at least seventy-five people were gathered under two canvas tents, an extra having been erected as shelter from the rain. August had insisted that Rebecca and her parents sit next to him on the first row of chairs. Nichole and Seth were to his right. Rebecca thought August looked remarkably composed. Nichole, on the other hand, seemed close to being swept away by a torrent of tears. She and Rebecca had exchanged a glance, but not a word.

Astonishing, miraculous even, that her parents had driven to Hillsboro to tell August that his granddaughter had done the unthinkable, that Nichole had helped send an innocent man to death row. Instead, they had been at his side to tell the dear man that his son was dead, that Russell had committed suicide.

When the officiant moved to the head of the casket, August reached for Rebecca's hand. His grip was strong and steady. "Russell loved you and Callie so much," he whispered, then kissed her cheek. "We will always be family, you and I. Always." And they would. Rebecca would be sure of it.

The preacher opened the service with a word of welcome and a brief prayer. His message was anchored on a verse often chosen for Christian burials. As a funeral director, Rebecca knew the scripture by heart. We would not have you be uninformed about those who have fallen asleep, or to grieve like those who have no hope. Officiants employed the passage as an opening to address the destiny of deceased Christians. In Rebecca's view, the latter part of the verse was too often ignored. The scripture offered the speaker an opportunity to underscore that believers need not grieve as those who have no hope.

A female vocalist sang a lovely rendition of Amazing Grace. At the conclusion, muffled sobs and indistinguishable whispers mingled with a sudden fall of gentle rain. The service was mercifully brief. The pastor raised his right hand and extended it. "And now, may the grace of the Lord Jesus Christ, the love of God, and the fellowship of the Holy Spirit be with you all. Amen."

Jake removed boutonnieres from the pallbearers' lapels and asked that they place the white carnations among the casket flowers before filing past the family. Then he moved to the side and said, "This concludes the graveside service. The family asked that I express their deep appreciation for the love and concern you have shown by your presence here this afternoon."

Some of the numerous mourners filed past the closed casket, pausing to offer sympathy to the family. Others opened umbrellas and went directly to their cars. Rebecca whispered to August, excusing herself. "I'll meet you at your house for the reception."

Open umbrella in hand, Rebecca was picking her way across the soggy grass when she heard someone call her name. She glanced over her shoulder. Nichole and Seth were walking toward her, arm in arm under an umbrella. "What do you want?"

The pair strode nearer, closing the gap with clumsy speed. "I need to get some things out of Dad's apartment. You had the locks changed. You had no right to do that."

"I had every right. I'm in charge of his affairs. Now leave me alone, Nichole."

Seth placed his hand on Rebecca's shoulder, gently, almost pleadingly. She shot him a warning look anyway. "You're not going to choke me this time?"

He removed his hand. "Please, Rebecca. Nichole needs to get her dad's life insurance policy."

Rebecca shook her head, her lips twisted in a smirk. "You two are unbelievable. His casket is not even in the ground yet."

"Rebecca, please," Nichole whined. "I'm the beneficiary. We need the money."

Rebecca resisted an overwhelming desire to be uncooperative, but she had a professional obligation to serve a client-family, even if it included Nichole. "I'll locate the policy and request a claim form."

"How long will it take to get the money?" When Rebecca grimaced in disgust and turned away, Nichole grabbed her forearm. "Please, Rebecca. You won't slow walk the claim, will you? I'm facing perjury charges. And Seth is in even worse trouble because of the lies Jessica told you." Words tumbled from her mouth. Tears streamed down her face, mingling with raindrops. "You don't understand, Rebecca. We have to get a defense attorney right away."

"Oh, I understand, Nichole." Rebecca's voice was sharp with sarcasm. "I just don't care."

◆ ◆ ◆

CLAY AND REBECCA leaned against the deck railing, elbow to elbow. He was dressed the same as the first time she met him, a little more than three weeks ago. Neatly pressed jeans. Black boots. And a button-down white shirt. This time, though, she had greeted the man with a warm, grateful hug rather than resentment and suspicion.

"What a proud old live oak." He tilted back his head, eyeing the top branches through aviator style sunglasses. "Hard to believe that grew out of an acorn no bigger than the tip of my thumb. How tall is it? Sixty feet maybe? And look at the crown spread."

"It's a treasure." Rebecca's gaze drifted from the Lone Oak to the patch of trampled grass where first responders had gathered around Russell's body. She cringed and looked away. Gazing out over the still, blue-green water, she recalled the day she and Myra had placed Callie's last drawing of the Lone Oak into her grave.

Clay was looking out over the lake now, still leaning on the handrail. "Rebecca, are you familiar with a song called The Dance?"

"Yes. It's Garth Brooks's signature song."

"I heard it on the way down here, and I thought of you. Part of it goes something like 'For a moment, all the world was right. How could I have known that you'd ever say goodbye? But now, I'm glad I didn't know the way it all would end. I could have missed the pain, but I'd have had to miss the dance.'" Clay turned toward Rebecca, his left forearm still on the handrail. His voice was quiet, tranquil, and earnest. "If you had never married

294 • LINDA AMEY

Russell, never given birth to Callie, if you hadn't loved them both so deeply, you could have missed so much pain."

Water rippled gently toward the shore, quiet as a whisper. The Lone Oak's leaves rustled in the breeze. "But I'd have had to miss the dance." Without comment, Clay looked away, leaving Rebecca alone with her thoughts. "What about you, Clay? What dance could you have missed?"

"My late wife was a concert pianist," he began. "Listening to her practice and play at home, watching her perform on stage was indescribable. She was elegant and gracious. But at the same time, she was ambitious and unbelievably disciplined. When she was fifty-three, Liza was diagnosed with ALS." Clay paused to clear his throat. "A year later, she killed herself with my service weapon."

Rebecca moaned. "Oh, Clay. No."

"For two years, I grieved so hard, I thought I would literally die. But I survived, like you." Clay patted Rebecca's hand. "If I had never loved Liza, I could have missed all that pain, but I'd have missed a dance that lasted twenty-five years." Clay drew in a deep breath, then released it slowly. "There is no shortage of suffering in this world, is there, Rebecca? You've suffered so much, and you see it every day at the funeral home."

Rebecca leaned away from the rail, walked across the deck, and stretched out on her favorite chaise. Clay was right. There was no shortage of suffering in this world. "Tell me about Jude Donovan. How is he?"

Clay sat at the table in the shade of an umbrella and removed his sunglasses, tucking them in his shirt pocket. "I talk to Emma and Lester often. Jude is in a bad way. He didn't recognize them when he finally agreed to see them. The poor guy is hallucinating. Doesn't even know where he is part of the time. Maybe that's a good thing."

"Why is he still incarcerated?" Rebecca demanded. "He's innocent. The State knows that."

"Damn judicial system. I hate it."

"But you were a detective."

"Yeah. I was a cop. Not a lawyer."

"Why did you offer to help Jude Donovan?" Rebecca asked, shading her eyes from the sun with her hand. "Did you think he was innocent?"

"I didn't have any idea. I just wanted Emma and Lester to know the truth, no matter what it was." Clay handed Rebecca his sunglasses, and she put them on. "You and I were after the same thing, Rebecca, but we didn't even know each other."

"I'm grateful we met." She gazed down at the shore. Her thoughts churned like water around the granite boulders. "Sierra Hollister's family must think Russ was a monster. I hate that. He was Callie's father. I'm thinking about writing them a letter. Not to explain or defend. I would never do that. But to apologize."

"You don't owe anybody an apology, but I think a letter is a good idea."

"I'll think about it. I don't want to upset anyone."

"Why would hearing from you upset the McKeon family?" Clay's tone signaled that the notion was preposterous. "You're the reason they know who shot Sierra. And they know why Russell did it. Most important, they know the threat is gone. The shooter isn't still out there somewhere. Think how relieved they are that you recognized Russell's fishing cap, how grateful they are that you came forward."

Rebecca had been so weighed down with what Russell did and so shocked by his death that she hadn't thought about things the way Clay just presented them. Yes. She would write a letter, a carefully worded letter.

Clay's phone pinged. He read the text message, replied to it, then set his phone aside. "Rebecca, I have an idea. I need to go to Austin to pick up something. Why don't you write your letter, and we'll deliver it to the hospital."

"Oh, no," Rebecca protested. "I don't think so. I don't want to go anywhere near the hospital. I might run into the family."

"Don't worry about that. Seton is a big hospital. And I would enjoy the company. What do you say?" He paused, not long enough for Rebecca to respond, then stood. "I'll go fill up my truck and pick up some lunch. What sounds good?"

Rebecca felt as if she were being swept along by a current. "Uh. Salads from the Highline. Grilled salmon or chicken, maybe?"

"What kind of dressing?"

She was swimming against the current but making no progress. "Lemon vinaigrette?"

"I'll be back in forty-five minutes. Write your letter. It'll do everyone good."

♦ ♦ ♦

WITHOUT A DEADLINE, Rebecca would have labored for hours over the letter. But after a final proofing, she was infinitely pleased. The tone. The content. Exactly what she had strived for. Now, she and Clay were in the cafeteria at Seton Medical Center. He had insisted that she come in with him, saying that he was thirsty and needed a glass of tea. He had already delivered the letter to the nurse's station. Rebecca was incredibly nervous and eager to leave. Why hadn't she just mailed the letter? Why had Clay insisted that they deliver it to the hospital?

Clay's phone rang. "Excuse me a minute. I need to take this." He pushed back from the table and disappeared into the hallway.

When Clay returned minutes later, a vaguely familiar couple was walking alongside him. The petite, auburn-haired woman smiled at Rebecca, then extended her hand. "Hello, Rebecca. I'm Emma Donovan."

"I'm Lester," the man said. "We're here to say thank you."

Rebecca swallowed over a sudden lump in her throat. She had not seen the Donovans since the trial. Why were they here? At a hospital in Austin? But for her nerves, she would have recognized Lester, but not Emma. She was wafer thin and alarmingly pale. Her hands were now clenched at her waist, like a nervous child.

"Emma," Rebecca stammered. "Lester. I'm so surprised to see you."

"We should have already reached out," Lester apologized, pulling back a chair for his wife. "But we wanted to thank you face to face." Once seated, he reached across the table for Rebecca's hand. "You saved our son's life."

"We will never be able to repay you," Emma added, her voice flickering like a candle flame. "How do you repay someone who saved your child's life?"

"I'm so sorry for what you're going through," Rebecca answered, her voice quivering, "for what Jude's going through. It never should have happened."

"No, it shouldn't have," Lester agreed. "But thanks to you and Clay, it's all coming to an end."

As they talked, realization dawned. Rebecca felt embarrassingly dense. "Clay, you planned this." He gave her a guilty-as-charged grin. "You knew Emma and Lester would be here."

"It all worked out perfectly." Emma smiled warmly at Clay, patting his shoulder. "Thank you for making this happen."

"And for everything else you've done," Lester added. "We saw Mac and Catherine a few minutes ago. Sierra is improving. They're eager to meet you, Rebecca."

"Oh, no. I don't want to intrude."

"Intrude? You couldn't possibly intrude."

Clay repositioned on the small metal chair. "Rebecca's having trouble separating what Russell did from what she did."

"I understand," Lester said. "But thanking you would mean the world to Mac and Catherine. They've even told Michaela, Sierra's daughter, about you. I'll let them know you're here."

Lester returned before Rebecca had time to calm her racing heart. The man with him was smiling as he walked across the cafeteria. Mac McKeon. He was five-ten perhaps, broad shouldered, trim, and fit. His appearance, the way he moved exuded the confident poise of a successful man.

"Hello, Rebecca. I'm Mac McKeon." He extended his hand, not to shake hers, but to grasp it. "I'm so grateful to have a chance to thank you."

Rebecca was speechless. She had absolutely no idea how to respond, but Mac McKeon did not seem to expect her to.

"Knowing that my family is out of danger. I cannot begin to tell you. I was about to lose my mind." He squeezed Rebecca's hand, then released it, freeing both his hands to hug her. "Thank you so much."

"No, Mr. McKeon. Thank you." Rebecca returned his firm embrace, as he told her to call him Mac. "I was worried that you — I'm just so relieved."

The five of them gathered around the table, Rebecca between Clay and Mac. Her nerves were beginning to calm.

"Catherine and Michaela are with Sierra," Mac explained. "They'll be here shortly. We want Michaela to meet you, Rebecca. She's almost five. Precious little thing."

"I would love to meet her, but I'm concerned," Rebecca confessed. "How much does she know? I don't want to say the wrong thing."

"For now, all she knows is that the man who shot Sierra was a dear friend of yours. I told her that your friend's daughter died, and that for a long time he had been miserable and depressed. I didn't use any names, other than yours. I told her your friend was taking medicine to make him feel better, but that it wasn't working. He lashed out and did a terrible thing. That seemed to satisfy her."

"Are you sure about this, Mac?" Rebecca pressed. "You've handled this crisis so well. I don't want to say the wrong thing."

"Just follow her lead," Mac said. "You're a mother. You'll know what to say." A smile swept over his face. "Here they are."

Catherine McKeon was a lovely woman, dressed in a crisp white shirt, black ankle pants, and stylish pewter flats. Her eyes were an intense blue, a stunning combination with her dark hair and light complexion. The child holding her hand was exactly as Mac had described. Precious. Messy curls held in place by turquoise barrettes. Cute little jeans, cuffed haphazardly. Multi-colored sneakers. And a white polo shirt with a logo. LSL&R.

Mac escorted them to the table. "Michaela, I want you to meet someone. This is the lady I told you about, the lady who—"

"I know." She released her grandmother's hand and stepped forward. "Hi, Miss Rebecca. It's very nice to meet you."

"It's a pleasure to meet you, too, Michaela."

"Thank you for helping the police." The child moved closer, so near that Rebecca could see a scattering of tiny freckles across her nose. "You were very brave."

"I tried to do the right thing."

"Granddad said you know the man that shot my mommy."

Rebecca cringed. The words were stark and brutal coming from this precious child's mouth. "I did. And I am so deeply sorry that my friend did that."

"It's not your fault." The darling little girl patted Rebecca's shoulder. "Just remember. Your friend did a very bad thing, but he was not a bad man."

Rebecca nodded, grappling for composure. "You're right, Michaela. I promise I won't forget." She managed a smile, her nerves gradually settling. What a precious child. What a lovely family. "Were you with your mom just now?"

"Yes." Michaela smiled for the first time. "Mommy's eyes were open. And she whispered my name. Tomorrow, she's going to her own room." The child leaned toward Rebecca and lowered her voice. "I hope it smells better."

Rebecca laughed. What an adorable little girl. "Michaela, I've been really sad lately, but I feel so much better now. Thank you for helping me."

The child leaned forward and put her arms around Rebecca's neck. For a moment, they were Callie's arms. Then they were Michaela's.

CHAPTER 38

ONE WEEK LATER

Graham Hollister was having lunch on the terrace with Michaela. Chicken quesadillas, freshly sliced avocados, and Cherub tomatoes. Mac watched them from the French doors, repeatedly checking his watch. The man would be there for another half hour. Sierra was sitting on a glider, rocking it back and forth with a tap of her foot. She was wearing sparkly sandals and a crisp cotton robe that zipped up the front. Her left arm was in a sling meant to give her some relief from the pain in her collar bone and shoulder. Her hair was twisted up in the back and held in place by a clip. Strands dangled on the back of her long, thin neck.

"Honey," Catherine said, standing now at Mac's elbow. "There's a saying that a watched pot never boils."

"What does that mean?"

"Watching Graham won't make him leave any sooner."

Mac ignored her but stepped away from the door and headed to his study. After Sierra had been released from the hospital, Graham had agreed that for the next two years, he would come to Austin for visitation. Michaela would not be required to travel to Plano. He had also consented to supervised visitation, insisting that the terms family member or appointed agent would not include Mac. In return for Hollister's signature, Mac had agreed to let the man inside his house twice a month to see Michaela. He still had to fight the urge to put the guy's life through a meat grinder, but his family needed him to close that chapter of their lives.

Mac was expecting an email from Ben Morrow. The closing on the Donovan ranch was coming up soon. Now that Jude was out of prison, his parents' financial crisis had eased, but it was not over by any means. Jude was in a psychiatric treatment center, but the length of stay covered by insurance was limited during a calendar year. The Donovans needed cash, but they were desperate to hold onto their home.

Mac had suggested a solution. With their approval, he had approached Ben Morrow. Emma and Lester would keep their home and a hundred acres, selling the prime acreage to Ben. It had beautiful trees, easy access, and a creek running from one side to the other. It was a perfect setting, Mac had pointed out to Ben, for him and his wife to build a ranch house perfectly to their liking. To enhance the deal, Mac had found five-hundred acres a few miles away where Ben could run a herd of cattle. The land was not for sale, but the owner was eager to lease it.

Mac was hopeful that the deal would work. Ben was a reasonable man, a family man. Mac had informed him of the unthinkable crisis the Donovans found themselves in. "If you help them out, Ben, you will save this family a lot of grief."

Rapid little footsteps in the hallway signaled that Michaela was heading his way. Mac waited for her gentle tap on the door. She had been taught not to enter his study without permission. Mac pretended not to notice her, giving her a chance to follow house rules.

Tap. Tap. Tap. "Granddad, excuse me. My dad's leaving. Do you want to say goodbye?"

"Wouldn't miss it." Mac swiveled his chair to face her. "I'll be right there, sweetie." He did a quick email search, but there was nothing yet from Ben. "No news is good news."

Graham was standing near the front door, chatting with Michaela and Catherine. Mac resisted the urge to laugh when the grandfather clock started chiming. It was one o'clock. Time for him to go. "Are you heading back to Plano?" Mac asked. "Or are you spending the night in town?"

"Think I'll head out," he answered, not looking at Mac. "Michaela needs time with her mom. Catherine, thank you for lunch and your hospitality."

"You're welcome. You'll be back in two weeks?"

"I sure will." For the first time in Mac's memory, Graham Hollister got down on one knee in front of Michaela and took one of her hands. "Have a good time at the pool with Anna Rose. I'll see you soon. And try not to worry about your mom, Michaela. She's going to be fine." As they shared a hug, Graham whispered, "Dad loves you very much."

"Love you too." Michaela stepped away and opened the front door. "Come on, Gran. Let's walk Dad to his car."

For a split-second Mac started to object but checked himself. No man with a gun was watching his family come and go. Russell Shane was not a threat. The man was dead. Graham was not going to snatch up Michaela and speed away with her. In the past weeks, Graham had experienced what fear was like. Mac had made sure of that, encouraging Bostic to keep the pressure on him during the investigation.

I must let this go, he insisted silently. For Michaela.

Sierra was sitting alone on the terrace. The sun was glaring overhead. Mac asked if she wanted to move into the shade. "I'm okay. Feels good actually. I won't be out here much longer."

Mac sat at a table, shielded by an umbrella. "How did things go with Graham?"

"Well enough." Sierra gave him a sly grin. "Brooke suggested Michaela and I meet him at her house. She was going to push him in the pool and hold his head under."

Mac snickered, noticing that Sierra flinched when she moved her arm. "Are you in pain?"

"No. He just left." Sierra's little laugh sounded raspy from the breathing tube, but it was getting closer to normal. "Brooke thought Graham was involved in the shooting. Did you know that?"

"She might have mentioned it."

"What about you? What did you think?"

"I don't want to talk about that." Sierra had been out of the hospital for a week, but Mac still had a hard time believing she was home. They had come so close to losing her. She could have died on the sidewalk when Shane shot her. She could have died on the way to the hospital, or during surgery, or from the infection. She could have suffered permanent injury, even brain damage. "You're going to be fine, honey."

"Of course, I am. So stop worrying." Sierra looked down at her sandaled feet and wiggled her toes. "I need a pedicure."

Mac shook his head in disbelief. "You were on a ventilator for three days. You have a drain tube in your chest. Your arm is in a sling. And you need a pedicure." Mac wadded up paper napkins and poked them in an empty glass. "Talk to your mother. I can't help you with that."

"Could you help me stand up? I'm ready to go inside."

Mac stood to his daughter's right and crooked his elbow. Sierra's hand, when it appeared around his arm, still bore blue-black bruises from IV needles. The abrasion on the right side of her face was starting to heal, but her torn eyelid would require plastic surgery.

Sierra groaned as she pushed herself up from the glider. Upright, she still held tightly to Mac's arm. "Would you do something else for me, Dad? The next time you slam me to the sidewalk, try to protect my face."

"Not funny, Sierra."

The French doors opened. Catherine and Michaela appeared from inside the house. "Where are you two going?"

Mac stepped to the side. "Would you take over here? Your daughter's being a little sassy today." With the transition safely executed, Mac said, "I'll be in my study. Michaela, you want to come with me?"

There was still no response from Ben Morrow. Mac was growing concerned. He put it from his mind and lifted Michaela onto his lap. "How was your visit with your dad?"

"It was good." She cupped her hand over the mouse.

"Don't mess with that."

"Sorry." She pulled her hand back and yawned. "He'll be back in two weeks. Where will we visit then?"

"Here, if that's what you want." Michaela leaned back against Mac's chest. The weight of her was comforting. An email popped up. It was Ben Morrow. "Cross your fingers, sweetie." He grinned when she complied, then read the email aloud. "Mac, tomorrow works for me. See you at noon. Confident we've got a deal." He gave Michaela a quick squeeze. "Looks like I'll be on the road to Kerrville tomorrow."

Michaela perked up and leaned toward the monitor. "Let's check the weather, Granddad. Might be a beautiful day for flying."

CHAPTER 39

ONE MONTH LATER

The afternoon sky darkened as Rebecca walked along a tree-lined path leading from the main building to the Conservatory. A courteous woman at the front desk of Oak Ridge Treatment Center had said that Jude Donovan was waiting for her by the pond. Rebecca had phoned Emma and Lester last week, asking if she might visit Jude. "Maybe talking to each other would help. I know it would help me." Jude's parents had required no convincing. "Jude is in a fragile state, Rebecca," Emma had warned. "You'll see that right away. Without you and Clay, though, our son would still be in hell."

The last time Rebecca had seen Jude Donovan was at his sentencing. She remembered him, the defendant, as medium height, five-feet-eight maybe, square shouldered and slender. He had one unforgettable feature. His eyes. They were wide set, their color as rich as caramel, and fringed with long, dense lashes. But the young man sitting slumped on a concrete bench at the edge of the pond looked nothing like Jude Donovan at all. He was dressed in black shorts and a white tee shirt, pathetically thin and frail. The seams of his shirt dropped inches below his bony shoulders. His hair was shaggy at the neckline and tossed by a gathering breeze.

When he heard Rebecca's approaching steps, Jude gradually angled his face toward her. Her disbelief turned to dismay. Jude's skin was as dull as the concrete bench, and his lips just as dry. His cheeks were sunken, and his beautiful eyes looked hollow and faded. Jude Donovan looked like a dying man, and Rebecca's heart sank.

"Hello, Jude. I'm Rebecca." The corner of Jude's mouth twitched. Was he trying to smile or to return her greeting? She couldn't tell. "What a pleasant spot. There's something soothing about sitting by the water."

The simple act of sliding over to make room on the bench seemed to take an enormous effort. Rebecca thanked him and sat, gazing out over the pond. A lone duck swam in their direction. Its compact body, dotted with deep brown spots, hardly disturbed the water's surface.

"My home in Sparrows Cove is on Lake Travis. I love it there." Rebecca looked at Jude, but there was nothing in his expression that she knew how to read, so she waited in silence for him to speak.

Together, they watched the duck gliding their way. The bird had a slate gray head and neck, and something like a white mask in front of its eyes. Most of the upper wings were blue-gray. Others were an exquisite, iridescent green. A drake, Rebecca concluded, decked out to catch the eyes of the ladies. As the duck neared the edge of the pond, his short, orange legs slowed their paddling. Comically, he waddled onto the bank and immediately shook the water from his feathers.

Long moments passed before Jude slowly swiveled his head and looked at Rebecca. He studied her face with tortured eyes.

She noticed that his long, thick lashes had thinned and looked brittle.

"Rebecca, would you take off your sunglasses?" Jude's voice, despite the brevity of the request, trailed away.

It was a peculiar request, but she complied, squinting in the sudden glare of an overcast sky. She knew her eyes were bloodshot and puffy. She cried last night. For Callie. For Russ.

Jude continued to study her face, looking puzzled. Then a memory seemed to rise out of the depths of his misery. "I remember you. I wasn't sure I could."

"It was a brutal experience. For both of us."

Jude looked away and resumed watching the duck. The busy bird was pecking at something hidden in the grass now, his long, black bill jabbing and poking.

"May I ask how you're doing, Jude?"

His chuckle came out like a grunt. "Well, I know that's a duck." The left corner of his mouth twitched. Once. Twice. Then again. "I know I'm in San Antonio, and what year it is. They tell me that's progress."

Rebecca placed her hand on Jude's forearm. His bones felt delicate in her grasp, his muscles like soft fruit. "I'm so sorry."

"Why? You got me out of that place." Jude jerked when the duck quacked loudly, the rapid series sharp and piercing. He seemed at the same time jittery and lifeless. "Why did you help me? Why did you do that?"

Rebecca squeezed his forearm gently, then withdrew her hand. She had fielded the question numerous times in the past month, sensing that most people found her response unsatisfying. She was not a philosophical or contemplative person, certainly not religious in the traditional sense. Talk of miracles, of God's plan, of divine intervention invariably propelled her down a path that led to more questions than answers. She preferred to leave that road untraveled. But throughout her life, particularly in the years since Callie's death, she had attempted to hear and heed the Still Small Voice.

She had responded to it, she believed, the day she parked her mother's Infiniti on the wrong side of the pumps at 7-Eleven. She could have suppressed her memory of going to the convenience store in Houston with her father two weeks after Callie was killed. She had repressed it many times before, but not that day. Instead, she had relived the emotional trip, remembering how her father had fretted over the positions of the vehicles and their fuel doors, how he had puzzled over the sketch. She had heard the Voice again, she believed, when Myra had said, Too bad you don't have access to Nichole's credit card statements. Rebecca could have ignored Myra's musing, but she had not. It was the Voice, she believed, that had urged her toward the truth through two singular, improbable occurrences. Then the truth had set Jude free.

Rebecca felt the light weight of Jude's gaze. "Sorry," she apologized. "My mind is all over the place. What did you ask me?"

"Why did you help me?"

"To be honest, Jude, at first I wasn't thinking about you at all."

"What do you mean?"

"Ever since Callie died," Rebecca explained, "I've tried to accept that I would never know the truth of what happened that night. But I couldn't seem to accept it. Callie was my daughter, and I wanted to know the truth. My friend Myra insisted that I deserved to know the truth."

"Do you know it now?"

"I know enough, yes." Rebecca paused, hesitant to express her next thought. Jude looked so fragile. Did she dare ask him to go back to that night? How much could he remember? "Do you mind if I ask you some questions?"

Uncertainty flared in Jude's weary, watery eyes. "About that night?"

"I understand if you prefer not to talk about it."

"It's okay. If it will help. I can try."

The left corner of Jude's mouth twitched again. It wasn't an effort to smile, Rebecca realized. It was a muscle spasm. A tic. Had he always had it? Was it a side effect of his medications? Or had it been brought on by living in hell? "If it's too much for you …"

"It's okay."

Rebecca was relieved that Jude had not said, "It's okay. I owe you that much." He owed her nothing. For more than two years, she had believed a lie, that Jude Donovan had been Calvin Canon's accomplice, his getaway driver.

Tragedy had caused their lives to cross paths, to intersect, but it did not have to define the connection that they would always have. "I have a question about Callie. Do you remember seeing her that night?"

"Of course. Yes." Jude spoke slowly, gathering words as if they were scattered about in his mind. "I was sitting in my car, digging coins from the console. I looked up, and there she was."

"Did Callie see you?"

"Yes. We glanced at each other. Just briefly. She looked nervous."

"Why do you think that?"

"She hesitated when she saw me. Then she looked over her shoulder, back toward the gas pumps."

Toward Nichole, Rebecca thought bitterly, and Seth Palmer. "Did you see Callie go inside?" Jude nodded. "Is there anything else that stands out in your mind about her?"

The corner of Jude's mouth twitched repeatedly. He reached up to control the tremor with his fingertips, like one would do to stop a bleeding cut. "Her hair. I remember her hair. It was swirling in the wind."

Tears pricked at Rebecca's eyes. Jude's description made her throat ache with regret. "Forgive me for this, Jude, but did you hear Callie scream?"

Jude flinched, then his fingertips slid up his cheek to touch his ear. "No. Only the gunfire."

Rebecca wiped tears from her cheeks. For some inexplicable reason, she found comfort knowing that Jude remembered Callie's hair swirling in the wind. "Thank you, Jude. You've helped me more than you know. How can I help you? Is there anything else you want to ask?"

Clouds, heavy and gray, shadowed Jude's face. "Before you knew the truth," he said haltingly, "did you want me to die?"

"No."

"Why not?"

"I don't know," Rebecca answered truthfully. It was the best she could do. "Honest to God, Jude. I don't know why."

There came a dash of raindrops. They painted gray dots on the sidewalk and on the surface of the bench. The duck, briefly forgotten, eased back into the water, then disappeared under the surface momentarily. His feathers glistened brilliantly when he reappeared and began his purposeful journey back across the pond. Rebecca closed her eyes and tilted her face skyward. The droplets were cool and tender, soothing her swollen lids.

"Can you ever forgive me, Rebecca?" Jude's voice rippled and wavered. "I should have tried to help Callie."

Rebecca opened her eyes, then looked tenderly at Jude. "That's the first time you've said Callie's name." She extended her right hand, silently insisting that he accept it. When finally he did, Jude's hand felt as small and delicate as a child's. "There was nothing you could have done. Nothing." A light rain began to fall. Drops rustled the leaves of live oaks and peppered the pond. It was a soft and beautiful sound. "You are not to blame, Jude. And neither am I."

ACKNOWLEDGEMENTS

Many thanks to my family for your love and support, especially to my mother Billie Brizendine who passed away in January 2024. You had a keen eye for details, Mother, and you were the best listener I have ever known.

To my longtime friends Peggy Nadeau, Karen Rhodes, and Jim Schooler. I appreciate and treasure each of you. You bring so much to my life. Thank you for the prayers and for the laughter!

Finally, love and gratitude to my dear friend Marci Henna, author of the Fireside, Texas series and other works. Writing is said to be a solitary journey, but not for us. We have each other.

ABOUT THE AUTHOR

LINDA AMEY IS A NATIVE TEXAN and lives in Austin. She proudly claims to have mastered spelling her maiden name, Brizendine, before finishing first grade. Linda graduated from the University of Texas at Austin, then practiced as a funeral director for nearly twenty years. Linda and her late husband John served thousands of central Texas families at their Austin funeral homes.

Writing novels, while primarily intended to entertain her readers, is an extension of Linda's long-held desire to lift the veil that has shrouded her profession with secrecy. To that end, she takes her readers behind closed doors in a funeral home, interweaving scenes with myth-dispelling descriptions. Such insights are offered to allay the reader's uneasiness about funerals and the funeral profession, and to provoke thought about life, loss, and human worth.

Linda enjoys time with family and friends. After years of playing mahjongg, she remains an enthusiastic rookie. Her passions are reading, traveling, serving as a Docent at the Texas Governor's Mansion, and, of course, writing.

Made in the USA
Coppell, TX
19 October 2025